THE
CADIS
EVENING

by

Lee McQueen

McQueen Press

Published by McQueen Press

Cover image and design, interior design, typesetting by McQueen Press.

Author photo by McQueen Press.

Logo is a registered mark of McQueen Press and should not be copied without permission.

The Cadis Evening novel is based upon the poem "Wild Hazy, Beautiful Crazy" (Things I Forgot to Tell You, 2nd ed, McQueen Press, 2007) short story "The Confessions of the Dreamers" (Imaginarium, McQueen Press, 2006) and the short screenplay "Stephanie" (The Dark Fantastic: 12 Short Screenplays, McQueen Press, 2013) by Lee McQueen.

ISBN 13 978-1-7352369-1-9
2nd edition

The 2nd edition of The Cadis Evening published with re-pagination, spelling corrections, a new cover, and a new author photo.

Catalong-in-publication

McQueen, Lee, 1970-
Cadis Evening, The/Lee McQueen
The Cadis Evening
1. Business intelligence--Fiction
2. Mind control--Fiction
3. Psychological abuse--Fiction
I. Title

WORKS BY LEE MCQUEEN

Short Story Collection

Imaginarium

Poetry

Things I Forgot to Tell You

Novels

Kenzi

Celara Sun

Windrunner

The Cadis Evening

Screenplays

Kindred

SUDAN: The Lion of Truth

The Dark Fantastic: 12 Short Screenplays

I Disappear: 3 Short Screenplays

Non-Fiction

Writer in the Library! 41 Writers Reveal How They Use
Libraries to Develop Their Skill, Craft & Careers

Road Romance: Tales From the Book Tour

TABLE OF CONTENTS

You Are More than the Mistakes You Made

For the Voyager Who Always Finds a Way Home

The stranger did not lodge in the street, but I opened my home to the traveler. Job 31:32. *The Holy Bible*. King James Version.

Some years ago

CHAPTER 1 SUNDAE

Sundae."

The handler's voice came from behind the white light shining into her face as she reclined in the soft leather dentist's chair. The tall, dark-haired man dominated the space around her like a football player en route to tackle. Though good-looking, the handler was neither nice nor kind. Nor was he a dentist.

So she answered, "Yes," and waited for further instructions.

"Open the door." Low and insistent, his voice vibrated and hummed past her eardrums and ricocheted inside her skull.

"Open," she confirmed, as she knew he expected.

The chair beneath her reclined backward in an oily smooth glide until she lay almost horizontal. The light and the hum and the vibration and the voice filled her insides until nothing else existed. No space for escape remained. She lay open and exposed.

"Even when you leave us, you are still with us."

"I am still with you."

"Even when it's over, it's never over."

"It's... not over." She died a little inside every time she agreed.

"Nothing that you hide, that cannot be found."

"Nothing."

"Nothing that you say, that cannot be heard."

"Nothing."

"Nowhere that you run, that we cannot follow."

"Nowhere."

"It is your privilege to do as we say."

"Yes."

"You were nothing before us. You are nothing without us."

"Nothing."

"Do you understand?"

"Yes."

"What more does life have to offer you?"

Pause.

"Answer!"

Silence

"Sundae."

"Nothing. There is no life without you."

"She's ready." Sundae's handler faded into the black mystery behind the light. The operator raised her seat back. Now her owner and master moved in front of the brilliance of the light like a doomsday eclipse. The older, silver-haired version of the handler dominated Sundae's dark brown eyes with his own crystalline blue gaze that burned like the cold fire of a laser deep into her brain. According to her master, she held no secrets from her master.

The recorder wheeled the bulky camera closer to Sundae's face, devoid of expression and free from thought. He adjusted the focus to further violate then steal her soul.

Ice-cold blue chips from the owner's eyes drifted over Sundae's vacant countenance. "You altered from my instructions. You disobeyed a direct order from me."

"Yes."

"Why did you disobey?"

"Ronny. Told me."

The handler stepped forward and whispered into the owner's ear. "She means Ronny Webster. He's a manager at Celara. King's guy."

The owner responded with a slight nod. He gestured for the handler to move back from Sundae's view. She had the capacity to deal with only one of them at a time. The owner returned his attention to Sundae.

"What did Ronny tell you?"

"He... he... said."

"What did Ronny say?"

"He said. He told me."

Her stumbles angered the owner. "Sundae! Open the door all the way! Open it! Now!"

Sundae blinked once. Twice. Her eyelids fluttered.

"She's fighting," the owner muttered over his shoulder. "Sundae! Listen to instruction. Tell us what Ronny said."

"No more."

"Ronny did not say that to you, Sundae."

"No."

A long silence passed while the owner considered various options to force Sundae to cooperate.

"My son worked very hard to train you, but your discipline has been lax."

The owner cut a significant look at the handler who moved his bulk further into the darkness beyond the light. The owner then returned his attention to the woman entranced before him.

"For every reward, there is a punishment, Sundae. You will be punished today. When you disobey instructions, you are punished. You know this. Tell me that you understand."

"Yes."

The owner thought a moment and then sighed. "I don't believe you, Sundae. You still seem... confused. I need for you to convince me." The silver-haired man nodded to the operator. "Do it."

The owner and the handler faded into the darkness behind the light. Once again, the operator stepped into position behind Sundae and fiddled with the dashboard that controlled and drove her like a car.

He turned dials and adjusted knobs. Sundae's body stretched to full horizontal as the chair flattened to form a long narrow bed. The operator then connected each of Sundae's limbs to a metal cuff at each corner of the rectangle while the recorder changed camera angles. When the recorder finished, he nodded to the handler.

"Ready."

The handler stepped forward and spoke in the monotone perfectly pitched to invade Sundae's mind and permeate every hiding place, every sanctuary inside her brain.

"Things fall apart. You are lost in time and space. Remember to forget."

"Forget."

"But you know the way home."

"I know. Remember."

"No! You know the way home."

"I... remember the way home."

"Sundae!"

"I am... Sundae."

"Come home now!"

"Now. Now. Now..."

"Sundae, we are going to count. Are you ready?"

"I... please... please... please..."

The operator flipped the switch that sent an electrical current through Sundae's body. She stiffened and jerked. The vacancy in her eyes resembled that of an abandoned house, the windows coated with a powdery film of dry dust. The lights were on, but no one was home and likely never would return.

A metallic taste of iron filled Sundae's mouth. The carousel whirled her and twirled her around. The carnies called out a cacophony of promises set to music from a calliope. And the lights flashed and danced like rainbows across the walls through glass prisms. The carnies told Sundae to believe in magic and so Sundae believed in magic.

"We're going to start from the beginning, Sundae," the handler told her. The operator waited for the next signal... should the jump-start prove necessary.

CHAPTER 2   STEPHANIE

Early on a clear and crisp Sunday morning in March, Roy paused in the doorway to his daughter's room at his condo on the outskirts of Lake City. He marveled at Mother Nature's ability to replicate his dark brown hair and light brown eyes in female form. Both he and his daughter had skin the orangey-brown color of pecans with eyes that ranged from sherry to honey to hazel depending on mood or weather.

John, his veterinarian buddy, often joked that it looked as though he gave birth to Marietta all by himself with no help from Susan. She seemed so much like him in demeanor, as well—studious, quiet, serious, sometimes given to daydreaming. Pretty low maintenance, for a teenager.

Roy sighed. Like him, Marietta would soon have to adjust to the soul-killing realities of life. He raised his voice over the Jodeci cassette tape blaring from the boom-box she brought with her.

"Marietta, we're going to have to cut the weekend short. Your Aunt Stephanie died this morning."

Marietta looked up from her poetry homework. "Aunt Stephanie?"

Her mother's identical twin existed only in sinister whispers on the fringes of the family circle. Her name hardly came up in conversation anymore. On the rare occasion someone said, "Stephanie," eyes looked left, right, and then downward.

An awkward silence would descend. "Think it might rain?" someone would ask with a puzzled glance at a crystal clear sky. "Who won the game?" someone else would inquire even as the score blinked in large red numbers on the television screen. "How did Susan get the potato salad so creamy?" another someone would wonder as Susan stared at the family-sized store-bought container without reply. And then more voices hurried to fill the dead silence.

Following the usual family protocols, Marietta looked left, right, and finally, down at her unfinished poem. "How did she die?" Even a sixteen-year-old knew that thirty-six was still pretty young.

"Susan's already on her way to pick you up. It's probably better that you hear it from her."

Her father hesitated.

"Marietta, she... Well, the funny thing is that Stephanie sent you something care of me. It arrived yesterday. I didn't open the box until this morning. It slipped my mind until I got the news. But I made sure it was okay." Her father handed her a thick book. "This is still in the wrapper, so it should be fine."

"A Bible?" Marietta hefted the weight of the book up and down. "That's weird. I mean, I didn't think she was religious." None of them were, really, except Grandma. No one else in the family bothered to pretend to fear or dread God.

Roy shrugged. "Well, there's a lot about Stephanie that no one ever knew. And now maybe never will." He hugged her. "Go ahead and get packed, sweetheart."

***

Low murmurs drifted up the stairs and whispered down the hallway towards Marietta's room. Roy's voice held a familiar tone of pleading that made Marietta's skin crawl.

"Susan, I'm... I'm sorry."

A long silence passed and then, "Really." One quiet word from Susan said so many things and yet left many other things unspoken because they were understood.

Marietta's ears strained to hear what she really didn't want to understand. "It... doesn't have to be like this." Marietta remembered that same whimper used to crawl from the master bedroom of the Brazil family home just before Roy left, banished to suburbia and weekend fatherhood.

"But it is like this. You made sure of that."

Cold. Final. Unforgettable, Susan. Marietta slung her duffel bag over her shoulder and hurried down the stairs. She loved her father. She did not want to see a grown man cry. Not again anyways.

***

Wide, open spaces on the road compacted as traffic increased on the drive back into Lake City proper. The weekend ended and it was time for everyone to gear up for the Monday grind. Spring winds wailed inward from the lakeshore and whipped against her mother's sedan, rushing them ever faster through traffic.

"Mom, what happened to Aunt Stephanie?"

Susan checked over her shoulder as she raced other vehicles towards the exit to the Brazil family home.

"There was an explosion at Cadis Industries where she worked."

"What?"

"She was in a meeting with a few other people and something ignited. Chemicals, they think."

Her mother sighed and smoothed a pale hand over her glossy raven hair, pulled back into a tight French twist. "Marietta, you remember that I told you Stephanie was unstable?"

"Yes."

"Sometimes, when you walk a tightrope, you make it to the other side. Other times, you fall off." Susan's dark eyes flashed as she shot Marietta a side glance. "Stephanie made it across many times. As a matter of fact, she got real good at it. But she crossed one time too many."

Marietta looked at Susan's creamy hands as she turned the steering wheel. "What are you talking about? It was an accident. Wasn't it?"

"One person survived the attack. The CEO at Cadis, Derek Robinette, though he was injured. His face was burned, they said. He says that Stephanie caused the explosion with some kind of chemical device." Susan's fingers tightened to a bloodless white color as if to choke and throttle her own vehicle to death.

"Marietta, it's probably going to be on the evening news. They're calling what she did terrorism. That's why I came early to get you, so you'd know ahead of time."

***

Marietta hid inside her room upstairs. Susan forbid her to talk on the telephone, listen to the radio, watch television, or answer the front door. She could listen to her cassette tapes or pop a movie into the VCR built into her thirteen-inch television, but she couldn't watch the news. But she did overhear the messages that filled the answering machine in the downstairs hallway. Her mother fielded more calls as the phone rang throughout the rest of the night.

Marietta crept downstairs to heat a plate of leftovers in the microwave. Between the flat Midwestern-accented announcement of Aunt Stephanie's death on television and the hum of the microwave, she overheard Susan talking to someone on the telephone.

"The deceased, Stephanie Madison purchased..."

"...threatened me just last week..."

"...a .22-caliber handgun, illegal within Lake City limits..."

"...something told me..."

"...family members that she had a history..."

"...last time I would see her alive..."

"...no further... Cadis Industries..."

Marietta poured a glass of juice and tried not to overhear Susan's telephone call through the kitchen door.

"...her wallet... a business card from an abortion doctor... I don't know... Stephanie..."

Susan's sigh slid underneath the kitchen door. "I was afraid for Marietta."

Marietta raced back upstairs and quietly closed her bedroom door.

***

Monday afternoon, Susan used her tried and true system to straighten the living room. She snapped up window shades, beat pillows into cooperation, and tied back loose curtains as if at an old-time lynching. She used the same relentless precision to clamp down the disobedient edges of her raven waves with quick-drying gel, a sharp-bristled hair brush, and metal clips.

Marietta didn't know why her mother bothered. Company only got as far as the foyer before Susan used a gentle but firm hand to herd unexpected visitors back through the front door. Life would go on. Marietta knew her mother disturbed a groove only in extreme emergencies. Stephanie did not count. Routines were not accidents waiting to happen. They were routines. And Roy needed to understand that.

"You should have asked me first, Roy."

"I probably should have, but I wanted Marietta to have a chance to see him. It was either dog or a falcon, like your father's."

"I married you so that I could get away from all that, not that it did me any good."

Marietta cringed at the quiet verbal war waged in her honor. Susan said something else that Marietta didn't catch because her mother spoke in the low, clenched-jaw cadence specifically-tuned to cut Roy into tiny bite-sized pieces.

To her surprise, Susan's weirding voice didn't work on Roy this time. Marietta's father didn't back down and the discussion continued.

Exasperated, her mother called upstairs, "Marietta!"

The fluffy, golden dog yipped and barked with the over-anxious eagerness of an animal shelter rescue that smelled cabbage stir fry on Marietta's hands. She couldn't help but laugh at his silliness.

"Oh, he's beautiful!" She hugged him. "He's so friendly."

Her mother made an impatient sound that her father quickly covered with, "He's yours, Marietta. You get to name him."

"How about Jesse?"

"Jesse Brazil." Roy repeated the name, pleased. His hazel eyes met Susan's dark brown ones square on as he answered Marietta with triumph. "Sounds good to me."

This exchange revealed a new dynamic to her father and mother's relationship that Marietta knew her mother did not appreciate. Roy would pay. Maybe not today or tomorrow, but Susan would present him with an invoice listing blood, sweat, or most likely tears for Roy to surrender to her in thirty days or less... or else.

"Marietta, this dog is your responsibility. You're going to feed him and walk him." Susan frowned a crease into her smooth cream-colored skin. "And he sleeps outside."

"Mom."

"Marietta."

"Can't he sleep in my room?" Marietta looked at her father who looked away with a don't push it, kid expression.

"Marietta, you don't know what he might be carrying."

"He has a clean bill of health from John," Roy announced in a loud voice.

"Alright." Susan still looked dubious.

"Susan, you're running out of reasons. He's fine."

"I said alright!" Shut up, Roy, her mother seemed to want to say. Instead, she turned to Marietta. "But Marietta, remember the rules."

Jesse raced from Roy to Susan back to Marietta as if he couldn't believe his luck with this group of suckers.

***

All day Tuesday, Marietta set up Jesse's backyard home. She made his dog house extra warm and cozy since March nights in the Midwest could still turn frosty. She hauled food and supplies from the store in the ancient, wood-paneled family station wagon, her first car, of which she was very proud. Riding shotgun on the passenger side, Jesse pointed his nose straight into the wind.

Outside the store, Stephanie's resemblance to her own mother felt creepy and so Marietta turned away from the enlarged color photo on the front page of the newspaper in the rack.

She'd missed two days of school so far so her teachers phoned in her assignments to the answering machine. Early evening, while she put the finishing touches on her poetry assignment, due on Friday morning, she discovered Stephanie's secret.

Marietta had removed the plastic from the Bible, noting that it wasn't the plastic that retailers used. Instead, ordinary plastic wrap hugged the book like a leftover pork chop in their refrigerator. Someone had gone over the clear plastic with a hot blow-dryer to make it shrink to fit.

Now Jesse nosed around her room all restless whining curiosity. A cold wind blew so Marietta sneaked him into her room. He repaid her generosity by knocking the Bible off her nightstand. And now, underneath Jesse's paws, the Bible that Stephanie sent her lay open. On the left page, Marietta saw the good word in enlarged print. On the right page, a neat typewritten sheet of white paper hid, glued into the spine, cut to fit between the book pages without sticking outside the edge.

> She's doing it again. How does she do it? I remember playing with fire in a vacant lot a long time ago. I pretended that I was a cave woman in prehistoric times. When I got home, Mama beat me like a slave. Like Kunta Kinte. Like my name was Toby. The only way Mama could have known was her. How did she do it? I hate Sundays.

Marietta slammed the Bible shut in confusion. What kind of creepy message did Aunt Stephanie want to send her? In the Holy Book of all things. Curiosity got the best of her, so Marietta allowed the book to flop open to a random page. The more she read, the more she realized that Stephanie was nuts. Walking a tightrope until she fell off, just like everyone said.

CHAPTER 3   MARIETTA

The strangest dream began that night. Surrounded by a white mist of water and smoke, Marietta heard splashes and gurgles. Someone called to her. But she couldn't see anything inside the white mist. The cloud closed in on all sides to smother her like a pillow. She couldn't breathe.

A voice screamed, "Marietta!"

Marietta gasped for air and jerked awake, sweaty and terrified. She drew the covers up to her chin and looked around her room. Silence settled over the Brazil house. Outside her window, the moon shone full and much too white, so bright it resembled an oncoming headlight bearing down upon her from the sky.

Jesse stood stock-still by the window at full attention, watching her. He gave a half bark that ended in a whine and a whimper.

Marietta hurried him down the stairs before her mother or a neighbor heard him and complained.

"Eeeeeeyowrrrr!"

The scream came from somewhere outside, maybe a cat?

By the time Marietta reached the kitchen and sent Jesse through the patio door, the enemy invader had left. She shushed Jesse once more and returned to bed.

***

Early Wednesday, the weather relented with great reluctance and warmed just enough for a harsh red haze to glare down like murder from the sun. The crimson glow painted the surface of the lake until it appeared bloody, and then rose higher in the sky to reflect off the windows of the downtown skyscrapers until they blazed like towering infernos.

The morning sun faded to a vague sugary pink and orange by the time Susan shoved Jesse's nose away from her while she finished trimming last year's dead leaves off her rose hedges. Their neighbor, Mr. Johnson, was of the classic nosy variety which is why Susan insisted that Roy plant the hedges in the backyard rather than the front yard in the first place. No matter. Mr. Johnson, who admired Susan's beautiful face as well as her rose hedges, soon found a small opening through the sharp thorny bristles and spoke through the hedge now.

"Poor kitty. I found it when I turned off my sprinklers and buried it so it wouldn't draw rodents."

"Disgusting. People are so irresponsible with their animals." Susan hacked with vicious precision at the hedge in hopes that Mr. Johnson would receive the hint.

Oblivious, Mr. Johnson nodded his agreement and peered with interest at Jesse who barked his love for life to the world and chased butterflies around the backyard.

"My condolences on your loss, Mrs. Brazil." He took another breath as if to hold forth on more of his musings.

Fed up, Susan turned away and thus rewarded Mr. Johnson with a view of her backside in a stiff, militaristic march towards the patio door.

Inside the kitchen, Marietta clunked into a chair and reached for a glob of honey to spread on her toast. Susan shut the patio door in Jesse's hurt doggy face.

"Mom, I was just thinking about Aunt Stephanie again."

Washing her hands, Susan didn't turn around. "You know you can always talk to me, Marietta. That's what I'm here for."

"When do you think they'll stop showing the video of Stephanie's... you know, the chemical attack?"

Marietta managed to sneak a peek at the television while Susan fought the rose hedges. Early morning news came to excited life with screams and cries and first responder commentary. Helicopters and news vans still buzzed with excitement around Cadis Industries like flies on diminishing piles of excrement. That's all she managed to see before Susan headed back to the kitchen.

"They will never stop," Susan said. "Not until the next fire or three-mile car pileup. Whenever police are around, that's when the cameras come out. Blood money."

"People seem so angry with her."

Susan sighed, finally finished with her hands, and sat down. "They're agitating for action against a dead woman. But I let all of them know that this family is not interested in scandal. It's over. Stephanie wanted to die, now she's dead."

"Why do you keep saying that?"

"Because it's true. There's nothing else to be done and there's nothing else to say. By the way, stop watching television, like I told you. And don't answer the phone." Susan paused. "Like I told you."

"Mom..."

"We have no comment."

"You already told me that."

"Yes, I did, didn't I? Now remember that."

"Mom, I know!" Marietta waited a moment. "Do you miss her?"

"Yes. Yes, I do. Despite all of the strange behavior and the negativity, she was my sister."

"When was the last time you saw her before she killed herself?"

Susan fiddled with the salt and pepper shakers. "Months ago."

...threatened me last week... Susan said that on the phone. Who had she been talking to? Grandma?

"She'd been drinking again. Probably drugs too. And there were always these strange bruises on her legs. She fell in with a bad crowd. Different men, likely." Susan shook her head with slow sorrow. "She had a destructive personality. I didn't want any of that around my house or my daughter."

Marietta waited to see if her mother would say more. Susan stood up and looked through the patio door. "She threatened to hurt you, you know. That's when I cut her off completely."

Marietta's eyes widened in surprise. Not long ago, a disheveled woman stood motionless across the street from her high school. The woman stared at Marietta while she sat on the front steps and waited for the bell to ring for first class.

"Look at that homeless lady." One of her classmates snickered and pointed.

"Yeah man," said another boy. "Looks like she keeps saying 'baby' over and over."

A spear of horror shot through Marietta where she sat frozen with dread. Not this again. Not her. She always knew her mother's sister at a glance. Not once, not ever, had Susan ever left the house with a strand of hair out of place or a wrinkle in her clothing.

"Dude, she wants you to be her baby, man. Go on over there and be her baby for her." The boys laughed together.

Marietta remained seated, full of consternation. Her face heated, fully aflame.

The other boy shoved the first boy. "Nah, look bro. Look! She brought a garbage bag full of sack lunch for you. Go get your lunch, dude!"

They boys jostled back-and-forth until Marietta couldn't take it anymore.

"Leave her alone!" she shouted and ran inside the school in fear that Stephanie would call out to her. Then she felt ashamed of that fear.

"Marietta..." one of the boys called after her. Marietta kept going.

She never told anyone about Stephanie's random visits to her school. She decided not to mention anything to Susan now. It wasn't like it mattered anymore anyway.

Susan spoke over her shoulder as she went upstairs. "Remember to feed and walk Jesse because I'm not getting back until about ten tonight."

Marietta dumped half a bag of dog food in a mixing bowl and filled the plastic sink tub with water. She shoved it all through the patio door.

***

Later in the day, after an afternoon of mall and movie adventures, she and Roy had dinner at their favorite seafood restaurant. Susan had flown home to Wayfarer right after breakfast to attend Stephanie's funeral service.

"Dad, did Aunt Stephanie hate me?"

Roy's hands stilled from cutting into his steak. "Stephanie had a hard time in life. She... often acted out her pain and anger because she didn't know a better way to deal with it. I wouldn't say she hated you, though." He frowned and shook his head, "No," he said, and then picked up his knife and fork.

"Is she happy now?"

"I don't know. I'd like to think so."

"Did anyone love her?"

Roy put down his knife and fork. "Of course, honey. She was loved." He picked up his glass of lemonade.

"Did you love her?" This time, Roy paused so long that Marietta didn't think he would answer. He finally remembered to take a drink and set down the glass. Her father seemed uneasy. It was something kind of strange, the stick with which he'd been beaten.

"She was part of the family," Roy said, at last. Then he changed the subject and asked Marietta about school.

***

The house was dark when her father pulled into the driveway beside the decrepit station wagon. Somehow, some way, it passed city inspections. As usual, Roy asked her, "You're taking care of the engine, right? You take care of your engine and your engine takes care of you."

"Daaad. Yes."

"Checking all the fluid levels like I taught you and the..."

"Yes!"

"What about the oil?"

"Daddy! I'm taking care of my car!"

"If you take care of your car..."

"Daddy, come on. You just said that."

"All right, all right." Roy cleared his throat. "Ah, look, I would wait for your mother to get home, but..." But you're afraid of her, Marietta finished the thought for him.

"...I've got to get up early for work tomorrow," her father finished in a rush. "You'll be okay?"

"Dad, I'm sixteen, not six. Mom's already on her way back. She said she'll be home by ten. That's what she said this morning."

"Right," Roy laughed. "Sixteen, not six. Okay, I'm sorry. See you soon, sweetheart."

After much melodramatic honking of his car horn and rolling down of his window and waving out of the driver's side, Marietta finally shooed her father away, then closed and locked the front door behind her. She didn't tell her father that an empty house meant opportunity. And that opportunity meant exploration. Or that exploration meant answers!

Maybe.

Inside Susan's medicine cabinet, Marietta found a half-empty bottle of what her mother called 'nerve pills.' Grandma warned Marietta early and often to not argue or talk back to Susan because stress made Susan feel bad, made her nerves nervous, or something. That's why Susan stayed home most days and didn't work. That's what Grandma said.

On the back of a mirror on the inside of the door to Susan's closet hung a restraining order against Stephanie dated a week previous to Stephanie's death. Marietta bit her lip and decided that she wasn't sure what that meant. Inside a barely visible slot built underneath the night stand beside her mother's bed, lay a small handgun. It looked like a toy. Marietta cocked her head to the side and blinked. The weapon at her mother's bedside didn't make sense. The gun had to be an optical illusion. Marietta reached out to touch it.

Headlights beamed across the walls of her mother's bedroom which faced the street and driveway. Marietta heard a familiar engine shut off. She used the early warning to race around her mother's room, shutting doors and cabinets and drawers.

From the driveway, Susan watched without expression as her bedroom light cut off.

***

Marietta jogged down the hallway towards her own bedroom. She yanked at her clothes, snatched those off, and stuffed them into the hamper. She turned off her bedroom light and dove into bed. She pulled the covers up to her chin and tried to slow her breathing just in case Susan came to check on her. Just when sleep finally arrived to carry her away to dreamland, she heard her mother's footsteps outside her bedroom door.

The door opened. Marietta deepened her breathing and waited to see what Susan would do. But nothing happened. Susan simply closed the door and walked down the hall to her own room.

In the still of the night, Marietta worked up enough courage to open Stephanie's secret journal again. She read by the night light. None of the pages had dates. She had no way of knowing when Stephanie had recorded her deranged ideas. So Marietta closed her eyes and let the book fall open to a random page.

> Papa, to me, was a superhero. Large and tall. Always helping people and fixing things. Sometimes he told us about the war. Two wars he fought. Three if you count the war at home for civil rights. He was like Captain America and Superman and Shaft and Luke Cage all rolled into one. I tell myself that. I like to think so. But not really. Back then he was Invisible Man eclipsed by Mama's so-called godly goody goodness. I hate Sundays.

Behind Marietta's closed eyes, images floated in and out of her body. The smoke drifted up and cleared away. She saw her mother. It looked like her mother? But no. This was not she of the metal clips and clamped hair, nor the chignon or French twist. Not Susan. The wild spread of bird's nest black hair and the near fanatic glitter in her eyes gave Stephanie away every time.

"Marietta! Where's my baby?" Stephanie screamed. "Where's my baby? Marietta!"

The voice intruded and clanged against the dreamscape. It no longer fit. The voice jarred her awake and, for once, Marietta felt grateful to hear Susan's yell up the stairs.

"Marietta! Wake up! You're going to be late for school!"

She groaned and looked at the clock. Great. She'd overslept. She'd have to make up time after school in the library with all the other social misfits. She didn't even want to go back to class today. And why should she? What was the point? Today was Thursday. She may as well have stayed home the whole week. Dad would have let her, but whatever.

"Marietta!"

"I'm up!"

"Well, get moving! You're supposed to feed and walk Jesse before school."

Marietta dragged over to the shower and slapped at her body with handfuls of liquid soap. She scrubbed a toothbrush through her mouth with a decided lack of enthusiasm, and then snapped a rubber band over her tangle of curly dark brown hair without combing through it. But per MTV, big-sized uncombed hair was the style these days.

Unbelievable. Susan was still on her lecture when Marietta emerged from the bathroom. "He's jumping around all over the kitchen. You need to..."

Oh geez, just take the pills, Susan. Take them all.

"Mom, I'm coming!"

Marietta rushed downstairs. She slung her backpack over her shoulders. Sure enough, Susan's bathrobe bore paw-printed evidence that Jesse had tried to climb up and over her. She looked unusually disheveled this morning. Jesse licked at Susan's face and hands until she knocked him away. Then he growled at her.

Marietta looked at the clock, which Susan noticed.

"Oh no, you don't..."

"Mom, I have to go." Marietta, all of a sudden, didn't want to stay home. In fact, she welcomed the chance to get out of the house. "I'm already late for class. You know how they are..."

"Marietta!"

Marietta grabbed fruit off the dining room table and made for the front door while Susan tried to shove Jesse out of the patio door.

"They're gonna make me stay after."

"Jesse, outside! Marietta..."

Jesse decided to make his stand at the patio door and barked his protest.

"Marietta!" The irritation in Susan's voice brought her up short. "I told you about this!"

Lady, who are you anymore anyway?

"Jesse, go!" Jesse growled louder at Susan's angry tone.

"Mom, just for today. Please?"

"Go!" Susan shouted.

Marietta decided that this last shout was for her. She shrugged and ran to the station wagon.

She pulled the old elephant of a car out of the driveway with a great creaking of the joints that she knew she'd better oil before her father said something. Snaps, crackles, and pops drowned out the radio as the old engine strained to haul the weight of the car up the hill to the main road that led to her school.

She knew about Baby Alicia. Most of the family did. They synchronized their stories. Everyone presented an unshakable, united front that no outsider could penetrate.

Forgiven, but never forgotten by those who knew her, even before her final breakdown, Aunt Stephanie had become urban legend. The whispers, the averted eyes, the insinuations, the tight clutching of newborns whenever she arrived in the vicinity... It had all become too much for Stephanie to bear.

Once upon a time, way back before Marietta's memory began recording her life, Marietta knew that she and Alicia played together. That's what everyone said. Well, that's what Susan always said. Their birthdays were only three months apart.

Marietta sighed and turned the corner. If Alicia were still here, Alicia would have understood her like no other. With Alicia as her best friend and cousin, things would have turned out so much better. Marietta could have been cool at school.

Marietta would call up Alicia. "What movie to you wanna see tonight, girl?"

Alicia would pop gum at the phone receiver. "I don't know. Are you and Darius still talking?"

"No! He's way too immature. All he wants to do is play basketball. But you know what? Reggie stepped to me the other day trying to see what was up."

Alicia would gasp in outrage at Reggie's audacity. "Reggie already got a girl!"

"He sure didn't act like it!" Marietta would giggle.

"Don't let him play you!" Alicia would advise with a high-pitched shriek.

Or... Alicia would hang out in Marietta's room. They would experiment with different hair gels and glitter and wear matching clothes.

"What do you wanna do?"

"I don't know. What do you wanna do?"

"I don't know. Girl, let's go to the mall," Alicia would say.

"Cool with me. I need some shoes. Dad already said I could go to senior prom even though I'm a junior. And if Darius doesn't have his game straight, then I might go with Reggie and be like..."

And then after a flirty wave to the fellas, girlish laughter would accompany her and Alicia's mutual social consultations and they would strut arm-in-arm through the food court at the mall.

Marietta parked in the school's parking lot. As the engine sputtered, she hurried off to the attendance office to check herself in, finishing her muttered conversations with Alicia along the way. But really, there was no Alicia. Neither was there a Reggie or Darius or even a senior prom. The woulds, the coulds, and the shoulds and what ifs didn't exist because they never happened.

There were only her thoughts, the ones she had while she sat at a lunch table by herself. She tried not to be noticed by the other students. Ten to one, she exceeded her own expectations in this regard. She hoped no one would ask her about Stephanie today. As Susan told her, she had nothing to say.

No one asked.

She and her aunt didn't have the same last name. They didn't look alike either. Though her mother and Stephanie were identical with the pale skin and long black glossy hair courtesy of Grandma Madison, Marietta's dark brown hair and pecan-like skin and hazel eyes remained her birthright from her father's family, the Brazils. She resembled her father more than anyone else.

So it should be okay at school for the rest of today, Marietta hoped. So why worry?

CHAPTER 4   SUSAN

The phone rang about one in the afternoon at the Brazil home. By then, Susan had showered, dressed, and clamped down her hair. All morning, Jesse rampaged through the kitchen. The dog bothered her and plucked at her nerves like a first chair violinist tortured the tautest of violin strings.

His dirt trails twisted and turned in a path of adventure and exploration back-and-forth on the kitchen floor and represented a total loss of her control over her household. And now, someone called her and put her further behind her disinfection schedule.

"Oh it's you."

"Yeah, I'm excited too." When all else failed with Susan, sarcasm served as Roy's last and most desperate line of defense. "Susan, I'm worried about Marietta."

"Aren't we all? She's not taking care of that dog you gave her like she promised, Roy."

"No. I mean she asked me about Stephanie last night."

"What about?" she asked.

But Roy overheard Susan's in drawn breath and homed in on her rare show of weakness. "That got you, didn't it?"

"Roy, don't even start with me."

"Whether Stephanie was happy and did anyone love her."

"Well, I guess you would know the answer to that." Susan could be a stone cold bitch when she really put her back into it. She was aiming for Olympic gold today.

"I'm moving on, Susan. This is not about you."

Silence.

"I think the Bible might have caused Marietta to think about it a little more."

"Bible? Marietta doesn't read the Bible."

"She didn't tell you?"

"Tell me what, Roy?"

"Stephanie sent Marietta a Bible to my condo last week, care of me."

"What? Roy! We discussed this before, didn't we? We weren't going to allow..."

"It was just a Bible, Susan. It was still in the wrapper."

"But still..."

"Susan, calm down! It was in the wrapper. I..."

Susan's voice sliced into his ear canal like a hot knife through butter over the telephone line. "Why didn't you tell me?"

"I didn't think it was that big a deal."

"Kind of like the damn dog wasn't a big deal, right? You wanted Marietta to have a chance to see it first. Right?"

"Susan, listen..."

"Right? Wait a second." Susan dropped the phone receiver, shouted something, and then picked it up again. "Let me call you back. He's barking again."

Half an hour later, Jesse quieted down and like any other married but separated couple, Roy and Susan picked up their argument at the same point with unerring precision. They continued the vigorous back-and-forth volleys at a steady pace for another hour and half.

***

Marietta, lost in thought at school, read Aunt Stephanie's hidden journal behind a textbook during dull moments in class:

> Mother, on the other hand, was a different sort. A mad scientist who built Frankenstein's monster in her secret laboratory inside the kitchen pantry. I used to pretend that. But when she canned fruit and vegetables with the kitchen blazing hot, she did look a little crazy. I have to be honest. Once, she slapped me at church. I told her it seemed like a nightclub with the lead soprano as lounge singer and the offering basket collecting the cover charge. All the women dancing for the men. So, apparently, I'm a blasphemer as well as a liar and a thief. I hate Sundays. Hate them hate them hate them!

"What!" Marietta shrieked into the school secretary's telephone receiver. The secretary paged her from the library where she made up time for being late to school. For the first time, when her name came over the intercom, her classmates noticed her. The other detainees in holding actually turned their heads around and looked her direction.

"Ooooh! Someone's in trouble with Mommy and Daddy," one of them said with a delighted smirk.

The librarian motioned for her to pick up her belongings and go amidst the hoots and giggles of the other bored children.

"Marietta, I'm your father. I know you've been through a lot with Aunt Stephanie's death and things. Now, you're going through puberty..."

"Dad. Are you kidding me? I'm at school right now."

"Well, you're at that time in life when everything changes."

"Oh my God. Daddy, please don't put either of us through this. I'm begging you." Marietta glanced around to see if any of her classmates could overhear, but she was alone.

Marietta lowered her voice and looked around again, still apprehensive. "Who told you I was on drugs? I mean, where is this even coming from?"

"Your mother and I talked it over and she..."

"Mom? Mom told you I was taking drugs?"

"Marietta..."

"Dad, it's not true! I would never do that, I promise! Drugs are stupid!"

"Marietta, I know the separation must be hard on you. Hard to understand."

"But Dad..."

"I promise you, Marietta. I'm not going anywhere. We'll get it figured out real soon. It's going to be okay, sweetheart." Somewhere in Marietta's vicinity, a toilet flushed.

"Dad, I gotta go!"

Marietta hung up the phone and waved good-bye to the school's secretary who walked in humming a happy tune, her last task for the day accomplished without a hitch.

Marietta walked to the school's parking lot where she sat shaking inside her station wagon. Something like a shower curtain separated her from the natural world. Not the windshield. A clear bubble covered in grey film gathered around her, inside the car with her. It wanted to stop her breath. Marietta coughed and clawed at the empty air in front of her like a wild animal trying to escape a cage. But the bubble wrapped itself tighter around her like the janky plastic that covered Stephanie's Bible.

"What would you do?" Marietta looked at Aunt Stephanie's Bible as if she waited for it to speak. She closed her eyes and allowed the pages to fall open at random.

> Arby used to look at me as if wondering the same thing. Did she? I always looked away. I hate that doubt in him and me. But there's nothing I can do. Nothing I can ever do! Sometimes I hate my sister and the things she says and does. We can't choose our family. We just love our family. Or, at least, we tell everyone we do.

Ever since she started reading Aunt Stephanie's journal, Marietta's head tilted off-center like a funhouse. She saw things that weren't there, heard things that weren't said, spoke to people who disappeared into white haze. She dreamed things that she knew she shouldn't think about while awake.

Life seemed just left of center. Off-kilter, for sure and in need of calibration. But Marietta knew for sure that she wasn't on drugs. This one thing she knew for a fact. And this meant that someone was confused. But the confusion didn't come from her.

A clear, warm afternoon brightened the grayscape of Lake City's greasy streets, slathered with mud and polluted snow. Determined, Marietta held the steering wheel in her fists as she drove home. Nerves or no nerves, the showdown with her mother would happen.

***

"Oh Marietta, Marietta. Your father is really not himself lately. I'm sure you've seen it. I think... Stephanie's death affected him more than he lets on."

Susan's dark eyes searched Marietta's hazel gaze with thorough care. Marietta neither blinked nor flinched. She could tell that Susan didn't like this situation. This confrontation with her daughter had no precedent.

"I've always had my suspicions, you know. I heard the rumors. The two of them." A pause went by as Susan tested the atmosphere of the room. "Stephanie was... obsessed with us. Me, Roy, you."

"Me? Why me?"

Susan nodded her head, pleased. "You represent the daughter she always wanted but wasn't woman enough to raise. You know what happened to Baby Alicia, don't you?"

Marietta looked at her own hands, nodding.

"Stephanie has always been... unwell, even when we were children. No one in the family trusted her. Even Roy. But I think, maybe, he still had feelings. I know that she did."

Marietta felt tiny prickles at the back of her neck. The thoughts in her head, the things she'd learned the past few days shifted, clanged, and scraped against her mother's words, resisting.

"Mom, I think if Aunt Stephanie got the help she needed, she wouldn't have hurt me."

Jesse barked again. Susan stood up with clear irritation at the double team and looked out of Marietta's bedroom window which faced the backyard.

"You're a child, Marietta." Susan waved away Marietta's protests, dismissing their significance to the conversation. "Yes, you are. You don't understand. Stephanie couldn't function in normal society. She was hostile and paranoid. All she had was that job. She'd go to work. She'd come home. Work. Home. Work. Home. She didn't have anything else. Couldn't hold a man. Or a baby. Dear God, she couldn't even handle a simple thing like reality. She thought she was saving the world."

Susan let out a derisive laugh and looked at Marietta, part of her face shadowed by the curtain.

"She was a robot! They used her. Used and used her. And then she just..." Susan turned away from the window and looked into Marietta's mirror, speaking to her own reflection. "That's why she killed herself and everyone else."

Marietta thought her mother never looked more like a mannequin than she did at that moment. *Susan works in mysterious ways.* Someone said it long ago. The air in the room seemed drier than normal. Marietta cleared her throat, nervous.

"Look, I mean... just as long as you know I'm not getting high, Mom."

Susan smiled, smoothed her tight bun of raven hair, and turned away from the mirror. She sat back down on Marietta's bed, patting the space next to her in an invitation. Marietta didn't move from her doorway.

"Of course not, Marietta. No one who knows you and loves you would believe something like that." Susan paused as if a new thought just occurred to her.

"Oh yes. Your father did mention one other thing--some sort of gift you received from Stephanie."

So, at last, they came to the real purpose of the conversation and the real reason she'd found her mother in her room.

"He was concerned that you felt the need to be so secretive about it."

Marietta felt thin, invisible filaments stroke her body like silk. The soft, light touches tested her, and then crawled across her scalp.

"I wasn't being secretive. I just didn't think it was important."

"Oh, then can I see it?"

The filaments moved down from her scalp and gathered at a vulnerable spot on the back of her neck. The strands pressed against her spine light as a feather. "I'm... I'm still looking through it."

Susan narrowed her eyes. "That's funny. I don't remember you showing such enthusiasm for the Good Book before."

Marietta's heart did something funny in her chest. Rarely, actually never had she ever defied her mother. It felt scary doing so today. The tension in the room drew tighter. The filaments gathered around Marietta's throat and tightened. She coughed.

"As a matter of fact, I seem to remember you telling me that the kids at church were phony and fake."

The soft pressure on her throat made Marietta's voice sound high and unnatural to her own ears. "Well, they are." She fiddled with objects on her nightstand.

"You say the same thing about the kids at your school."

"It's true."

"Marietta, Marietta, Marietta. You'll never make any friends with that uppity attitude, miss." Susan laughed. "Remember your twelfth birthday, how just the family showed? Remember that boyfriend you nearly had? And now look at you."

Marietta's eyes widened. "Why are you bringing all that up? That's the past. I don't care anymore. No one does."

"Own up to your mistakes, Marietta," Susan advised with calm.

"I'm more than the mistakes I made, Mom."

"No. You are the mistakes you made Marietta. We all are."

The cobwebs that covered Marietta felt sticky and gross. They smothered.

"Your father's going crazy trying to figure out how to please you despite it all. I'm doing all that I can. And you can't even keep your promises to us. Now you're hiding secrets and God only knows what else. When I think of all you could have been and chose not to be, I lay down and cry sometimes. I do."

Marietta felt herself begin to shrivel inside, but Susan wasn't nearly done.

"You act so much like your father's side of the family sometimes. Those people..." Susan curled her lip. "Remember that summer program at your father's firm?"

Marietta's voice wobbled despite her effort to control it. "Mom, you're not even allowing me a chance, are you? I did a good job at work last summer. Dad said so." Her begging sounded so much like her father's and she hated the sound of it coming from her own mouth.

Susan smiled with a great show of sorrow and suffering. "Just determined to create a nervous breakdown out of thin air, aren't you?"

"I am not having a nervous breakdown! I'm just..."

"Calm down the hysterics, Marietta."

"I'm not hysterical!"

"Aren't you?" Susan tut-tutted. "I think I'll talk to a doctor about your antisocial behavior. I should have a long time ago because you may need medication. But we'll see."

"Mom, being shy is not anti-social."

"And denial is not just a river in Egypt."

"I'm not in denial! I just..."

"Soooo defensive, Marietta." Susan smiled, finally satisfied. Marietta in the corner pocket. "As I've told you before, more listening, less talking."

"Stop it!" Horrified, Marietta backed two steps away and choked back a sob. "Just stop, Mom."

"Marietta!" Susan exclaimed. "I think you'd better calm down before you end up like Stephanie."

Marietta gasped as if she'd taken a two by four to the face. All the air drained from the room. And still her mother sat with no change of expression even as her words knifed deep into Marietta's soul.

"Shut up!" Marietta ran down the hall to the stairs. "Shut up! Shut up!" She yelled it over her shoulder as she slammed open the front door and threw herself across the threshold.

CHAPTER 5   ROY

From the backyard, Jesse's barks rose in volume as a distant reflection of Marietta's own frustration. She started the station wagon, and then dragged the old behemoth up to the top of the hill. Once on the main road, she drove an aimless path. Finally, she parked near Lake City's airport for an hour. She watched airplanes take off and land, bright lights streaking up and away, or down.

Just last night, Susan landed here and brought back some new kind of mood from Wayfarer with her. And last night, Marietta learned some secrets about her mother. But she still didn't know what it all meant. So she picked at the cold remains of a fast food takeout meal.

At last, she admitted her real fear. Is Susan right about me?

Marietta opened Stephanie's Bible to a random page and read by the station wagon's interior light. The hopeless words of a crazed, dead woman advised her from the grave.

Mama used to look at me so sad as if she didn't know how such a crazy child came to live in her house and what should she do about it. Nothing I said ever got through to her. Or, if it did, she took the easy road. She always thought the worst of me and she expected the worst from me. Pretended she didn't see. I AM NOT CRAZY!!! I hate Sundays!!!!!

Marietta slammed the book shut, heart pounding. Stephanie... Stephanie... That's why you sent the Bible to me!

I'm moving out.

Marietta spoke aloud to the darkness, her mind made up. "I'm gonna go home, pack up, and move out. Take Jesse with me. Live with Dad."

Susan was right on one point, at least. She hadn't looked after Jesse like she should. Poor boy.

"She's a liar! All that stuff about Dad. How could she? Just fourteen months and I can leave this place and never look back. I just need to make it to eighteen, that's all. Finish high school and then ghost."

Marietta crumpled the food wrappers littered across the front seat and stuffed them into the takeout bag.

"I am not a drug addict. I am not an alcoholic. I am not anti-social. I am not uppity. I am not irresponsible. I am not in denial. I am not crazy."

Marietta took a deep breath, and then yelled it across the airport landing fields. "I am not Aunt Stephanie!" The shout died down to one last sob. Marietta realized that if she didn't act soon, she would, indeed, become Aunt Stephanie.

"That's how she gets you." She turned the key in the ignition. "She whips you with your own emotions. That's how she got Stephanie. That's how she got Dad. Don't let her get you, Marietta." She's not gonna get me.

Marietta made the turn off the main road and headed down the hill to her family's home.

"Play it cool for fourteen more months. That's nothing. Just stay calm." Marietta muttered the words like a mantra. "Don't go out like that. Maintain your composure"

Distracted by the dark and her own agitated thoughts, Marietta didn't notice Susan until the tail lights of the truck in front of her on the downhill decline swung left. The headlights of Marietta's station wagon marked Susan as a target while she dumped something into the trashcans by the roadside. Marietta gasped and slammed her foot onto the brake.

The brake stuck to the floor. The heavy station wagon submitted, as all things on Earth must, to the laws of gravity. Once in motion, it stayed in motion. The creaky vehicle picked up speed. Marietta screamed and stomped at the brake, which remained immobile.

Marietta yanked the steering wheel. But the station wagon lost confidence and no longer obeyed its driver. The old elephant decided to obey physics instead and swerved this way and that, and then back to its original trajectory.

Susan screamed at least once before impact. Marietta heard her. Then scraped and gouged by the brick corner of the garage at sixty miles per hour, the station wagon screamed. Marietta lay across the car horn. Susan lay across the driveway, where the station wagon tossed her out of its way like a sack of lumpy potatoes.

***

Pain.
No. Not quite pain.
White mists and drifting smoke hid the pain behind a cloudy, foggy light. Was she alive? Marietta lay still for a few moments and tried to figure it out.

Something helped her to breath. But someone else nearby breathed too. She heard the breaths.

"Where am I?"

A familiar voice answered, "Marietta, you're in the hospital. It's Friday morning."

She focused her eyes on Roy who looked back at her, grief-stricken. "Do you remember the accident?" he asked her.

Yes, she remembered. That was the reason she didn't want to wake up.

"Mom?"

"Honey, Susan..." He swallowed. "Your mother is dead."

Marietta closed her eyes. Where were her mists now when she needed them most?

"You were hurt too."

She didn't answer him. The pain in her middle already told her that she'd been punished.

"Marietta, what happened?"

Finally, she broke. The tears came and increased the pain. "Daddy," she whimpered.

Roy pushed the buzzer next to her bed. Marietta tried not to shake because movement hurt her so much.

"Daddy." She used to call him that all the time when she was a small girl. "The brake. I tried the brake. I tried. I tried! Daddy, I'm sorry!"

The nurse came into the room at a run.

***

"Eventually, she'll have to give us a statement."

Friday evening, Roy Brazil sank back onto the sofa of his suburban condo with the weary confusion of a single father of a teenage daughter. The news affected Marietta badly. He should have waited. And now, this.

"Please allow my daughter the time she needs to recover from the accidental death of her mother and her own injuries.

She is suffering severe pain and trauma right now. She just had surgery."

The two policemen exchanged a glance. "We're just doing our job, sir. I mean, what with the restraining order and the death of her sister..." The other cop coughed and picked up the thread. "Your wife's neighbor, Mr. Johnson, said he saw Mrs. Brazil hitting the dog with dog food from the patio door almost midday yesterday."

"Look, you guys. Marietta just woke from the surgery a few hours ago."

"He also reported someone screaming and the dog barking about three hours or so later the same day."

Roy stared at the cop in silence.

The cop gave it another go. "He said he's pretty sure he heard a gunshot."

"What?" Roy said, with an incredulous shake of his head. "That guy... he's... somewhat senile. Trying to make his life more interesting than it actually is."

"Well, okay. None of the other neighbors corroborates that account. And we saw no sign of the dog."

Roy shrugged, helpless to provide additional information.

"Sir, does it concern you at all that the dog is now missing?"

The cop actually had the nerve to allow his question to sound like a reprimand. Roy closed his eyes and heaved a great sigh. "I can tell you that Marietta said something about her brakes before she went under. That's it. That's all she said."

The cop who took the lead raised an eyebrow and opened his mouth to ask more questions.

At this point, Roy threw up his hands. "I can't do this right now. I just came home to change clothes and then I have to get back to the hospital to see about my daughter."

Roy stood up. He walked to the front door and held it open. "Please leave my home."

"Sir, I apologize, but..."

"Please, just go." Still, the officers hesitated. Roy opened the door wider. "I'm asking you. Please."

"We'll stay in touch, sir." Putting their hats back on and tipping the brims, they left.

While Marietta slept through the night, Roy drove back into the city. He remembered the layout of the Brazil house. Even more important, he still had a key. After all, it had only been nine months since Susan pointed him towards the front door.

That night, years of enmity, buried and smothered under a shallow layer of false, brittle forgiveness burst forth in a hideous, monstrous display of pure, raw, undiluted hatred. He'd had a front row seat at a private screening of the live-action horror movie that played out in the master bedroom.

For one terrifying moment, something in Susan's eyes seemed not quite human. Then the ice came down again and his marriage returned to its default wintry setting. He left his family on his wife's terms. He had no choice. She would have taken him to court. She would have told her tales and cast her spells. She would have told Marietta anything and everything... and then some. He would never have seen his daughter again.

Susan was gone now, but her shadow endured and blackened the night. He would have to make sure that Marietta knew it wasn't her fault. She would never be to blame. Susan's death would not ruin his daughter's life. Not on his watch.

If Jesse managed to escape, then that made him the lucky one of them all. Unlikely to have happened though. Susan practiced vigilance in keeping him penned up in the back yard. Jesse figured out in just a few days what it took years for almost everyone else, including him, to finally see. Susan's beauty meant nothing to Jesse who had a direct line on Susan's soul or lack thereof. Animal instincts remained unmarred by the false human comfort of pretense.

Roy's own mother, father, and older sister tried to tell him about Susan's unique personality. They'd recoiled from his wife from the beginning. Something was very wrong, they said. His relationship with his people grew more distant every year when he chose to bury common sense under his love for, or maybe fear of, Susan.

He defended his wife with such vigor that he drove his family of birth away. Marietta only knew her maternal grandparents.

Even now, in the midst of his pain, despite this recent tragedy, he did not reach out to them. Neither did they reach out to him, if they even knew what happened. No one called or came to visit in a familial show of support for Susan's death. The distance that pained him was his own fault because he'd rebuffed them time and again. By now, they got the message.

So he and Marietta were on their own. How would he continue to raise and guide a teenage daughter by himself? He had no clue. Not a single one. Well, first things first.

Roy found a flashlight in a kitchen drawer and used it to search the back yard for openings in the fence. No openings in the fence. He planted the rose hedges too close together for a dog to get through. Jesse would have hurt himself on the thorns if he made an attempt to escape Susan's custody. Well, maybe discouraged him, but not necessarily prevented him.

However, Roy did find a freshly-dug mound of dirt around a tree that he planted at least ten months ago... at Susan's insistence. Once he got a look at what lay under the dirt at the base of the tree, he knew he would have to wake up John, his veterinarian buddy.

***

The clock radio's glowing red display explained that nine o'clock in the evening caused the darkness of the hospital room.

Marietta spoke into the intercom. "Nurse, please help me. I need to find my Bible but I can't move."

The nurse entered the room with a ready smile. She turned on the light and began to poke around. She opened a small cabinet beside Marietta's bed with a flourish of triumph.

"Found it!"

The twist to Marietta's mouth appeared more of a grimace than a smile.

"Oh honey, would you like something for the pain?" As she expected, the nurse's patient answered in the affirmative. Pain medication was rarely a hard sell in a hospital.

Marietta reawakened at five the next morning. The back cover of Stephanie's Bible lay open. Inside the back cover, behind a map of the Middle East, Marietta found another sheet of the secret journal:

> Today I pretended that I was normal. I pretended that I caught Susan's baby before she fell. That I had a daughter and a husband who loved me. I wanted to be better, you know. I did try. Someone always there to remind me and everyone else who I was. What I did. What I let happen. It was an accident! She was my niece and I loved her too! I begged and begged Susan to forgive me. For everything. You were the best thing that I ever did with my life. I promise you this. But I had to make it right. And that is the only reason why. It is over for me now. No more babies. No more nothing. I just can't wake up to face it anymore. I used to hate Sundays so much. But not anymore. But even though Arby

doesn't know, I know you will be all right. I
just have this feeling. I love you Alicia.

Behind this journal entry, Marietta found a creased,
yellowed letter addressed to Stephanie. The writing was shaky.

Trust in God, Stephanie. Except His will be
done. She have took to Susan. She never
told you and Susan apart. Let them live. You
will be blest and so will she. We all love you.
Mama.

She. She. Who was... she? What?

The morning hospital routine interrupted her thoughts.
The nurse checked her. The doctor checked her. Then the
nurse came back for hygiene. Then the orderly came with
breakfast.

Marietta usually spent every summer in Wayfarer with
Grandma and Grandpa Madison. But last year, Marietta put
on a grown woman's dress shirt and slacks with pride in order
to work as an intern in her father's financial services firm. She
had her own little desk and telephone. No one called her
except her dad to summon copies of documents and coffee, or
to stuff envelopes, or to fetch a box of paper clips. However,
she developed keen expertise at unjamming the copy machine,
and the shredder, and the fax machine, and the laminator.

She'd even met a boy at work, but the relationship hadn't
gone anywhere, which impressed Susan not at all. Thoughts of
Susan shriveled Marietta's insides. She preferred to focus
more on the mysteries inside Stephanie's journal right now
and less on what she'd done to her own mother.

Anyway, so last year, she spent a rare summer in Lake City.
Rose and Michael Madison trekked north on the slow road to
spend a week at the Brazil home. Then, at the Brazil's first and
last annual Fourth of July barbecue, a disheveled, wild-eyed

Stephanie arrived unannounced only to be restrained and escorted away from the stares and whispers of family, friends, and neighbors.

"Marietta, my baby!"

No. It couldn't be. No! Not her.

"It's not true. It can't be true," Marietta said aloud.

Drunk, high, and crazy--all of the above, all at the same time--that's what everyone said about that incident. Susan wept with misty beauty on Roy's shoulder as everyone rushed across the backyard to comfort her and her nerves. Then that quiet whisper slid across the potato salad.

"Susan works in mysterious ways."

The look on Grandma's face was not senility. That was the look of guilt. Then later that night, after the barbecue and after Grandma and Grandpa chugged away in the old RV, angry voices floated down the hallway from Roy and Susan's bedroom.

Then Roy left, her father gone, gone, gone. She saw her father only on weekends after that. The arctic silence between her parents burned Marietta's heart like frostbite. Marietta never asked them why. Susan never told. And neither did Roy. No one said a word.

The cold blanket of clouds burned away. Thoughts no longer scraped and shifted against each other. They slipped into place with the quiet, smooth glide of well-oiled hinges.

Arby. R.B. Roland Brazil.

No wonder she and Alicia looked so much alike in their photo albums. They would look alike. Their mothers were identical twins. The same man fathered them.

Did Roy suspect his daughter had been exchanged like a thing? Like a favorite sweater? Did he?

"How could they?" Marietta whispered. "Who am I?"

When she could not answer the question because she no longer knew, she laughed and laughed some more. Then she exhausted herself with tears. The sounds of her panic carried down the hallway to the nurse's station. Over the wails that echoed off her hospital room walls, she heard her nurse's shouts. The nurse rushed in with a needle at the ready. Marietta felt a prick on her arm like that of an insect bite. Soon after, the mists came back down and floated her away from such nonsense.

***

Roy found the letter crumpled in a ball inside Marietta's hand. Now he sat with his head in his hands, scarcely able to comprehend the monumental trick played on him (and Marietta) by Susan and Stephanie.

The fact that Susan failed to inform him that their birth daughter died went so far beyond decent and moral behavior, that he couldn't fully comprehend the sheer depravity behind it. He tried to follow the reasoning, but his mind kept shutting down before he completed the logic behind the cold equations.

The fact that Susan blackmailed Stephanie into giving up her own daughter and neither of them said a word... Everyone but he knew. And no one, not even Susan's mother found an inner conscience to tell him. Roy's mind finally shut the door on what he could never understand in ten lifetimes. He needed to focus on the here and now. And that was Marietta.

His daughter, for Marietta was the one person in this twisted world that he still understood, slept like the dead. Good thing because he was pretty sure she wouldn't welcome the sight of him sobbing over her. She didn't need to see all sorts of fluids leaking from his eyes, nose, and mouth. Disgusting. He grabbed a tissue off the nightstand.

No wonder the nurse sedated her. He could barely handle the information he just learned himself. All of their adult flaws exposed to teenage scrutiny had proven more than she could bear. How much would she hate the memories of Susan and Stephanie? How much of that hatred would she take out on him? He'd better brace for it.

Roy wadded the letter up in his hand with the used tissue and threw them both into the trash can with disgust. How would he get Marietta through all of this by himself? Stephanie's death. Susan's death.

The accident.

For that is what happened he decided with a fierce expression. No matter what anyone else said, Susan's death was an accident! The buck stopped with him and he would make damn sure that buck went no further.

Marietta said something about her brakes, didn't she? Yes, she did! It was a horrible, unexpected accident.

And Jesse. Marietta loved her dog, the dog he gave to her. He finally ended up doing something right and then... Susan, why? Why did you do such a thing? How could you?

Because Jesse made people happy and Susan couldn't stand that, that's why. The bullet lodged inside Jesse's skull came from a twenty-two, a woman's gun, John said. And that's when Roy knew. Susan. He'd left the gun next to Jesse's body at John's veterinarian clinic. His old friend agreed to take care of everything. No one would know, including Marietta.

Somewhere, somehow, Susan acquired the gun, even though it was illegal to carry or possess inside Lake City limits. But when had Susan ever cared about limits? Anything or anyone that got in her way...

Oh God.

Roy leaned forward and rested his elbows on his knees. He stared at the floor and tried to concentrate. He had no choice but to take more time off from work, which shouldn't be a problem. They knew his family was going through a tough time.

He could finish some things at home by phone and fax. If he did nothing else for the rest of his life, he would fix this. He and Marietta would still be a family. He needed to be a better father to her anyway. So then he would be a better father!

Roy stared in despair at the cold, white squares of the hospital floor through his fingers. Oh God, why have you forsaken the Brazils? Where are you now? Can't you spare any pity for us today?

A pair of thick, white shoes entered his periphery. Roy sighed but did not look up. He didn't feel in the mood for more small talk with the cheerful nurse. Tomorrow maybe. Not tonight.

"Sorry, sir," a quiet male voice said. "I just have to do a quick check here."

Roy frowned and lifted his head at the low-pitched voice. "But the other nurse just checked her. She's sleeping now."

A tattooed arm, inked with a dark blue sleeve of wild designs whipped across his vision. A shiny syringe filled with something murky flashed in an arc to stab into Marietta's intravenous line.

"Wait!" Roy stood up in protest. "What are you doing? The other nurse was just in here. She's already sedated. She doesn't..."

The man who Roland Brazil decided was not a nurse turned towards Marietta's father and pounced. After a struggle so brief that it broke the heart, Roy knew no more.

CHAPTER 6   GRANDPA

Even in April, the cold remains of winter held Lake City captive in a dirty, gritty, grayish oatmeal of snow and ice and pollution. The sky provided a dim gunmetal cover at dusk. Still, Grandpa Madison's ancient RV ground its steady way down the highway, battered by cold rain and greasy road splatters as cars and trucks roared past them, their drivers impatient and scornful.

Michael Madison's fuzzy white head raised so he could glance again at Marietta in the rear view mirror. One hour south of Lake City, he and his granddaughter still had twelve more hours on the road to Wayfarer. She'd scarcely said a word since they drove away from the hospital.

Sunday, Monday, and most of Tuesday--it took him three days to settle her affairs while she healed in the hospital room from the car accident guarded in shifts by hospital security and Lake City police. Clearly still in pain, she lay down now on the first row of seats behind him. The pain from her injuries would fade in a few weeks the doctors told him. But the psychological turmoil might take longer.

"How long?" he'd asked. No one knew the answer to that. But in the meantime, the hospital required Marietta's room. And it was past time for them to leave Lake City anyway, Michael Madison decided.

Marietta grew tired of meeting her grandfather's anxious eyes. She hated the sorrow and pity that she saw looking back at her. But most of all, she hated the unspoken questions. Both of Grandpa Madison's daughters perished in horrific manners one week apart. Stephanie died during her notorious suicide attack on Cadis Industries. Susan died when the grill from Marietta's station wagon knocked her into the next week.

Then Marietta's father met his maker also in a horrific manner. The family dog? Missing. Only Marietta remained of the House of Brazil with no clear explanations for anyone.

She wanted her grandfather to shout and to beat his fist upon the dashboard. That way, she had an excuse to shout back. Why didn't he point his finger at her? Why didn't he demand to hear the truth? She wanted to fight, scratch, throw and kick something! But Grandpa said nothing.

Well, so what? He was a hypocrite! So whatever! When Marietta felt tired from laying on her back, she gingerly eased up and stared out the windows as Midwestern prairies rolled under a dark sky like the ocean at night. Five hours on the road now, the waves undulated, rose, and twisted upwards until they formed a mountainscape.

Winner by default, because there was no one else who wanted her, Grandpa Madison drove the slow road up to Lake City to collect her from the hospital where someone murdered her father while she slept, oblivious. Marietta's nurse had run into Marietta's room after hearing a commotion down the hall. The nurse repeated once, twice, and then thrice to Lake City police that Marietta had been sedated and unaware of the events that transpired beside her hospital bed which resulted in her father's death. All Marietta knew is that she woke up in a new room with a flurry of activity outside her door. She received plenty of whispers by hospital staff, stares from hospital security, and glares from Lake City police.

"I don't know. I don't know. I don't know," was all that Marietta could answer between the crying jags that racked her injuries with sharper pain. Then the tears ran out and all she had left was a wounded, confused, dull sadness that bordered on catatonia.

Marietta stared at the hospital room wall until Grandpa Madison arrived to talk to the doctors and police. He left the hospital for hours then came back and reported to the back of Marietta's head that a realtor put the Brazil home on the market. All their fake family memories, including her father's condo, went to charity, estate sales, or rode with them to Wayfarer inside the olden times RV. Grandma stayed behind in Wayfarer to arrange services for Roy and Susan and to get Marietta's usual room ready for her arrival.

The bodies of Susan and Roy made the journey to Wayfarer separately. Marietta's dead parents would soon join Stephanie in the Madison family plot. The Brazils had indicated no interest in Marietta's whereabouts or welfare, nor that of Roy's.

Grandma's southern sugar honey ice tea voice made a quavering attempt at cheer over the hospital's telephone line. "Instead of visiting for the summer, Marietta, you'll finish high school here. And isn't it great that you already know some of the kids here? Like Tony from across the street? You remember him... "

Marietta's thoughts faded. Grandma rambled onward. "...can help Grandpa with the falcons and the orchard. You're old enough to make deliveries in the truck now..."

Marietta sickened at the thought of sitting behind a steering wheel ever again. "...and if not that, then you can help me peel and shuck and skin. Okay? You remember how we bag and box them, don't you?"

"Um, yeah..." she said at last and handed the phone to Grandpa. Then they hit the road.

Marietta shuddered. Everything in life would have been so much easier for everyone if she'd died too when her car impacted the garage. Why hadn't God just put an end to it all? Those mysterious ways of his that Susan borrowed for her own use from time to time. Oh, Grandma, you're a lying bitch and a hypocrite too. Marietta wanted to scream and not stop until the RV reached Wayfarer city limits.

She didn't want any more false assurances because everything was not going to be all right. Everything was going to be all wrong, very strange, and very sad and wrong and alien. Everything changed, especially Marietta. She had changed and she wasn't sure what she'd changed into, which is the part that made her feel so angry and afraid.

She didn't want to see the uncertainty in Grandpa's eyes anymore, wondering what she knew, wondering what she had done, wondering what she refused to say aloud. Nor did she want to hear anymore lies. Why did they still call her Marietta when they knew it wasn't true? Why did her grandparents call her by the name of a dead girl? Instead of conversation, silence accompanied Marietta Brazil and Michael Madison as the third passenger on the road trip.

Seven hours on the road now, the RV creaked up and groaned down the sides of mountains. Marietta lay back down and stared at the interior of the RV's roof. She tried to sleep in the deep dark pitch blackness of predawn. But the look of twisted triumph on Susan's face the moment she realized that Marietta would be the death of her, terrified and frightened

Marietta from daring to dream. Her mother, no, her fake mother, which is what Susan was, seemed almost pleased in those last few seconds of her life.

Susan wore a smile on her face. That is what Marietta could not bring herself to tell Lake City police when they questioned her. She would never tell anyone. How could she describe such an expression of sly cunning that seemed to almost say, "See Marietta? I win again!" But then, Susan always did win. Didn't Stephanie say so?

As for the girl that Susan raised--the girl behind the steering wheel--what had she become? Susan twisted and bent Marietta into a shape that finally won approval. Not until moments before impact had Susan shown such pride in Marietta. Tears seeped beneath Marietta's eyes. She learned Susan's lessons well enough to kill her own mother. No. Her lying cheating fake mother.

Grandpa Madison cleared his throat. "Your father's death has been ruled a homicide by person or persons unknown. They have no information to go on, really." He paused to gather his thoughts. "They're still investigating your mother's, ah Susan's death."

Fake mother.

Marietta glanced towards the front of the RV. Her grandfather's hands held the steering wheel in a tight grip as if he thought it might try to get away from him. Maybe it would. Sometimes steering wheels got away and did bad things. She should know.

He saw her looking at him and relaxed his hands and tried to smile at her in the rear view mirror. "Your grandmother's gonna take you to Wayfarer High School next week after you heal up some more and get you all set for summer school." He blinked a few times, uncomfortable with her stare. After watching the road for a while, he continued. "You'll be enrolled as Mary Madison, just to..." his voice faded.

Marietta looked through the RV's windshield. Only the white line on blacktop provided any guidance through the darkness. Why didn't Grandpa wait until morning to travel like normal people? She cleared her throat, her voice roughened from crying followed by long periods of silent rage.

"What happened to Jesse, Grandpa? Where is he?"

"Jesse?"

"My dog. What happened to Jesse?"

"We, ah well, the police think the dog ran away."

"No. He never would have run from me."

"No one's seen him since..."

"I don't believe you, Grandpa. Jesse loved me. He was the only one who did."

"Marietta..."

"He wouldn't have run away from me. Maybe he's at the pound. Did you check?"

"We..."

"Everybody lies." Marietta choked back more tears. "He was my dog!"

Grandpa sighed. That pretty much ended all conversation for the remaining hours on the road to Wayfarer. Softness appeared in the eastern sky to provide relief from the long, dark night. Morning would usher them into Wayfarer. But neither Marietta nor her grandfather said another word for the rest of the journey there.

***

In the privacy of his sanctum, the beast with the large red puckered blotches over his face and hands struggled to breathe. The dry air raked over the rawness of his throat like steel wool. The humidifier helped, but not much.

The mirror on the wall behind his desk helped not at all, but pride didn't allow him to cover the silvered glass that glimmered whenever he moved. Instead, wrath inspired him to face his new appearance as an inspiration. Gazing into his reflection, he summoned the demonic terror that dwelt inside of him to the outside of him. Red rheumy eyes, the eyes of a dragon, blazed back unholy promises.

CHAPTER 7   GRANDMA

Marietta felt well enough to help Grandma with bagging and pricing last fall's healthy crop of pecans. Since they sat in the backyard now, her grandmother snapped gauntlets on both of Marietta's arms. The falcons circled overhead watching for squirrels, mice, and pest birds that interfered with the fruit and vegetables. Once in a while, they swooped down for a landing on a human arm or shoulder.

"Grandma, thank you for fixing up my room." Marietta filled the large scoop with pecans and dumped the nuts into a plain brown paper bag.

"I do that every summer, Marietta. Except for last year." Her grandmother folded the top of the bag twice and set it onto a cart.

"Grandma, you know," Marietta paused for a breath, "Stephanie sent me her journal before she died."

Rose Madison neither answered, nor moved.

"I read it," Marietta continued.

Grandma's hands twitched. "What did Stephanie say?" she finally asked after a stubborn silence.

Marietta stared with intensity at Rose Madison's profile and tried to find her courage. "Who is my mother, Grandma?"

Silence.

"Please tell me," she whispered.

Silence.

"I don't mean my mother. I mean, who gave birth to me?"

Grandma put the paper bag she'd just folded down on the ground.

"Grandma?"

Rose Madison stood with the slow, arthritic deliberateness of the elderly.

"You know, don't you?" Marietta's voice shook at first, and then grew stronger. "I know you know."

Rose Madison turned and walked towards the kitchen door. Marietta stared after her open-mouthed and frozen still. Her grandmother opened the kitchen door and stepped inside. The screen door slammed shut behind her.

The backyard became a vague blur of green. The wind watered down to a suffocating blanket of warmth. Marietta felt as though she were drowning inside her dreams again.

As I've told you before, more listening, less talking.

The sound of ripping flesh snapped her out of the spell. One of the falcons carried off the stupidest squirrel ever. They never learned. Tiny bits of bloody fur fell at Marietta's feet. The raptor and its prey screamed together. Then no sound except the rustle of leaves. Such was her life now.

Marietta finished bagging the huge pile of pecans. Fall would bring another large batch and they had to make room. She sold produce by herself for the rest of the afternoon at the roadside stand in the lot next door. She put the cash and the tally sheet inside a strongbox hidden inside the kitchen pantry.

Then she walked upstairs to her bedroom, closed the door and wept.

***

Tony's stealth crush on Marietta flourished during the summers she spent across the street with her grandparents and endured steadfast during the school year when she returned North to Lake City. So pretty with clear brown skin and honey eyes and curly brown hair, his fascination and her appeal grew stronger each time he saw her. Now, his mother Annette Jennings told him that Marietta would finish high school in Wayfarer. He liked the sound of that.

But he gathered that a cloud hung over the family. "Some things had happened," as the townsfolk said. He sympathized because he already knew about the sinister side of family life. Anxious to be Marietta's friend again, he showed her the ropes around summer school. But she didn't act the same.

"So how do you like Wayfarer High?" he asked her after they rode their bikes up the Madison driveway.

"I don't know. It's a school. I mean, some of the kids already know me from when I came down the other summers."

Marietta leaned her bike against the porch and sat on the bench in the front yard. She stared up and into the crape myrtle like she never saw one before.

Tony, graceful and limber from track practice, dropped into the place of honor beside her. "Just one more year to go and we graduate," he said just to make conversation.

"Yeah, after I make up all the work left over from junior year..." Marietta's voice trailed off like she forgot what she wanted to say.

An awkward silence fell between them. It didn't use to be this way, but, well... some things had happened. He decided to try again.

"I can't believe you and me finally went out."

"Just to see the movie downtown."

"And to get sandwiches."

"Yeah."

"And an evening bike ride with plenty of fresh air."

"Okay," Marietta laughed at last, to his relief. "You really don't notice all these mosquitoes?" She slapped at her arm.

"They can't see me. I'm too dark!" Tony held out an arm the color of the darkest chocolate with pride. "Actually, citronella. Bugs hate it."

"Oh yeah. Smells nice."

"I'll have my mom make up a batch for you."

"Oh, gifts!"

"You're welcome. Hey, let's go to my house. Our Catahoula had puppies about a week ago. You have to see them!"

Tony tugged her across the street to the Jennings home, a near mirror image of the Madison's two story. As tall and dark and lean as her son, the still young Annette waved the teens inside with a smile. Seated on the kitchen floor beside an enormous pillow, Marietta looked at the wriggly pups competing for space near their mother's body.

"They're so cute," she finally had to admit.

Tony smiled like a proud father from the opposite side of the mother Catahoula. "You can have one if you want one. I don't think we can keep them all. You know, they might remind you of Jesse."

The smile disappeared from Marietta's face. "How do you know about Jesse?"

Tony looked up. Annette met his eyes. An uncomfortable silence passed. The mother dog sensed the tension in the room. Wary, she glanced from one human to the other.

Marietta stood. He stomach felt sick. Her grandparents told them, of course. Either her grandfather or her grandmother or both gossiped about Jesse's disappearance, which was family business.

And what else did they decide to put on the local grapevine? Prickles walked down both of her arms. If Tony and his mother knew, then likely everyone else knew. Marietta was already a freak and fall term hadn't even started yet. It wasn't fair. The whispers and the averted eyes and the innuendos came next, just like with Stephanie. Good ole small town Wayfarer. Marietta bit her bottom lip.

Miss Annette held Marietta's hands in hers and squeezed. "Marietta, we are always your friends in the Jennings house. I've known you almost all your life."

"Jesse was private." Marietta eased her hands away. "They shouldn't have said. They had no right to tell anyone about that."

"I'm sorry, Marietta. So sorry. But we won't pass it on, right Tony?"

Marietta didn't bother to wait for Tony's answer. "I don't want a dog," she called over her shoulder in a rush out of their front door.

Marietta ignored Tony for the next two weeks at summer school though she knew he wanted to talk to her. Unfortunately, she discovered that the previous summer when she stayed in Lake City, Tony became her grandfather's part-time helper in the orchards. So she kept an eye out for him from her bedroom window and waited for him to leave as she got dressed for her own shift. She would pull her own weight. But not a lot, since she was still healing and she didn't want to talk to Tony.

Irritated overall, rather than indulge Tony with the opportunity to apologize, Marietta continued to punish him with her silence in the neighborhood and at the school. Susan taught her so well how to freeze a man to a standstill. He had no idea how bad it could get, how hard she could make him cry if she really tried.

Tony watched her walk down different hallways to avoid him. She ate her bagged lunch with a quickness and even carried food away with her if he sat down before she finished. She hid inside the library between classes and took a different route home from school on her bicycle.

When he called out, "Marietta!" she pretended not to hear him and kept pedaling home.

***

Late one evening, like any other summer evening, Marietta sat with her grandparents at the dining room table. A vegetable mixture of garden-grown tomatoes, onions, okra, summer squash, and beans accompanied store-bought brown rice.

Grandma, as always, started off the evening's conversation. "Marietta, your grandfather and I opened an account for you at our bank because of all you sold at the stand."

"Oh good," Marietta responded in a lifeless tone.

They ate the meal in silence. The repetitive melody of cicadas and beat-boxing by crickets, members of the backyard menagerie, provided musical accompaniment for the quiet chewing around the dining room table.

Once again, Rose Madison smiled with cheer. "We're thinking about asking Annette for one of the puppies for you."

Startled, Marietta dropped her fork on the plate with a clatter. Then she shook her head. "Puppies have to be careful of the falcons, Grandma," she said in the same lifeless tone as before.

"You could keep him inside or in a pen until he's bigger."

"No."

"I know you like dogs, Marietta. You've always been good with Annette's."

Marietta shook her head again. You gossiping old hag.

"You sure?" Shut up, Grandma!

"No! They're not Jesse!"

Marietta pushed away from the dining room table and ran upstairs. "They're not Jesse!" She closed the door to her room and looked at a photo of herself and the world's most faithful retriever. Tears ran down her face.

"Jesse, where are you, boy? What happened to you? What did they do? I'm sorry, Jesse. I'm so sorry."

She spent the rest of the night trying to think of a way that she could run away back to Lake City. She knew if she tried hard enough, she could rescue Jesse from the pound. She could put up fliers in her old neighborhood. Ask some of the neighbors to help her search for him. If he ran away from the pound, he would return to their back yard. He might be there right now chasing butterflies and sniffing at roses. Or maybe he was cold and lonely and scared like herself, waiting for someone to show up and rescue him.

Marietta closed her eyes. She didn't have enough money to travel and live by herself. If she didn't show up for class at Wayfarer High, the school would alert her grandparents. Rose and Michael Madison might get in trouble with the county or state. And besides, they told her to always ask permission if she ever did anything else besides attend class.

The logistics of the trip, the expense, and the fact that she was a minor who might get sent to juvenile hall if caught by police made her feel so tired.

That night, she had the white cloud dream again. It pressed down, surrounded her. Then somehow, the cloud invaded her. Now it poisoned her...

CHAPTER 8   THE SISTERS

Days and weeks and then months passed. Fall term arrived. Never really an extrovert, Marietta's trauma rendered her nearly mute to the point that other students decided English must not be her first language. Others thought her slow and treated her as such. Some of her classmates knew her because of her past summer visits, but didn't really know her.

Marietta stuck to her low-profile routine through the grind of her last year of high school. She bent her head and focused on the computer screen for typing class because pretty soon no one would use typewriters anymore, so the instructor said. Just like the constant click of the keys on the keyboard, she remained background noise, like a television show that no one wanted to watch, but didn't bother to switch off.

Her teachers saw her but didn't remember her. She wasn't an outstanding student or a problem student. She did the bare minimum of participation preferring to return as quickly as possible to Wayfarer Orchards to fly the falcons, rake straw from the falcon house, build fences and trellises, rake up leaves and brush for compost, prune the fruit trees, and sort seeds for spring planting. No one asked her questions because she kept herself too busy to answer.

Tony remained the only other student who really knew her at Wayfarer High. Marietta unclenched just enough to be civil towards him when they passed each other in the hallways. The school year passed in a blur of her apathy until spring arrived.

On a rainy afternoon of sorting and cleaning and sharpening tools in her grandfather's tool shed, Marietta turned around to see Tony's tall, athletic frame leaning against the doorway where he watched her. Built long and lean, he didn't take up much space, but his focus on her seemed so intense, she stopped grinding metal.

"Look Marietta," he told her. "I'm sorry that me and my mother interfered about..."

"Don't worry about it, Tony. You didn't know. It's fine." Marietta returned to the tools while he continued to watch with the weird look still on his face.

Tony cleared his throat in order to recapture Marietta's attention. When she looked at him, he could see that the broken pieces of hazel in her eyes had melted, which signaled the all clear.

To his surprise, she accepted his invitation to prom. "I have some money from the work I've been doing around here. My grandparents started my account for me at the bank," she said. "I'm going to look for a really nice dress at the second-hand store the next time they're open."

"Will they have something available?"

"I already know which one I want."

He smiled with triumph. So she'd been thinking about prom too.

"It's gonna be pink, just so you know," she said with a casual shrug. Then she went back to the tool work. He helped her sharpen and sort out the equipment for the rest of the afternoon while they discussed their plans.

The next afternoon, to Marietta's delight, she was just in time to lay claim to the light pink confection that made her feel like a delicious piece of divinity candy. She telephoned Grandma from a phone booth to let her know that she planned to track down shoes next.

"Marietta, while you're in town, stop by the hair salon."

"For what?"

Grandma allowed a significant pause to pass. "Oh honey, I'll come to town and meet you there if you need me to since you don't really know them."

Just that morning, after Marietta mentioned her invitation to prom, Grandma had stared at Marietta's huge upsweep of frizzy, nappy brown curls with a slight upturn to her top lip. Marietta loved her natural hair even more for that reason. Besides, she missed her father and wearing her hair the same texture as his, helped her to remember him.

"I don't need you to do that, Grandma."

"Oh, well, bless your precious heart," Grandma said, her voice sweet and cloying with southern-fried magnolia gentility.

Marietta took a deep breath and shifted inside the phone booth. Don't yell at her. Don't yell at an old woman.

"Grandma, sometimes you act like..." Don't do it. You'll be the one who looks bad. "I mean... Grandma?"

"Yes?"

"No, really, I can handle it. It's too hot outside for you to come down here. I'll stop by the beauty shop before I come home."

Grandma said something else that Marietta didn't feel like listening to so she disconnected and grumbled all four blocks to Lady Tia's. She locked up her bicycle, grabbed her bagged dress, and walked and into the salon's front door with its tinkling bell. Lady Tia herself greeted Marietta.

"Miss Rose just called me, baby. She wants an extra special press and curl for you. Shampoo. Deep conditioner. And then she asked me to go to work with the hot comb and curling iron. You know Miss Rose's credit's always good with Lady Tia."

Marietta put an extra dose of sugar honey ice tea in her own voice to cover her fury. Through clenched teeth she replied, "Actually, Miss Tia, would you please do me a shampoo and condition with two-strand twists under the hairdryer? That's what I've really been needing in my entire life, I declare. If we can do that today, I would be ever so grateful."

Lady Tia raised her arched brows with amusement at Marietta's exaggerated, slurred southern accent. She inclined her head with her own drawled, "Yes, ma'am, we can sure can, Miss Marietta. Right away, Miss Ma'am."

Lady Tia started with a vigorous shampoo. A warm spray of water rushed past Marietta's ears. Lady Tia worked her magic hands coated with conditioner through the long corkscrews on Marietta's head. Marietta relaxed, pleased to let someone else deal with her problems. More water rushed past Marietta's ears, but she still heard the bell over the beauty shop door tinkle again and again as more women plopped down to wait their turns.

The water stopped. The bell sounded again as Lady Tia sat Marietta up in the chair. This time, a group of middle-aged chatterers stepped inside.

"Well, I had heard that when she came down for Stephanie's service..."

Marietta frowned while Lady Tia used a strong hand to wring extra water from her huge mass of dripping wet hair.

"...not one single solitary tear was shed. And then she had the nerve to wear sunglasses chile! Though she didn't need them..."

Lady Tia grabbed a clean towel which muffled most noise, but not all.

"...Giiiiiirl, I'm saying though, something was always strange about all of them."

"Even Miss Rose?" someone asked the happy chatterer.

Lady Tia's hands stilled on Marietta's head. Too late, the hairdresser turned to the gossips and snapped her hand in a cutting motion.

"Especially Miss Rose!" the chatterer finished with a divaesque flourish of her hand and a toss of the wig on her head.

Lady Tia broke into the conversation, desperate to end it, "Now Miss Linda, you know better than to say things you don't mean when children are present."

Multiple eyes zeroed in on Marietta. A charged silence passed. Lady Tia guided the other women towards a safer subject.

"Besides that, who's gonna bring dessert to church this Sunday? I'm not bringin' nothin'! Ya'll see how many heads I have to do this afternoon. Please!"

Marietta wished she had a hundred hands on each arm with which to slap them all. She untied the bib from around her neck. Over Lady Tia's hushed protests, she stood up from the chair and counted out bills, while thin trickles of water ran down her face. Lady Tia set down the bottle of moisturizer she'd just gotten ready to spread through Marietta's hair onto the counter and shook her head in consternation.

Marietta dropped the bills on the counter next to the moisturizer and then focused her energy on placing one foot in front of the other while fifteen sets of eyes watched. Once again, she wondered why she had not perished instead of Susan in the car accident. She hated Wayfarer.

The water from her scalp ran into her eyes and she blinked a few times, but she made it through the shop door before actual tears joined the drips on her forehead. Then she ran for her bike. She placed the bag with the prom dress in the basket and headed for home.

She made the call to Tony from the telephone in the kitchen. Not even thirty seconds passed before he showed up at their front door and yanked it open.

"Is this because your grandmother told us about your dog?" He huffed and puffed. Is that why you don't want to go to prom with me?"

She didn't answer.

"I told you I was sorry, Marietta. So is my mother."

Marietta shook her head but couldn't meet his eyes. Her stomach churned from what she overheard in town. "It's not that," she whispered.

"Are you sick?" he asked her. "You look funny."

"No. I just want to stay at home tonight."

"But we talked about this. You said you wanted to go with me." He looked confused. "And why is your hair wet? What's going on?"

Marietta shrugged.

"I said what's going on here, Marietta?" he demanded and grabbed at her arm. "You said you weren't mad at me anymore. We made plans together."

"I just..."

"Say it!"

Just then, her grandparents entered the kitchen door from the backyard. Marietta didn't want to face them and Tony too. She snatched her arm away.

"Leave me alone!" she shouted at them all. Then she ran upstairs to her room. She spent the rest of prom night attempting to repair her hair which frizzed and tangled into a spectacular afro which would have sent Grandma screaming to the nursing home if she saw it.

***

The next morning, Grandma walked into the kitchen with a grim look, but this time, not for Marietta's two-strand twists.

"Sit down, Marietta," Grandma said.

Marietta sat. Here we go.

"Tony took another girl to the prom since you changed your mind at the last minute."

Marietta's face flamed.

"Miss Annette called over here and told me all about it. Told me you put that boy down for no reason. I saw the way you flounced up them stairs. Real siddity-like."

Marietta opened her mouth to answer back.

"No ma'am," her grandmother waved a hand in dismissal. "Let me tell you something, Miss. Those Jennings are friends of this family. We go back. There have been Jennings over there about as long as there's been Madisons over here. We get along and we respect each other."

"What about me?"

"What about you?"

"I'm your granddaughter, Grandma."

"I know who you are. But just because you feel bad, there's no call to treat others like dirt under your shoe. You owe that boy an apology."

"I know I do."

"Then get to it! You're not the only one who had something bad happen to you. Don't you know that boy's daddy is crazy? He went to prison on aggravated assault and armed robbery. Left the boy and his mama broke with bills from every whichawhere. Grandpa gave Tony that job so he could earn some money and keep the roof over their heads. Law was about to put them in the streets!"

Marietta looked at the table.

"Tony's a good boy. I don't know what's wrong with you, girl. You come down here and sashay all around him like he's nobody, but let me tell you. He does the work of ten men out in the orchards. He's helping your Grandpa save his back before old Arthur takes it, for one. For two, you need to start walking in the real world, young lady."

If the lecture stopped at this point, both Marietta and her grandmother could have gone about their mutual businesses satisfied that open communication resolved many of society's ills. However, Grandma continued one step too far and the conversation veered right off the rails.

"Your mother, Susan, was the most popular girl in high school and she never pulled a stunt like this. She never did nothing like that."

Marietta accepted the challenge. She stiffened her back and shoulders, and then plowed right through the red flag, snorting away. "Since you're going all around the neighborhood gossiping about me to everyone who wants to listen, why don't you let me in on all of Susan's secrets too?"

"What are you talking about, Marietta?"

"You know what I'm talking about."

Grandma frowned, so Marietta helped her out.

"There was a letter to Stephanie inside her Bible. You wrote it, Grandma. 'Trust in God, Stephanie. She never told you and Susan apart.' That's what you wrote to Stephanie. You wrote it and you signed it." Marietta took several breaths. "You were talking about me, weren't you?"

Rose Madison didn't answer.

"Oh no you don't. Not this time, Grandma. I want to know which of your daughters gave birth to me. Tell me! I know you know." Marietta's face crumpled, but she rallied. "Who is my mother!"

Rose Madison walked to the kitchen counter and pulled off a few sheets of paper towels for Marietta and sat back down.

"All right, Marietta. Since you want to be grown and you want to know grown folks business, I'll tell you."

Marietta waited.

"Stephanie's journal is true. She is your mother. She gave birth to you. But Susan raised you up."

"Why did Susan raise me and not Stephanie?"

"Stephanie had that accident. She dropped Susan's baby."

"And then?"

"And then she felt obligated so she gave her own baby to Susan."

"Me."

Grandma nodded.

"Why did Stephanie feel obligated to give me away?"

"To make up for what she did."

"But who made Stephanie feel obligated to give me away?"

Grandma shook her head and shrugged.

"Grandma, who told Stephanie to give me away? Who?"

Grandma's expression seemed stricken now.

"It was you, wasn't it? You told my mother to give me away like trash."

"No!" Grandma slammed her hand on the table top. "No, Marietta. It wasn't like that."

"What about me? What about how I felt?"

"You were just a baby. You didn't feel anything." Shocked, Marietta could only stare at the woman who raised Susan and Stephanie. So much explained. So much still unexplained.

"It seemed like the right thing to do to keep peace in the family."

"You took my mother away from me. And you took Stephanie's daughter away from her. What about Stephanie's peace?"

"What about it, Marietta?"

Marietta shook her head. "You shouldn't have done it, Grandma," she whispered. "You hurt her so badly. Me too."

"Well what about Susan?" Grandma demanded.

Marietta had no response for her, still stunned by her grandmother's callousness.

"When Stephanie left here to go North, all she wanted was to prove something to the rest of us."

"What did she want to prove? To the rest of who?" Marietta could barely conceal her disgust.

"To all of us down South. That she could be somebody without us. That she didn't need us and that she was better."

"Better than what?"

"Her family. Well, me really. Her father, Susan. Everybody."

"What?" Marietta shook her head. "Okay, let me get this straight. Stephanie went away to college up North, near Lake City, and you couldn't stand that. I don't get it. Most parents are proud when their children are successful."

"Marietta..."

"No, Grandma. You couldn't stand it. Then what?"

"That's where she met Roy Brazil."

"You mean Stephanie met my father first?"

"They attended the same college, Marietta."

"Oh." Marietta hadn't known that. Why didn't anyone tell her? Because she never thought to ask? "But what about... Susan?" Marietta refused to call the pale-skinned creature who smiled as Marietta's car accelerated forward, 'mother.'

"Susan went up to visit Stephanie at her fancy know-everything school. And so she met Roy too."

"But my father married Susan."

"Well... life happens."

Susan always gets her way. Marietta thought about Stephanie's frustrations with Susan and how Susan always managed to come out on top, until the last and final time she didn't. Roy had never been a match for Susan's maneuvering, nor that of his mother-in-law's, likely. Certainly Stephanie had not.

"So Stephanie had an affair with my father after he married Susan and I was born."

"Three months after Marietta was born to Susan. The real Marietta."

Marietta pressed her lips together to keep herself from shouting at an old woman. Now that Grandma was talking, she wanted to keep her on topic.

"Then Stephanie had the accident with, 'Marietta,'" Marietta made finger quotes, "And you and Susan forced Stephanie to give up her own baby, me."

Grandma sighed. "The way you tell it, you make it seem like..."

"Stephanie graduated college, which you hated. Yes, you did. And she started work at Cadis Industries so she could... what? Forget about me? Forget her own daughter?"

"No. So she could show us that she was still better than us. All of us here in Wayfarer. Well, Susan mostly."

Marietta frowned. "Who said that?"

"Susan talked to us about it. Stephanie always made better grades than Susan. And she liked to brag on that. Then she started making more money and she put that in everybody's faces too."

Even within the fantastical, unbelievable, wacky world of the Madisons and the Brazils, this part of the story sounded ridiculous.

"Why do you talk about her like that?"

"Like what? How am I talking?"

"Like you never loved her. Like you don't even recognize her as your daughter."

Grandma sighed. "Oh Marietta..."

"When Susan came down for Stephanie's service, did she tell you why Stephanie attacked Cadis and killed all those people?"

Grandma shook her head.

"Why did she kill herself? Why did she leave me?"

"I'm trying to tell you. That's Stephanie." Grandma shrugged. "I don't know what on Earth drove that girl. I never did. Susan always said..."

"Susan works in mysterious ways. That's what you said. You said that about Susan last year at our barbecue. I heard you."

"Steady in grown folks business, Marietta. You need to be in kid business where you belong."

"The horse already left the barn on that one, Grandma."

"Clearly."

"Well, what do you say about Stephanie? She was your daughter. You must know something besides what Susan told you about her."

"Marietta, Stephanie has always been something of a mystery to me. Susan always said something wasn't right about her. But we never understood what exactly."

"I just don't believe that Stephanie would have killed herself for no reason."

"But she did, didn't she?"

"Grandma," Marietta choked out, "Why didn't she stay alive for me, at least?"

Grandma sighed, "Marietta." And then a long silence permeated the kitchen. "Lake City police considers that case closed and so do we. Since we're on the subject, in case you wondered, Susan's death was ruled an accident. Lake City police consider that case closed too."

Grandma Madison stared at Marietta with firm finality. "And so do we. You will too. Leave it because I am your elder and I'm tired of your constant questioning of me."

Marietta shrank back as if Grandma had reached out to slap her in the face.

Grandma continued, "You will not speak of this any further while you live in this house. I don't want to hear it. Or hear of it."

Head down, Marietta backed away from the kitchen table and joined her grandfather in the orchard. A long, silent weekend passed at the Madison home.

CHAPTER 9   THE DEATH

Grandma Madison died of a stroke a week prior to Marietta's graduation. Because Rose Madison put in decades of her time as a lifelong resident of Wayfarer, and as an active participant in church and community activities, quite the crowd turned out for her homegoing.

Mourners trekked past Michael Madison and his granddaughter to express their condolences. Rose Madison's fellow church members provided the after-service meal in the church basement. In a nasty moment, Marietta wondered whether they planned the menu at the beauty shop.

The Madison home seemed so quiet and much too big now. Marietta went to the mailbox and collected a large stack of cards and letters. She got down to the business of responding to the sympathetic who were unable to travel to Wayfarer to help see Grandma off to magnolia glory in the sky.

Her grandfather headed out to the orchard, as usual. Late spring felt more like the hot blaze of early summer. Grandpa had to use many gallons of water from the rain barrels to keep the orchard from burning.

As she wrote, Marietta wondered if her interrogation of Grandma caused her death. Had she given her own grandmother a stroke? Marietta wiped the tears from her eyes and then dried her hands on a paper towel so she wouldn't smudge the cards. Did Grandpa know about their conversation? If so, did he think Marietta stressed Rose Madison to the breaking point? Had she killed her grandfather's wife? What must he think of Marietta when everyone around her kept dying? What if Grandpa was next?

Marietta used more paper towels to wipe her face. Her hands trembled. Once again, she stopped writing to rub them together.

Everyone around me dies.

A knock at the front door interrupted Marietta just as she picked up the pen to sign the fourth standard response, "Thank you for your blessed prayers, Michael Madison and Mary Madison."

The front door opened and Tony stepped inside. He'd changed from the suit and tie he wore to church back into his regular work clothes.

"Marietta, I'm sorry about your grandmother. Miss Rose was like a second mother to me. She was always kind to our family."

Marietta nodded, polite. Although I may have killed her because I wouldn't stop asking her questions.

Tony cleared his throat. "Look, I don't know what happened between us..."

Marietta closed her eyes and shook her head. "Please, I can't. Not right now..."

Tony bit his lip. "Okay, I'm sorry. Look, I just came over because my mother told me to see if you and Mr. Madison needed anything."

Marietta stared at him.

Tony looked down at his hands. For the first time, Marietta noticed that he carried something in them, a triple stack of large plastic storage containers. "She made these dishes for you all."

Marietta didn't move. My grandfather is in danger. From me. I'm bad luck.

Something about Marietta's expression spooked Tony. "Well, I'm gonna put these in the refrigerator for you," he said in a clear, slow voice as if to a special needs child.

He backed towards the kitchen. Finally, Marietta returned her gaze to the cards and letters spread before her.

Everyone around me dies. The list is getting longer. I have to leave here so Grandpa doesn't die.

That decision made, she continued to sign the stack of response cards with determination. Tony exited the back door into the orchard with a worried look, likely to help Grandpa with whatever tasks he'd found to stay busy. There was always something to do on their small homestead.

Grandpa would be okay if Tony was still around.

Too late, Marietta remembered that Grandma's last order for her was to apologize to Tony about prom. But the moment passed. He didn't seem to want to be around her anyway.

***

Marietta found Grandpa in the living room which had a large panoramic view of the street in front of the Madison home. He and Grandma used to sit in their recliners together and since old habits die hard, Marietta knew Grandpa would continue to do so.

"You know, we planted that crape myrtle out front the year you were born," he said still staring outside.

Me or Alicia, Marietta wondered.

Grandpa turned from the window and gestured for her to sit beside him in Grandma's old chair. "Marietta, you turned eighteen a while back."

"Yes sir."

"I don't know if you're aware, but you inherited quite a bit from your parents, from Stephanie, and from Grandma. Insurance and property. Things like that."

Marietta crossed her arms. She felt cold inside. "Grandpa, I'd give it all away if I could have everyone back again. I would."

Grandpa chuckled. "Bless you for saying that."

She burst into tears and got up to look out of the large window at the crape myrtle. She knew what she had to do. Her grandfather, ignorant of what was about to happen, waited for her to calm down.

Marietta took a deep breath. "Grandpa, every day that you knew me, you lied to my face. Your only granddaughter and you lied to me all my life."

"Marietta, please."

"I don't want to live here anymore."

"Your grandmother forbid me from ever telling you about... that. She didn't know you already knew. She didn't want you to have the burden of knowing that your mother was..."

"Was what? A mass murderer? A terrorist?"

Grandpa flinched.

"Well she is. That's what they're saying."

"Who's saying?"

"My mother, my real mother, is a killer. People on the news said that. She was crazy."

"That's my daughter you're talking about," Grandpa replied in a quiet voice.

"And the woman who raised me, my fake mother, well she was a bitch."

"Marietta!"

"She hated me and I know she hated me!"

"Stop it, Marietta. Don't you use that language with me, young lady."

"And I hated her right back!"

"Oh Marietta. Marietta..."

"So, I killed her!"

"That's enough!"

"I did it!"

"No!" Grandpa Madison roared and surged out of the recliner. Marietta, startled, took a full step backward. She'd never seen her grandfather so exercised. They stared at each other for almost a full minute of silence.

"I'm a murderer too, Grandpa. I did it because I didn't like her. I didn't love her like a daughter loves a mother. And I stressed Grandma."

"No, Marietta. No."

"We never spoke about it, but I'm old enough to take responsibility. I can admit it now." Marietta's voice broke. "I'm sorry."

"Is this what you've been thinking all this time?"

"I'm going back to Lake City to face this. I'm an adult now."

"Marietta, you cannot return to Lake City. Ever."

"You can't hide me forever in this stupid little town. People know there's something wrong with me."

Grandpa shook his head, rejecting her statement.

"I see them, the way they look at me. They whisper and they talk. I can hear them."

"No."

"You can't stop me." Marietta raised her chin. "I'm legal age and I have train fare."

Michael Madison looked at the floor. His shoulders sagged with defeat and he sank back onto the recliner. Marietta frowned, puzzled. She took Grandma's old seat beside him. A silence passed.

"Something you need to know. Since we're speaking on the truth. Susan's death was an accident, Marietta. A terrible, terrible accident. And as for Grandma, well," Grandpa ran a gnarled, veiny hand over his fuzzy hair. "She lived a long full life, as God intended. She did God's work. And now her work is done and she's gone to collect on that reward He's been holding for her."

"Please, Grandpa." Marietta put up a hand. "Don't do this anymore. I... ran Susan over with my car. Even though I've tried to forget that night, I can't. I remember... I remember what happened."

Grandpa's gaze sharpened.

"I can't pretend any longer. I won't. How can you ever forgive me?" Marietta's eyes filled with tears. "I'm sorry about Grandma," she said and covered her face with her hands. "I'm sorry about everything!"

"Marietta, there's nothing to forgive," he told her in a quiet voice.

"Grandpa, please stop."

"What else do you remember about the night Susan died?"

"What do you mean what else?"

"Think about what happened, Marietta. Think very carefully to over a year ago."

Marietta closed her eyes and shivered. She wrapped her arms around herself. Then she shook her head. "I..."

"You were driving downhill towards home. You must have tried to use your brake. Don't you remember? Something went wrong. The brake didn't work."

Marietta summoned forth the nightmare of the darkest night of her entire life. Gravity sucked the station wagon downward. She stepped on the brake. It stuck to the floor. Her old elephant of a car gathered speed. The taillights of the pickup in front of her drew closer. She stomped and stomped the brake, but it wouldn't budge from the floor.

She braced herself to rear-end the pickup, but the red lights in front of her swung left as the truck turned from her path.

And then... and then... Susan's shocked pale face flashed out of the darkness like a warning beacon in the white light cast by the station wagon's headlights. And then the screams, hers and Susan's. And then Susan smiled.

Marietta stared at her grandfather. "The brakes, yes. I tried them. I tried over and over."

"You tried to brake when you saw Susan?"

"I did, but they didn't work and..." Marietta stopped. She couldn't go further.

"I have something for you," Grandpa told her. He stood up, picked out a key from the large set at his waist and took a step to the old mahogany secretary. He unlocked the ancient piece of furniture, hidden beneath his record player, which Marietta never noticed until now, and pulled out a piece of paper.

"What is it?" Marietta asked.

"You need to read it. There's answers."

Marietta sat forward and held out her hand. She gave the official document a swift glance, and then sucked in her breath. "It's a police report."

Grandpa Madison nodded. He walked into the kitchen and returned with two cold glasses of ice water. He sat down to wait for her to finish.

Marietta re-read the report. "It says... the brake fluid in my car..."

"Right," Grandpa answered.

"But... I don't understand. I put brake fluid in my car. Dad always told me to make sure, so I did. How could this happen?"

"How indeed." Grandpa nodded. "They went over your car piece by piece after the accident, inch by inch, and that's what they found."

"Someone... but how could this happen? Who did this to my car?"

"No one knows, Marietta. There were too many mysteries left over from Stephanie and Susan and your father. Too many questions with no answers. The only thing I cared about was getting you out of the city and as far away from that horrible place as soon as possible."

"Is that why we left at night?"

Grandpa nodded. "I didn't waste any time. I didn't start breathing easy till we hit the mountains. We changed your name to make it harder for anyone to..." He stopped talking and fidgeted.

Marietta frowned. "Harder to what?"

"We kept you close. Safe. Right here in this house. In a town where everyone knows you and cares about you."

"Where everyone gossips about me."

"Well, it's a small town."

"You thought someone..." Marietta sat down next to him. "Oh my God. My brake lines," she whispered. "But why? Why would someone do this? How? When?" She shook the police report.

"It could have happened at night while everyone was asleep. Or while you were at school. We didn't know what was going on either, your grandmother and me. The police didn't know either. So..."

"So... what happened to Susan... wasn't my fault?

"No." Her grandfather enunciated with firmness. "It was never your fault, Marietta. You didn't kill your... Susan. In fact..." He stopped again and pressed his lips together.

"In fact," Marietta blinked as truth dawned. "I was the one who was supposed to die."

"But you didn't. You're okay. It was a tragedy what happened to Susan. We lost our daughter. Both of them in less than a week. And we miss them and our son-in-law, your father. But your grandmother and I thanked God every day that you lived."

"Someone tried to kill me," Marietta said with wonder.

Grandpa sighed. "Don't go back to Lake City, Marietta. Please. As long as I've lived, I never begged anyone for anything a single day in my life, but I'm begging you, my only granddaughter, right now. I'd get down on my knees if I thought it would help, but old Arthur's finally got me. Stephanie... wanted a different kind of life from what she had here. And we... we... let her go after her dreams. But..." Grandpa shook his head. "Lake City is a bad place. Terrible and evil. We don't know the people up there."

"Well, I can't stay here."

"What do you mean you can't stay here? Why can't you stay here?" The indignation echoed around the room. He even huffed a little. "Who says? This is your home!"

"Why did you wait until now to show me this police report? I can see the date, clear as day."

"Your grandmother said we shouldn't talk about it with you."

"Grandma said that?" Marietta felt shocked, but the longer she thought about it, the more she understood that, yes, of course, Grandma said exactly that.

"She thought... well..."

"She thought what?" Marietta shook her head with a laugh. "Nevermind. Of course she thought."

"Anyway, once I saw how you took things, I decided you had the right to know."

"Right." For whatever reason, Marietta felt empty inside. Empty and tired.

"Grandpa, I'm so tired of all the secrets and the lies in this family. I just can't take any more. Are you really my grandfather?"

"Yes."

"Roland Brazil was my father?"

"Yes!"

"Who was Alicia?"

Grandpa exhaled and ran a hand over his scalp of sparse fuzz. "Alicia was your original name at birth. Susan renamed you 'Marietta' for her birth daughter that died."

That story checked with what Grandma told her and what Stephanie wrote.

"So... Susan's birth daughter was my cousin 'Marietta.'"

"Right."

"And I was Stephanie's birth daughter... 'Alicia.'"

"Yes."

"And now my name is Mary Madison so no one connects me to 'Marietta Brazil.' I'm so mixed up and confused." She stood up and walked to the window again.

"This place is making me confused. Grandpa, I have to get away. I can't stay here any longer. There's too many memories. People look at me funny. I keep thinking about things and I... I don't feel right here anymore. I want to feel normal even though I don't remember what that is anymore. I have to get away from here, at least for a while."

"I understand." Grandpa leaned back in his recliner with a look of defeat.

She took a step towards him. "Look, I changed my mind. Now that I understand about Susan, I'm not going back to Lake City, okay? At least not right now. But I still can't stay here in Wayfarer. I've been meaning to tell you that I applied for an overseas volunteer assignment. They found a position for me. They like that I have agricultural experience so I can really help people."

Her grandfather swallowed.

Marietta took a breath and braced herself for another go. "I'm going to be gone for two years. It was either this or military service. I just have to go."

"That... that... sounds like," Grandpa paused. "Okay," he said. Sadness shadowed his face. A long moment of silence passed.

"Marietta, I need for you to understand that you had nothing to do with your grandmother's passing."

"I understand," she told him, and then she turned away. "I still have to go."

CHAPTER 10   THE LEAVE

In Marietta's mind, she was already gone. She hated Wayfarer. People inside the power structure crushed the life and happiness of others. Opportunities disappeared. Unless, like her grandfather, and Lady Tia, people made their own opportunities. Those without that type of inspiration left for shiny new bright lives elsewhere.

Graduation came and went as a quiet, subdued affair at the high school auditorium. All around Marietta and her grandfather, youthful jubilation provided a theater of colorful excitement for proud celebratory families.

In contrast, she and Grandpa sat in silence until the school official called her name. She walked across the stage, smiled for the camera, and then returned to her seat with little fanfare. She did accept a hug from Grandpa and hugged him back.

Annette Jennings and Tony nodded their way, but neither of them approached Marietta or her grandfather. Instead, Marietta watched as they and two other families made lunch plans and then left the high school auditorium as a group.

And then, Marietta was gone.

Dear Marietta,

I so regret to inform you that your grandfather, Michael Madison, has fallen ill and is no longer able to maintain Wayfarer Orchards, the trees, the grounds, production, processing, or distribution.

For this reason, he has hired me to manage the business. In addition, since I have also been working towards my law degree, I manage his personal affairs and household expenses.

However, I do know that he misses the joy of having family near. In light of the fact that you are nearest and dearest to his heart, I am hopeful that you might return to the United States and come home as soon as your volunteer assignment has ended. In fact, we all miss you. My mother continues to speak of you often. I hope to hear from you soon so that I might pass on a good word to Mr. Madison and others.

All the best,
Tony Jennings

So, Marietta thought. Tony found his niche in Wayfarer. Her niche. The opportunity that would have been hers had she stayed. Marietta responded with a postcard with a photo of a field of rice on the front. She drew a random string of smiley faces and exclamation points across the bottom.

Thank you for your update on Wayfarer life!
I have taken on another assignment in the
same location. Two more years!!!!!

Mary

Tony read the postcard, stunned by her indifference. Something in their communication was off, he decided.

Marietta,

I may have been remiss in my previous letter in not sharing with you my very real and immediate worry about your grandfather's health status. While I have managed Wayfarer Orchards for the past year and half, I have not been able to manage the day to day personal care that Mr. Madison requires for his well-being.

I have taken the lack of acknowledgment on this matter as the authority required for me to hire a nurse to ensure that the welfare of your grandfather, Michael Madison, remains a priority.

As you are Mr. Madison's next of kin, please contact me so that we may discuss these matters as they develop. I happen to have an email address if that is more convenient than telephoning from overseas.

Otherwise, communication by regular mail is paramount. as soon as possible.

Tony Jennings

Tony,

I'm so sorry! Halfway around the world! Won't be stateside for another two years. I trust your judgment.

Mary

Several days passed before Tony got his fury with Marietta down to a workable level. By the time the blaze of fiery anger inside him died down to cold ash, he replied.

Miss Madison:

I regret to inform you that Mr. Michael Madison has passed away. A copy of his death certificate, obituary, and funeral service program is enclosed along with a copy of your grandfather's will.

You can trust that he found comfort in the last days among his friends and the community of Wayfarer who cared for him deeply and held him in high esteem.

You will also find in his will that he has appointed me executor of his estate, in light of the fact that I am familiar with his affairs and I have obtained my law degree. All affairs of Wayfarer Orchards and the residence and buildings and surroundings properties will be managed by myself until such time you are prepared to take that responsibility.

Also enclosed, please find an update on the Brazil property and estate and accompanying funds. I am also willing to manage these holdings on your behalf for the standard fee. Please review the contract at your earliest convenience. Sign, and return to me.

Tony Jennings

Marietta read through this last letter with a heavy heart and a sense of loss and abandonment. Even though she left home and tried to defy fate by creating distance between herself and her grandfather, he still died. It didn't seem fair. In this whole wide world, no one who ever loved and cared for her remained.

She flipped through the documents, understanding Tony's increasing disdain for her. He truly didn't like her anymore, which was par for the course because she didn't like herself much anymore either.

Nor did she want to think about her family. Thoughts about her family and her origins made her feel bad. Out here in the Third World, no one cared who she was. They didn't stare at her with pity or horror. They didn't ask a lot of questions either. They didn't whisper behind their hands when they thought she couldn't hear.

People didn't lie to her or play games with the truth. Sometimes for political reasons, yes. And she could handle that. But she didn't have to deal with games on a personal level. She always knew exactly where she stood. They wanted clean water, she made sure they had it. She provided a service. She fulfilled a need. People appreciated her. She felt proud of her accomplishments even if no one else did.

Tony didn't have to like her ever again if that was more than he felt like doing. And that would be just fine with her. Still, Marietta felt twinges of sorrow. She'd pretty much burned her very last bridge to Wayfarer. Maybe that was a good thing.

But where did she belong anymore? Her last known family member died. She was truly alone now. Not quite homeless, but... without a home and a family who cared. In other words, truly alone.

Marietta signed Tony's contract and returned it to him, as instructed, without a response to his letter.

Two more years passed before she dropped another postcard in the mail.

Mr. Jennings:

I am touring various countries to learn new business practices in sustainable agriculture. Please contact me by email, if necessary.

Mary Madison

"If necessary?" This time, Tony didn't bother with a personal reply. *As requested*, he sent regular updates on her holdings and accounts, once per month by email while she found herself.

Finally tired from two more years of suitcase living and ready to focus on her professional life, Marietta sent Tony a letter.

Mr. Jennings:

I have enrolled in a four-year college program. Classes begin this fall.

Enclosed, please find a brochure, along with a breakdown of tuition and room and board costs, payable to the school.

With appreciation,
Mary Madison

Full of disgust, Tony obeyed Marietta's instructions and took care of her college costs. Christ, Marietta would always remain a piece of work. If not for his promise to Mr. Madison, Tony would have dumped her as a client years ago.

He owed his life, his loyalty, and his career to Mr. Madison who stepped in when his own father stepped out to become a criminal. If not for Marietta's grandfather, he might have followed the elder Jennings into the prison system.

Dealing with the selfish, self-centered brat that Marietta had become seemed a very small price to pay in exchange for all that he had received.

> Mr. Jennings:
>
> Thank you for taking care of school costs.
> Will return to Wayfarer in two weeks to pick
> up things for school.
>
> Mary Madison

***

Once, he was a tall, dark, debonair prince of industry who strode his large frame into rooms and owned them. With power as the most potent aphrodisiac, women craved him and gazed upon him with hunger and desire in their eyes. He dominated and disarmed all challengers by sheer force of personality and charisma and strength of will.

Now, a gargoyle lurked alone inside a gated inner sanctum of apartments on the highest floor of the tallest tower.

The rise of the Internet allowed the gargoyle to issue a blizzard of marching orders and edicts sight unseen via email, or fax, or phone, or by proxy via his favorite majordomo. He either growled his instructions or roared them from the deepest darkest depths of his diaphragm and fed upon the fear that stirred in the wake of the last dying echoes. He watched his rats scurry to and fro via a complicated set-up of electronic surveillance of the floors below him.

He no longer exercised at his health club or anywhere else so his fabled girth grew legendary. He declined to update his haircuts to the latest styles. Instead, a well-paid and reliable barber visited and maintained the same style as the years passed and sometimes attended to the occasional white strand.

He decreased his attendance at social and business functions. He relinquished that life. He could not stand the sight of fear and revulsion upon the faces of others he encountered. And so, he wore replicas of the same suit and shirt and tie rather than submit to current fashion trends.

In a world of increased communication and expanded social networks, he became a phantom and a boogeyman. Fear grew his legend. Wealth became his avatar.

Why did he now see on his computer, in the random chat rooms he monitored, rumors of Celara Electric's interest in joining the Consortium? And how had Celara achieved the lead position for consideration?

Someone's head needed to roll. He could make that happen, had done it before. Days like these, he felt like climbing to the top of the roof and breathing rare air while swatting airplanes out of the sky. He would avenge his father if it meant this whole tower fell down upon him and everyone below him.

CHAPTER 11   THE RETURN

Tony Jennings thought she was full of shit. Marietta knew this even as she informed him of her brief return to Wayfarer to pick up personal belongings to transport to her Midwestern university in time for Fall term. Yes, she enrolled at the same institution for higher learning where Stephanie Madison and Roy Brazil studied, where her birth mother and father met. For what reason? Marietta still wasn't quite sure.

But now, after the taxi dropped her off, here she stood again on the front porch of the Madison family home with no Madison family inside.

Marietta noted when she walked up the driveway that someone had installed a sturdier, higher fence to guard the orchards. The trees matured a great deal in the six years she'd been away. Fruit hung heavy on the tops of the peach and plum trees whose trunks and branches thickened considerably. This summer's crop held much promise. Someone did a good job. She wondered who?

The apples and pears still had a month to go before they ripened. Some of the trees produced well into November. Who would harvest the fruit and nut crops? Who would package and transport and sell the produce? Who prepared the orchard trees for winter and maintained the orchard floor?

And what about the falcons? She could hear the occasional dying scream of some foolish animal that lost the game of life to the raptors. Who fed and trained them and secured them at night? Who cleaned the falcon house?

Curious about that, she walked to the gate and tugged on the handle. Locked. The front door to the house was locked too. None of her keys worked. She gathered the rest of the bags from the curb where the taxi driver left them and dumped the whole load onto the front porch. She crossed the street to knock on the front door of the Jennings house with its placard announcing the double function of residence and law office. Those who started their own businesses remained in Wayfarer. Others like herself...

When she knocked, she heard a dog answer with a *woof!* Some things remained the same. Probably one of the puppies she'd rejected had grown to become the guardian of the house and law office.

A car pulled to the curb behind her. Tony Jennings.

Tony checked the mail, and then advanced up the walk to his home and law office. He immediately identified Marietta's size, shape, and build from memory. Her large spread of hair had grown even larger and longer than he remembered, falling in a heavy curtain past her shoulders. When she turned, he realized that Marietta was no longer the pretty little girl he remembered. Everything about her had become "more."

She had more curves underneath skin that was even more the rich creamy orange brown of pecan nuts. Dark brows and lashes framed eyes the color of honey, but with more knowledge in them, which made his heart flutter, nervous now. He wondered how her hair would look fanned around her face like a cloud while she lay her head on his pillow. Who had been lucky enough to grip all that cottony-soft hair inside his fists while...

"Well?" Marietta asked with a look of expectation.

He realized that she'd asked him a question that he missed. He stared back at the clear irritation in Marietta's expression in silence because he wasn't sure how to respond. And now, he noticed that his mother also stood in the doorway frowning at his discomfit, her own expression puzzled.

"Of course he can get the keys for you, Marietta," Miss Annette declared into the awkward moment. Behind Marietta's back, Miss Annette raised her eyebrows in inquiry when he lingered on the porch.

So he hefted the groceries he brought back from the store inside and set them down on the dining room table. "Come on in," he gruffed over his shoulder. Then he stepped to fetch Miss Thing's house keys.

He overheard his mother invite Marietta to dinner, which she accepted, of course. He groaned inside. Just get it over with, he thought. She'll be gone soon enough and then you can forget about her again. He found the keys and walked Marietta back to the Madison property.

Marietta noted his hostile demeanor. She realized the only thing keeping him civil towards her on the walk back over to her house was Miss Annette's eagle eye.

"I noticed that the trees are really producing," she said.

Silence.

"They've really matured. Someone's been taking good care of them. I should get back there and help out."

"That's not necessary," he told her. "I already hired two guys from the neighborhood to take care of everything."

"They do a good job."

"They should. You've been paying them for years. If you paid attention to the account statements, you'd know that you pay their salaries."

"Tony, I..."

"You really should start reading your statements."

"I do read my statements, Tony. I just..." Marietta's voice withered and died in the face of Tony's utter scorn.

"He deserved so much better than what you gave him, Marietta."

"Look, Tony." Marietta turned to face him as they stepped together onto the porch. "I just returned here to pick up some of my belongings that I need for school. That's it. Let's not make it more than it has to be."

"God forbid."

"Really?" She hated the sarcasm in his voice.

"Right. Well, if it isn't asking you too much, please update me with your new address at school as soon as you can."

He cut off Marietta's response. "So that I can send you your statements to read."

Marietta took a few deep breaths to calm herself while Tony opened the front door for her. He held out the ring of keys. "I'll need these back from you before you leave," he said.

She snatched the keys from his hand. "Of course you do, Tony. And if it's not asking too much of you, I need to pick up a car to drive myself up to school. It can be used. I just need something in good repair so that I can haul some of my stuff with me. I only want to make one trip."

Tony shrugged. "No. It's not asking me too much. That's why I'm here. That's my job, Marietta. That's always my job.

To do the things you want and need done and don't feel like doing yourself."

Marietta wanted to slap him across the face. She could feel her hand twitch. The keys she held actually jingled a little. But by the time she got her hand into position, Tony had already turned his back on her and walked across the street without a backward glance. Then he shut his front door none too softly.

Marietta shook her head and shrugged. She explored throughout the rooms, noting the barrenness. She went through the house using the keys Tony gave her to access various cabinets. She opened her grandfather's secretary, now empty, the record player missing. The other furniture remained, but all personal touches like photo albums and papers and small electronics were gone.

Marietta frowned when she entered her old bedroom to find the same. There was her bed and chair and chest of drawers. That was her table that she used as a desk. But what happened to her books and drawings and little doodads, like her clock radio? In the attic? She certainly hoped so. Because otherwise, Tony would receive an earful.

Returning downstairs, Marietta jingled through the key ring until she found the set that allowed access to the attic through the kitchen pantry. First, she had to unlock the pantry door. In the pantry, she found the cabinets and old strongbox where her grandparents guarded cash from produce sales, also empty. Then she unlocked the optical illusion of a door that led to the attic staircase, invisible to anyone who didn't know it existed.

At the top of the narrow staircase, she used another key to open the door to the attic. She flipped the light switch. Coated with a light layer of dust, here hid all of the family secrets and skeletons. There was the record player and Grandpa's old radio. His old eight track player, her television and VCR combo, her clock radio, and then her boom box with cassette player. Everything. Tony must have put all of this up here for safekeeping. Her grandfather would have been too weak to haul all the boxes and equipment upstairs by himself.

In that case, Marietta wondered what Tony must know about her family. Would he recognize the discrepancies even if they manifested in old, yellowed photos and documents? Did he rustle through their deepest sorrows and turn up his nose? How much had Grandpa told him? Marietta sighed. Why did she keep thinking about it? The past was no longer her problem. It wasn't her fault and she had her own life to live.

She returned to her room to get dressed for dinner with the Jennings. If she had to jab herself with a fork to keep from letting Tony really have it in front of Miss Annette, then that's what she would do. On her volunteer assignment, she hauled buckets of water under a blazing sun for four years. Even though he deserved a good talking to, she would fake civility and just ignore him the rest of the time. She could handle Tony for about an hour. After an hour, no promises.

***

"Marietta, oh bless your heart, you look so thin," his mother exclaimed.

Tony wondered what on Earth his mother was talking about. Marietta was thin only in some places. But pretty phat in others. The maturity in her eyes reminded him that she had known the touch of a man other than him. Which excited him and pissed him off at the same time.

"It's all the work I've been doing overseas, Miss Annette." He watched Marietta's eyes light up as she explained her work with potable water.

"It's funny you say that," Tony answered. "We've been working on the irrigation system in the orchard."

"Oh really?" When Marietta turned towards him, his stomach wobbled a little. But he managed to update her on the new water tank and rain gutters that kept the trees supplied during summer drought.

"And that's not all," he went on, not caring if he bored her, "I arranged monthly orders to grocery stores, churches, schools, day care centers, restaurants. You name it."

"But what's left for the produce stand?"

"We haven't used it lately. There's no one to staff it and the monthly orders bring in more income."

She frowned at that. He shrugged. Fuck her, if she didn't like it.

His mother quickly interjected, "Any extra produce, I help Tony take up to the homeless shelter. They're very grateful to Wayfarer Orchards. Aren't they, Tony?"

"Yes, they are."

Marietta seemed especially pleased about the last part. "I think that's wonderful," she said.

He caught himself smiling back at her, pleased that she was pleased.

"That was all Tony's idea," Miss Annette announced proudly.

The atmosphere around the table lightened and seemed almost pleasant, but then...

"Marietta, did you know Tony's seeing a nice young lady?" Miss Annette asked.

Marietta blinked, not sure what Miss Annette meant since Tony sat opposite her right now. He was 'seeing' Marietta. Looking right at her, in fact. But then she understood because now he looked at his mother with an expression of horror.

Oblivious, Miss Annette chirped on, "You remember Carla, don't you? She and Tony attended prom together."

The statement clattered into the discussion like a broken plate, leaving an uncomfortable tension behind.

Not sure how to respond, Marietta glanced at Tony. Even though his skin was dark as chocolate, it seemed to grow rather purplish in tint. He took a drink of water and said nothing.

"How interesting," Marietta commented with a stiff smile for Miss Annette. "I don't know if I told you Miss Annette, but I have some news of my own."

She felt Tony's eyes on her face, swift and intense, waiting. "I just enrolled in a four-year university program up North." Tony relaxed somewhat.

Marietta went on to tell Miss Annette and Tony about her business major. She chose not to mention that she would attend the same university that Stephanie Madison and Roy Brazil attended. She considered that a family secret. Miss Annette exclaimed about the opportunity and heaped praise upon Marietta.

"Remember, I'm gonna need your new address when you have it," Tony said, at last.

"I know, Tony!"

That pretty much ended dinner. Miss Annette shooed Marietta home when she offered to help with cleanup. Tony disappeared into his office.

***

The drive through the mountains towards rolling prairies recalled the pain and anguish-filled drive in reverse that brought Marietta down to Wayfarer years ago with Grandpa in the ancient RV. She cringed when she remembered her gloomy mood in the aftermath of the death of her parents. Still a high school teenager, it never occurred to her to ask about or even notice her grandfather's pain... and fear.

Just because you feel bad, there's no call to treat others like dirt under your shoe.

Marietta gripped the steering wheel. She knew this trip back to Wayfarer would prove difficult, but the old memories continued to emerge like malevolent ghosts.

The times she snapped at Grandma. The times she ducked her head and stared at her desk when other students at Wayfarer High tried to engage her in conversation. The way she ran or biked back to the Madison property to bury herself in orchard work. How she ignored her grandfather's pleas and left him alone while she traveled the world. How she rebuffed Tony every time he reached out to her. How Miss Annette still invited her over despite it all. Admitting her own culpability made her feel bad.

So instead, for several miles, Marietta tried to think of all the things she should have said to put Tony back into his place as her employee. With Tony's grudging assistance, Marietta had finally purchased this second-hand sport utility vehicle with which to transport her belongings northward to her small town Midwestern university. But he really overstepped himself. Not only that, he'd pretty much won each exchange of words between them while they conducted business.

"Wow. Way to really show off the legal training, Tony," Marietta told him. Then she stopped talking to him about anything other than the business at hand, signing vehicle title transfer, registration, insurance, and then returning his precious house keys.

She'd been tempted to either throw them at him or drop them onto the ground for him to pick up. But there had been a light of warning in his eyes and besides, she wouldn't do that in front of Miss Annette. So she took the higher road and placed the keys into his outstretched hand. Their fingers brushed and the thrill she received in return bothered her. But that was just biology she told herself, nothing more.

As far as she was concerned, Tony was no longer a friend. He was a self-righteous, full of himself, know-it-all, arrogant, pain in the ass. One of these days, she would fire him and treasure the experience when it happened.

Marietta's mouth trembled. Despite her efforts, more than a few sobs escaped. She straightened herself when the SUV drifted across the double yellow lines that marked the mountain road. She needed to focus. All of that was then. This is now. She had work to do. She had a life to live.

***

Derek Robinette threw the newspaper across his large, dark wooden desk at the man opposite. "Rumors of an impending consortium of industrialists in Lake City," the title on the front page of the business section read, from where it lay crowded among mementos of his past glory.

"They don't deserve it," Robinette rasped. "They didn't build it and they didn't fucking earn it. They took it away from me and my father. They stole it from us!"

"The son seems different."

"Nah. Well yeah. But not in a good way. The son's an obnoxious piece of shit and a literal sonofabitch. People praise him like the second coming and the arrogant motherfucker eats it up like cornflakes. His public relations people probably wrote that press release themselves. And then paid someone to leak it to the paper as news. And he dares to call himself king of the city."

"Okay, but the new blood might be your opening to get some back."

Whenever Robinette laughed, really laughed, a rough, dry yet phlegmy growl rose from the back of his throat.

"Nah. I already met him. His father was a crook too, but at least he had some discretion and decorum about his ways. Alex King is a greedy, grimy, climber. He's crooked, but without the social graces of his father. That's the difference."

"Mm."

"I can't let him take my spot when the Consortium forms. Celara's not fit to lick Cadis's boots. You'll see to it."

"I'm your man, twenty-grand. You know this."

"Then you need to get started."

"It's already begun."

Robinette raised his brows, causing a deep furrow in the craggy, scarred landscape of his visage. His shoulders shook. Another laugh began to form. He threw back his head and yawned wide to reveal a deep black cavern filled with wet, yellowish stalactites and stalagmites. From within the cavern, another growl rattled, and then roared forth.

CHAPTER 12   THE CITY

Four years later, Marietta joined the staff at the university while she worked on her master's degree in business. She found that she excelled in the business program due to her work with her grandfather's orchards plus her overseas volunteer experiences. Best of all, no one complained that she sounded like a newscaster when she spoke. In the Midwest, everyone spoke like a newscaster.

She settled down for another few years of work and study for her doctorate. However, waves of sadness overcame her now and then, especially when it came time to collect her degrees. In a room full of congratulating families, she stood alone with a tight, frozen smile on her face.

No one discovered her connection to two former students. She never spoke of Stephanie Madison or Roy Brazil, though she found their yearbook pictures in the library and stared at the two people who created her.

She made copies of all the photos she located of Roy and Stephanie, but she liked to see the originals from time to time. So she visited the university's archives just to smile at her birth mother and father. They seemed so innocent and unaware that soon Marietta (Alicia back then) would make her grand entrance into their lives in just a few years. And so would Susan.

If they knew then, what they would know a few years into the future, would they have ever bothered with each other? The sight of her parents as teenagers melted her heart and made her decision to settle in the Midwest, less than an hour's drive from Lake City, worth it.

Marietta dated among the faculty and staff at the university and participated in community events. She traveled for work and for pleasure. She enjoyed the single life of an educated professional woman. Granted, none of her relationships lasted more than a few months, but no harm, no foul at the amicable parting of ways. She had no children, but then, she didn't want any. Surely she would wreck any child's life and she didn't need that on her conscience along with her other past mistakes.

Ever faithful, Tony's updates on her holdings arrived, dry and legalistic, delicately-flavored with distaste. Marietta read through the documents, searching for things to complain about, but she found nothing to say about them except, "Steady as she goes." But one day soon, she would fire him and enjoy doing so.

Whatever.

Life was fine as far as she was concerned until the day she realized that she'd finally arrived to the age of forty. She'd been so careful to live a quiet, ordinary life. Stephanie had burned so bright that she didn't last past thirty-six. Marietta felt no need to repeat history.

She had no husband or boyfriend, just occasional dates. She had no close friends, only acquaintances. If she slipped and fell in her shower, only her work colleagues would notice her absence from the world, and even that might take a couple of days.

But the important thing was, she felt safe, if not happy.

Despite her appearance of success and confidence, severe self-loathing greeted her at the door of her small one-bedroom, one bath house every night. A few glasses of white wine usually made all the bad memories go away. Sometimes she feared that she inherited nervous nerves from Susan and/or Stephanie.

Marietta decided that she needed a project to take her mind off the shadows and echoes. Why not clean out the clutter in her basement from top to bottom? She needed to get rid of outdated academic detritus--the ghosts of business classes past and whatever else she hadn't missed over the years. She would clean the cobwebs from her basement and then her mind and soul.

Beneath a stack of dusty books, Stephanie's Bible and the secret journal it contained surfaced. Stephanie's secrets had gone straight from the Madison home's attic into Marietta's basement when she hauled a car load of personal belongings north from Wayfarer.

Marietta hesitated. In some respects, Stephanie's secrets had ruined Marietta's youth and turned her girlish world upside down. Marietta searched herself. She was no longer a little girl. She was no longer afraid of what she didn't know. Was she?

Heart beating a little faster than normal, she read through the hidden journal again with the keen eye of a woman who had lived a life and had the benefit of wisdom through adult experiences. However, the questions still remained because the journal didn't answer them. Why did Stephanie kill those people at Cadis Industries and herself?

This time, she decided that she deserved the full story. She wanted answers and not just what other people wanted her to believe. It was her right to know. Stephanie had some explaining to do. She carried the journal upstairs, dumped out her second glass of wine, and flipped through the pages yet again.

Stephanie's writings, sad and tragic, and to be honest, horrific in their hopeless desperation, only revealed part of the story. She needed more. Marietta used her home computer to go online. She wanted to read through newspaper accounts of Stephanie's attack on Cadis. But the attack occurred during the infancy of the Internet. Online newspaper archives didn't go back that far. All she managed to gather was a list of citations. There was nothing else. Not even random mentions on obscure amateur websites.

If she wanted the full journalistic account, she would have to make the hour-long drive into Lake City to the historical center to find the newspaper archive on microfilm. But should she? Grandpa told her never to return to Lake City. For years, she heeded his warning. But the frustration of not knowing the answer to the riddles in Stephanie's life overwhelmed the voices of yesteryear, long dead and buried now. She simply had to know.

It should be okay. Whoever, tried to kill her by sabotaging her brake lines must have forgotten her by now. That saboteur might be senile and sitting in a diaper in the nursing home. Maybe they'd died or moved to a different city. It should be fine. It had to. She would be in and out of Lake City so fast, no one would even know she set a foot down inside city limits. Marietta arranged a day off from work and planned for a day trip into Lake City.

Now, as she stood outside the dark brown brick building just north of the Lake City River. Marietta hesitated. Perhaps she should just get back into her SUV and drive herself home. Maybe she should finish cleaning out her basement and let the memories fade away. She could slip right back into the routine of university life and continue with her committees and research and writing and still be great. No one had ever bothered her. Whoever wanted her back then had forgotten her and moved on to something else. Maybe Marietta should move on too. She could increase to an extra glass of Riesling on the weekends, if she needed to, and wait for forty-one. Let the past stay the past.

But was that really living a life? And did that make her a punk? No. Because she wasn't a punk. Marietta squared her shoulders and marched up the steps into the brick building.

She already knew which articles she needed and so she whipped through the rolls of microfilm like lightning, checking each title off her list as she printed. "4 Dead, 1 Survivor in unprecedented chemical gas attack," caught her attention. She remembered this headline because it showcased a large color photo of Stephanie above the fold. She'd seen this paper inside the newsstand.

Susan hadn't allowed newspapers inside the Brazil house in the aftermath of Stephanie's rampage. She'd ordered Marietta to not turn on the television or radio either. They didn't have Internet access back then. And Marietta missed all the chatter at school those first few days. In obedience to Susan, Marietta remained the most ignorant of anyone about what occurred in Lake City that horrific day. Even now, she felt somewhat defiant of Susan's twisted authority.

She scanned the article. Surprised to see Susan's name, she read Susan's statements to police. "Stephanie had a history of emotional instability. She wanted to die." Open and shut. Crazy woman goes postal and kills self plus four others. Investigate for what? Bing, bang, boom, case closed.

Marietta, you remember that I told you Stephanie was unstable? Sometimes, when you walk a tightrope, you make it to the other side. Other times, you fall off. Stephanie made it across many times. As a matter of fact, she got real good at it. But, she crossed one time too many.

Unforgettable Susan.

Marietta snaked more microfilm through the reader. From a follow-up story, she learned about Kate Winterset. The article's writer revealed that the woman befriended Stephanie at Cadis. No quote, just passing mention of a name, and then the writer returned to more salacious descriptions of gore and mayhem.

For what it was worth, at last, Marietta knew of someone other than a member of the Brazil or Madison families, or the gossips in Wayfarer who knew Stephanie and could shed light on her mentality. Marietta exhaled. Kate Winterset was her lead.

She printed more stories that included statements from the bereaved of others who died in the attack. She wouldn't contact them. But nothing else shed light on the circumstances. Except... that police mentioned that Stephanie had purchased a .22-caliber gun. But no gun was found on her person or at her residence, the police said. Marietta's mind clicked and a puzzle piece *snicked* into place. Under Susan's nightstand, a tiny toy-like handgun...

Derek Robinette expressed his pain and anguish at such mindless evil and destruction via a public relations representative. Marietta checked for anniversary accounts at the one-year, five-year, and ten-year marks and printed those as well, though no new information emerged. The doer died. Case closed.

She checked for the twenty-year anniversary article, but didn't see anything. Lake City and Cadis Industries had moved on, supposedly. It was now twenty-four years later. Maybe next year, some hotshot junior reporter would follow up. But Marietta certainly wasn't going to wait for that.

***

Inside the quiet office lined with dark wood trim that met dark wood floors and housed dark wood and leather furniture, the interior putting green and exercise equipment remained idle. The enormous flat screen television, well-stocked bar, and Cuban cigars received far more attention.

Derek Robinette scrolled through an older news article on his computer screen, "The sun also rises on Celara Electric." The rumors had become reality. The electrical construction firm moved into solar construction.

> Due to the acquisition of key solar photovoltaic cell designs, Celara Electric advanced its position within the energy sector. For years, in back rooms and boardrooms, industrialists have whispered that the electrical construction company would emerge as a leader in the alternative energy construction market. Heavily connected within the business, banking, and government contracting sectors, today to no one's amazement, only the sky is the limit as the fortunes of the new division, Celara Solar, rise like Apollo running his chariot over the Lake City metropolis...

"Christ, King and his public relations people really spread a thick pile," he muttered to himself. The article continued with only passing mention of Cadis Industries. The chemical attack had proven bad for their company's public profile. The death of Paul Robinette created a wave of uncertainty and a lack of confidence. All of which Paul Robinette's son knew first hand.

He read aloud now, "In addition, Cadis failed to develop the necessary technology to keep abreast and so fell behind Celara whose new developments in research and technology

THE CADIS EVENING 113

allowed Celara to dominate with strategic strides towards solar construction."

Furious, Robinette called Kowalski into his office for a half hour rant.

"Anything they got, it's because Cadis let them have it," he concluded and tossed the newspaper on his desk.

Kowalski started to protest.

"Nah. It's okay. Tough to admit, but it's true. But those days are over. We're back in it. King's confident, but it's all a show. Deep down inside his gut, he knows that he's not capable of going balls deep and dirty. He has no idea the things I'm willing to do and the places I'm willing to go. He doesn't know me like that. He's gonna pay for what he and his father did to my father and to Cadis, turning our own bitch against us. No. King will never understand how I hide my hand. He will never see me coming."

Kowalski waited.

"I need some legwork on Celara."

"I'll make contact today."

***

Marietta left the microfilm reader to use one of the computer terminals at the historical center to access the Internet. She found a photo of Kate Winterset in the directory of Celara Solar's website. Beside the photo, Marietta noted Kate's title. Executive Assistant, her phone number, and her email address. Marietta checked for her father's veterinarian friend and found his obituary instead.

She left the historical center with the stacks of articles. Her heart pounded because she knew the call to Kate would announce her presence in Lake City and possibly alert an old enemy. But she had already committed to following through on this quest. So she made the call from her cell phone while she sat inside her SUV. She tried to prepare herself for voicemail or a lot of rigmarole in case someone screened the call.

But a rough, Demi Moore-like cigarette voice answered, "Celara, this is Kate," on the second ring.

Startled, Marietta coughed then responded, "This is Mary Madison. I wanted to ask you about Cadis Industries. Specifically a former employee, Stephanie Madison."

The throaty voice answered back, "Mary Madison." An awkward silence passed. Then Kate cleared her own throat, without noticeable improvement. "Are you related to Stephanie?"

"I'm her niece."

This time, a longer silence passed. "No. You're not her niece. Stephanie had one niece and only one niece. Her name was neither Mary nor Madison. Nice try. No comment, bitch."

Taken by surprise, Marietta sucked in her breath. She quickly rallied. "Marietta. Marietta Brazil." She heard Kate's in-drawn breath and prayed the woman wouldn't disconnect the call.

"Marietta?"

"Yes."

"You're Marietta," the raspy voice whispered.

"Yes."

"How old are you?"

"I'm forty."

"That sounds about right." Silence again.

"My grandparents changed my name to Mary Madison and moved me out of state to keep people from harassing me."

"And now it's twenty-five years later and you're harassing me instead," Kate's no-nonsense Midwestern tone responded and flattened further.

"Yes, I..."

"Not over the phone... Marietta."

She and Kate arranged to meet at a downtown coffee shop after Kate got off work that evening.

CHAPTER 13   JESSE

Summertime in Lake City showcased a breathless celebration of people, sun, and nature. Winter demoralized and violated the citizenry with such brutal force that they partied as hard as they could during the warmer months. Today, nature exploded with the mardi gras of earth magic. Birds, butterflies, bees, trees, flowers-- everything popped in riotous, vivid color surrounding Marietta's old home.

The scene of Susan's death... the scene of what Marietta once thought was her unnatural crime of matricide... was beautiful in its wild abandonment. Mother Nature seemed determined to reclaim the sinister scene of her family's undoing.

All Marietta knew of the Brazil home these days lay in the rows and columns of Tony's detailed spreadsheets that he continued to email to her. Apparently, she paid the taxes, maintenance, and upkeep. In return, she received very occasional rental income.

She stared at the vacant shell and tried to remember the happier times in her life while she lived here. In spite of the flowery abundance, the longer she looked, the more the house appeared haunted and ready to devour the unwary who peered behind the floral mask. What type of degradation in someone's life would ever force such a desperate soul to rent this spooky house?

"You thinking about renting?" The thirty-something brown-haired man walked up from her left.

"I don't know." Marietta turned towards him. "Should I?"

"Well now, I don't know." The neighbor took his hands out of his cargo shorts and crossed his arms. He looked at the house with pity. "People say this place is haunted. No one ever stays for long."

"It looks so abandoned."

"Yeah. They say a nice married couple lived here once. Upper middle class. They had a daughter. Dog. Whole shebang."

"How long ago?" Marietta asked, though she knew.

"Before I moved in next door. I inherited from my uncle who passed. That was... uhm..." He thought a moment. "Eleven years ago. So way back before then. Some of the other neighbors told me the daughter went crazy and killed her parents."

Marietta gasped and flushed.

"I know, right?" the neighbor squealed, pleased with her reaction to his free guided tour. "Ran the mother down with her car over there." He pointed to the curb and demonstrated the trajectory.

"Then she crashed into the garage. You can see where they repaired it. The mother died and the daughter got taken to the hospital. When the father visited her, she poisoned him somehow."

"Wow," Marietta responded, too furious to defend herself.

"It's horrible," the neighbor replied nodding his head. "What's the world coming to?"

"Why do you think she did it?" Marietta asked.

"Don't know. Something in the water. Maybe she was abused, or something. She even killed the dog! Can you believe it?"

Marietta sucked in her breath. "The dog?"

"Yeah. Which is even more horrible. I mean, sure you don't like your parents. Some kids don't. I mean, really, who does? I sure didn't. But what'd the dog ever do to her? I don't get it."

"What... what happened to the dog? Did she... run it over too?" Marietta braced.

"Nope." The neighbor waited with expectation.

Instead of shaking him, she went along with this bit of street theater, playing her part in the neighbor's one-man, one-night-only show. "How'd the dog die?"

Right on cue, he whispered, "Well! My uncle told people... he was a nosy sort you see... the kind who always looked through the curtains to see what other people were doing."

Marietta remembered that Susan used to complain about Mr. Johnson's nosiness every once in a while. Several times a week, in fact.

"He says," and here the neighbor paused to look both directions to see if any latecomers wanted to join the audience, "The dog was shot! He heard the gun go off!"

"Shot? But..." Stunned, Marietta blinked. A pain seared through her chest. She remembered the anger she felt towards Grandpa, that something in his story didn't ring true.

What happened to Jesse?

The police think the dog ran away.

He never would have run from me. I don't believe you.

The lies, all the lies! They sickened her.

Marietta shivered. "I see."

"Exactly! They never found the dog's body though. Or a gun. So he couldn't prove it." The neighbor threw his hands into the air. "Nobody ever stays long in this place."

And, scene! Applause. Bow. Lights. Curtain. Please tip your waitress.

The small, toy-like gun under Susan's dresser? Susan disposed of something in the trash. And then... and then... she smiled. Jesse... Jesse... Jesse...

Three deaths, four including Stephanie. Jesse was alive when Marietta drove away from the house. She heard him barking after her confrontation with Susan. She ran to her station wagon. *Bark, bark, barkity bark!* Then she drove to the airport... leaking a thin trail of brake fluid drip by little drop.

Then... Susan shot Jesse. She shot a helpless dog penned in the backyard with no possible escape. Marietta struggled not to cry in front of this annoying man. Because then he'd just add her drama to his script for the next visitor to this house of horrors. Maybe even start acting out the multiple roles as performance art.

Susan walked out to the trash cans with... something. Marietta drove down the hill. She braked, but still accelerated. She stomped the brake into the floor, pushed the pedal all the way to the metal. The station wagon stampeded up the curb. Susan screamed and then... she smiled. The garage approached closer through her windshield.

When Marietta woke at the hospital, she saw her father at her bedside, distraught and confused. And then...

"Are you okay?" Mr. Johnson's nephew seemed more excited than concerned, as if pleased that his ghoulish Halloween tale brought the house down. Maybe the audience wanted an encore? Marietta had no doubt that his storytelling skills had direct correlation to the scarcity of renters. What next? Costumes? Hand puppets?

"Sure," she said. "I'd better go."

Shoulders slumped, Marietta took slow steps back to her car to finish her thoughts, the ones she'd trained herself over the years to never think again, as well as to process the new information she just received.

No more hiding, she told herself. No more running away from the truth. No more white wine weekends.

After she saw her father at her bedside, she woke again and found Grandma's letter to Stephanie. And that's how she discovered that Stephanie was her real mother. If she had not read that letter, if Stephanie had not reached out to her from the grave, no one would ever have told her. She would never have known the truth of her real identity.

Marietta dampened the quick flash of anger and betrayal that rose inside her. And where was the letter now? She had no idea. Stay focused.

She opened her car door and sat at the steering wheel, almost in the same spot where... Susan smiled with such eerie delight just seconds before she flew through the air.

What did that smile mean?

The triumph in Susan's eyes seemed almost an indication of some twisted victory. The knowledge that she had corrupted her sister's daughter to the point of murder, maybe. Marietta flinched as familiar prickles ran down her arm. How much had Susan hated her? Marietta felt an acrid taste in the back of her mouth. She took shallow breaths because she could feel a gathering of saliva in her throat. Her neck muscles tightened. She knew that feeling from Saturday evenings when she hadn't yet learned her beverage limits.

What did it make her that a ghoul, an eater of souls raised her? And what about Stephanie, her real mother, who delivered her into the arms of evil? What did that make Stephanie? How much of the degeneracy trait did Marietta inherit? Did degeneracy circulate even now through her veins, in and out of her heart, like sewage flowed through the brackish channels of Lake City River? Maybe degeneracy pushed its way up her esophagus right about now. Marietta tasted sourness in the back of her throat. Degeneracy. If it spewed across her dashboard, white and poisonous like the smothering cloud of her dreams, then she could study it. Perhaps come to understand it.

Marietta gagged and rested her head on the car's steering wheel.

An abrupt tap on the driver's side window made her jump. Mr. Johnson's nephew, just as obnoxious as his uncle, made a rolling gesture for her to lower the glass. Marietta pretended not to understand him. No matter.

"Hey, are you all right?" he mouthed through a circle of fog on the window.

Marietta frowned, as if confused. She started the car and strapped on her seatbelt.

No! What else do you remember about that night? Think about that night, Marietta. Think very carefully... you tried to brake. Don't you remember? Do you remember something wrong with the brakes on your car before Susan died?

"I remember," Marietta whispered.

Susan was wrong. Marietta was more than the mistakes she made. Susan had been wrong about many things. This annoying man beside her car was wrong too. Marietta shifted into gear.

Marietta would prove it. Scowling, she glanced over her shoulder to check traffic. The ice water that flowed through Susan's veins did not flow through Marietta's. The crystals that encased Susan's frostbitten heart did not freeze Marietta's. Still, as Marietta drove off, she did hope that the back wheel would catch Mr. Johnson's nephew's foot, making a good story great, but he jumped back in time. Pity.

Roy loved her. He told her so many times. Stephanie loved her. She said so in her journal. Grandpa loved her. He showed her through deeds, rather than words. Maybe Grandma loved her, though the jury was still out on that.

For the most part, Marietta had been loved. She had to believe in that love because she had nothing much else besides that. And still, that was much more than some could say. Her overseas volunteer assignments put that much into perspective, at least.

She'd reawakened in the hospital to chaos. Someone had killed her father. Not a suicide. And not an accident. A murder. Police swarmed everywhere. People yelled. *Poison.* They whispered the word in front of her as if she couldn't hear. And then they looked at her with questions in their eyes. And she didn't know. She really didn't know anything.

Four deaths.

Grandpa Madison came and took her away. He changed her name and helped her to bury the memories. But now, she wanted answers. Because someone destroyed her family.

All the mysteries began with Stephanie's death. Her real mother was the key, the catalyst for all that followed. Stephanie's chemical attack on Cadis unleashed a chain reaction that demolished almost her entire family.

Why did Stephanie kill all those people at Cadis Industries and herself?

"I'm more than the mistakes I made," Marietta whispered again as she drove from her old neighborhood with its residential idiots. "And I've made mistakes. But I did not kill Susan," she said in a louder voice. Grandpa proved that with the police report. He likely saved her from insanity when he finally told her the truth.

"I did not kill my father." The nurse at the hospital proved that with her medical chart. Neither was she responsible for

Grandma's passing. Grandpa said so more than once and she chose to believe him. She didn't kill Jesse because her wonderful dog perished from a gunshot. The neighbor revealed that with all of his soap opera narration. She'd never fired a gun in her entire life.

Then why was she hiding?

Why was she running?

She wasn't! Not anymore.

All of the lies and the secrets and all of the questions without answers had crushed Marietta's spirit and driven her into a corner where she hid from life. The shadows of destruction crept closer towards her every year and reached out like falcon talons to snatch her under.

But the time arrived for her to fight back against the shadows. The evening would soon begin. And then after the evening, she would bring the light of day to drive away the darkness from her life. She would fight to destroy the lies with the truth.

That's why she needed to talk to Kate Winterset as soon as possible.

CHAPTER 14   KATE

Marietta descended from the bright lights of Lake City's street level with its designer clothing stores, expensive hotels, and slack-jawed and bedazzled tourists to the second level underneath the train tracks and bridges and freeway overpasses.

Trains and cars and people crisscrossed overhead. The infrastructure above provided a safe haven below for the locals who desired their happy hours tourist and suburbanite-free. In a coffee and wine shop where raucous voices and train whistles drowned out the acoustic guitarist, Kate ordered a glass of red.

Her green eyes glittered in the low light across the table. "Why am I here? Why are you here and what are you trying to do... should I call you Mary or Marietta?"

"Mary's fine. I've been Mary the last twenty-four years, I'm used to it."

"I'll tell you right now, if this is about Stephanie Madison, then I've got nothing to say."

"Then why are you here, Kate?"

"Because you're buying."

Right on time, their drinks arrived. Marietta started a tab and took a hefty slug of ginger ale, almost wishing she'd gone for something stronger. But she needed to keep her head clear in order to work Kate, her only lead towards the mystery surrounding Stephanie. Red hair framed the hard beauty of Kate's face, both artificially-enhanced, along with the fingernails that reminded Marietta of falcon talons, which she'd learned from experience to always treat with caution.

"What do you remember about Stephanie? You claimed that you were her friend."

"I was her friend, Mary. I've never denied that. But I know that you can't win this, whatever you're trying to do." Kate started on her drink.

"Why did she hate Sundays?"

Kate choked. "Nice, Mary. Real nice." Her nostrils flared and her eyes narrowed. "You don't want to know why she hated Sundays. Trust me on that."

"I don't trust anyone. Stephanie taught me that."

"Did she?" Kate's lip curled to a slight sneer. "Playing Nancy Drew detective, eh? What's that gonna get you, I wonder?"

Marietta didn't answer.

"I highly recommend that you leave that door closed," Kate continued, "Because it's not going to end well, I promise you. This is the City, Mary, whoever you are, whatever you call yourself."

"I know it's the City, Kate. I'm from here."

"Then you know that you could either end up dead or alone and crying and wishing you were dead. I'm not lying."

"Is that what happened to you? Alone and crying?"

Kate's mouth tightened. Her talons drummed the table. No fool, Marietta kept the talons inside the periphery of her vision. The older woman's nostrils flared again. She took another drink of wine. Marietta responded with another drink of ginger ale.

"Whatever's bothering you about Stephanie, pretend it never happened. Pretend that you never knew her, Mary. Just like you've been doing up till now, and just... move on. Like me."

"Kate, I can't. You know I can't. I'm Stephanie's last remaining family, her only living relative. I have to know why she did what she did to herself and all those other people. They keep saying she was crazy. That's how people talk about her. I don't believe them. But there has to be a reason. I have to know for sure."

"For what?"

Marietta's mouth trembled, bravado gone, which Kate clocked.

"Yeah. That's exactly what I thought. I'm sorry, but no. For your sake. No."

"Please." Marietta's voice broke. "I've lost everyone. I don't know who else to ask."

"Fuck!" Other customers in the loud coffee shop glanced over. Kate glared right back at them, Lake City gangster-style. "Shit. Are you really gonna start fucking crying right here in front of all these people?

Marietta's stubborn side forced her shoulders back. She straightened up and waited. Kate huffed again and looked around the coffee shop. No one paid attention to them anymore.

"Mary, when you look back on this conversation, recognize and remember that you," Kate's talon extended forward, "were warned. Clearly warned. In English. Right to your face."

"I'm not going anywhere."

"Oh really?" Kate considered her a moment, then shrugged. "What? Gonna stalk me, or something?"

Marietta finished off her ginger ale, and then set the empty glass on the table between them with a firm *thunk*. "I do happen to have your home address."

Kate's mouth dropped open. "Goddamit. Jesus fucking help. You remind me so much of her." Kate sighed then finished off her second glass of wine. "You asked for this. Okay? So here we go. "

She leaned in closer to Marietta. The thick mane of hair swung forward and shadowed her face. "Stephanie wasn't crazy, Mary."

"She wasn't?"

Kate shook her head. "She was trying to survive crazy circumstances." Again, Kate tapped her fingers on the table. Again, Marietta waited her out.

Kate looked left, right, and left again. Marietta automatically mirrored her movements. Kate, at last satisfied that it was safe to continue, lowered her husky croak to a whisper. "I know because I've been there."

"Where?"

"In the basement at Cadis. It's all in the basement, Mary." Kate leaned back. "Way back in the good old days, I used to be a stripper," she said.

While Marietta blinked at the random change in topic, Kate put up a finger to signal another round.

"Oh yeah," Kate shrugged. "I know that surprises you. But before I got hired on as the file clerk at Cadis, I danced. After I left high school, I didn't know what the fuck to do with myself. My parents sure didn't know. So I had a great idea. I'll dance. Did that for a while. Then I left that life, so I thought. But word got out around the office. Some of those people used to be my regulars. They treated me like shit at Cadis. All except for Stephanie. She always looked me in the eye. Talked to me like normal, real respectful. Even though Stephanie was a superstar, she was always kind to me no matter what anyone else said. That's why I hated how they treated her which was worse than me. Well, that is until I faked stupid well enough to get away from the freak show."

The waitress arrived with their drinks, Kate's third, Marietta's second. The waitress left and Kate continued.

"That was right after..." Kate pulled a pack of cigarettes out of her purse and shook one out. She looked at the cigarette with impatience, and then placed it back into the pack. She opted for a healthy swallow of red wine instead. "Anyway, there was so much confusion after the killings that no one noticed little old stupid ex-stripper me heading for the exit. By the way, I forgot to ask. How did you find me?"

"One of the newspaper articles mentioned that you and Stephanie were friends."

"Yeah." Kate let out a snide laugh. "Boy, I dreaded the day someone would figure out I wasn't as dumb as I made myself out to be. Cause I tried real hard to be convincing. Look," Kate pouted. "You got me stressed out. I need a cigarette. Can we, uh..."

Marietta settled the bill and they relocated to a small park tucked between the skyscrapers. The warm clear evening and the block-sized canopy of trees made the light pollution that washed away the stars seem not so hard on the eyes.

"Where was I?" Kate asked.

"You made yourself look stupid and dumb."

"Oh yeah." Kate chuckled and lit up. "Thanks. Despite my best efforts to pretend retardation, Celara Electric snapped me right up, I think for any business intelligence I could bring about Cadis. Joke was on them. I didn't have any intelligence, none that I planned to share. But anyway, they let me stay and be the receptionist. Can you imagine they made me the phone jockey, even with this voice of mine? Go figure. Or maybe that was the whole point. Some people find it sexy. I don't like it. Anyway, then I moved up to executive assistant, and there I remain. I have kids in school. I keep my head down. I shut up and I do as I'm told. I live to talk about it."

Marietta flinched.

"Jesus, I'm sorry, Mary. What's wrong with me? How many drinks did you buy me?"

Marietta waited a beat. "What's in the basement at Cadis?"

"Hmmm." Kate's smile seemed wistful. "Just like her. Always have an eye on the ball. I was fresh off the block in those days. Didn't halfway know how to act or how to carry myself in an office. I'm probably just a few years older than you, Mary."

Marietta hid a smile. She was pretty sure that Kate had more than just a few years on her.

"I admired Stephanie. I wanted to be professional just like her. Dress like her. Talk like her. She really seemed to have it together." Kate tapped the ash from her cigarette. "But they gave that woman a special kind of hell that I wouldn't wish on my worst enemy."

Again Marietta waited her out, sensing that truth was near.

"Everything's in the basement at Robinette." Kate took a drag off the cigarette and stared into the trees.

"Everything like what?" Marietta asked to help her focus back on topic.

"Told you. I was their file clerk. They kept all their files in the basement. Derek called me into the office that Sunday morning. I removed her files after she..." Kate side-eyed Marietta and flicked some more ash. "After. Derek told me to find every single file on Stephanie Madison and put all of them into the incinerator. Every last one. We didn't have a shredder in those days, so we burned sensitive files. I was supposed to burn everything, her files and a bunch of other stuff. And I did put her files in the incinerator. Only..."

"Only what?"

"They didn't burn. He didn't ask me about it and I never told him or anyone else otherwise. Till now."

"So they're still down there in the basement?"

Kate's eyes shifted. "What?" She asked with a harsh laugh. "Oh, I get it. So Nancy Drew wants to have a look for herself. Is that it? That's the big plan? Oh boy, I guess that makes you the hero."

Marietta stared at Kate's profile. "There has to be a way."

"What way? Tell me that, Mary." Kate took another puff. "How you gonna do that?"

"I don't know. How am I gonna do that, Kate?"

Kate coughed and waved the smoke out of her face. She stared at Marietta, surprised. A silent standoff developed which Marietta broke.

"You showed up here tonight and met with me for a reason."

Kate gave another rough laugh that led right back to another coughing fit. "That's the spirit," she croaked. "Never back down, Mary. Not even an inch. Just get right in my fucking face though you've never met me and..."

Kate chuckled again. "Yeah. I get it." She threw the butt of her cigarette on the ground. "Gonna get yourself killed or jailed just like her. I can already tell."

"Maybe. Maybe not."

"You musta been hell on wheels as teenager, Mary." Kate ground the butt into the dirt with her foot and stared glittery green eyes into Marietta's hazel gaze, waiting for a tantrum, any show of weakness as an excuse to break off the discussion.

"I did all right for myself." Marietta's eyes flickered, but she held steady. "Kate, please."

"Oh, I like you." Kate laughed. "Yeah. Even though you're headed straight for a heart break, I like you a lot. Well, just because I don't want to see you standing outside my living room window staring at me at midnight."

Kate shifted towards Marietta. "Okay, just listen up, you. Cause I'm only gonna say it once. One, and then we're done. Got that? We don't talk no more. I don't wanna see you."

Marietta nodded, not trusting herself to speak. She waited with no show of the impatience she felt while Kate lit up again.

"So happens there's a job opening at Cadis that you might find helpful to your cause. I always keep track of what's going on over there, just on principle. That's a company you never wanna turn you back on. Ever." Kate flicked the ash. "Nope. No ma'am."

"You're talking about me getting myself hired there."

"Hey, unless you got something better." Kate shrugged. "At least the job will get you into the building and past security so you don't have to break and enter, or fuck your way, or whatever brilliant plan you had, hero. Quite frankly, I don't even know what you'll find. No guarantees. I mean, God, it's been like what? Twenty-five years. All the ones who knew, Stephanie took with her, except for..." Kate's voice trailed away to silence.

"Except for Derek Robinette," Marietta finished.

Kate waited a beat, then tossed away her cigarette and ground it. "Like I said, you're headed straight over a cliff. You won't like what you find. Oh, and by the way, whatever you're planning, don't say anything about me. You keep your mouth shut. If you get caught, if you bring my name into it, I'll throw you under the fucking bus, shift gears, and back that bus right over you. Then I'll put the bus in park and walk away. I'll tell them that you're lying and I don't know what the fuck you're talking about."

Kate looked square into Marietta's face. "See me and believe me that I'll do it, Mary."

"I won't say anything about you, Kate."

"Well, that's certainly all I got to say to you. So don't ask me for anything else. Look, it's getting late. Let's wrap this up. Stephanie hurt a lot of people, but she deserved better than what she got. She was my friend. She treated me nice. Not everyone else did." Kate's voice caught, and then she pressed forward in a rush.

"Don't call me again cause I don't wanna hear it. I got kids of my own and they mean more to me than you ever will. Sorry, but there it is. I wanna forget, just like I did before until you showed up out of nowhere. I told you all you need to know. The rest is up to you."

Kate stood and whirled to treat Marietta to a hard green stare that jabbed at her like shards of broken bottles. "We don't know each other."

She walked away, leaving Marietta alone and slightly dazed on the park bench. Minutes passed before she shook herself out of the stupor. Once she stood up, she noticed a strange set of keys on the bench next to her. One, two, three, four keys. She looked around the park, but Kate had vanished.

***

Though she felt totally drained, a nervous energy kept Marietta sharp and alert on the hour-long commute back home. Never a fan of night driving, Marietta pressed the accelerator harder. The SUV's engine surged her faster along the white line of the road's shoulder as if it snorted a line of cocaine. She felt the keys in her pocket to make sure they were real.

In the course of one day, Marietta learned so much. She was exhausted from the effort it took to track down the articles at the historical center, then having to endure the next-door neighbor's drama, with the final chore being the interrogation of Kate.

A thrill raced through her. She was on the right track. Soon, she would know all.

Soon, I'll find you, Stephanie. I'll know you. Soon... soon...

CHAPTER 15   CADIS

The next morning, Marietta used her laptop to find the job posting with Cadis Industries, her first test of Kate's veracity. If Kate was a liar, then that stopped this investigation right in its tracks. Marietta would return to the university and live a quiet, if uneventful life.

But there it was! Digital Archivist, the only job for which she qualified anyway. This was her gateway into the Cadis building and to the answers for all of her questions. She had to get that job.

Ashley at the employment contracting firm called her in for an interview. After brief introductions, Marietta launched into her spiel.

"I'm looking for a career change because I feel somewhat disconnected from current events in the business world. All the publish or perish research demands in academia can't replace real life experience."

"Well, your resume speaks for itself. You obviously do have a lot of experience. But this is an entry level position. How will it help your career?" Ashley asked.

"It is entry level, yes. But it is also an entry point into the private sector which is what I'm searching for. Cadis Industries is a chance for me to work my way up through the ranks of a recognized organization in the Lake City area."

Ashley considered that a moment. "Okay," she said. "The job is for a month. They need someone to digitize a large number of documents with a scanner, and then create a database of the files."

A flare of excitement rose in Marietta. This job picked up at the point where the position of file clerk became obsolete through technology. "I can do that, Ashley," she declared with confidence. "No problem."

The next day, Ashley called to tell her she'd passed the employment agency's background check which included fingerprints, driving record, credit report, and past employment references.

"You start a week from Monday which puts you into early September."

Ashley went on to explain time sheets and payroll and other administrative details, but Marietta's mind raced ahead. She made the appropriate listening noises while she created her own plans.

The next week, she arranged a six-month leave-of-absence and subleased her home to another faculty member and his family. She found a small studio apartment in Lake City available with a month-to-month lease. Then she loaded up her SUV and made two trips into Lake City with her personal belongings.

She didn't know how long it would take to figure things out or how long she would remain in the City. But she felt the need to stay close to follow any more leads that developed during her investigations.

And so, she would digitize documents at Cadis. At the same time, she would begin the second phase of her investigation into Stephanie's attack on the Cadis employees, her suicide, and the subsequent destruction of Marietta's family.

***

"Can I trust you to handle this? That's what I'm asking."

"Done and done. She starts next week."

"You have one month to pull this shit together. Like you told me, we need that database ready to launch for the Consortium. It's all we got over Celara. That's what you said."

"Right."

"No fuckups. If we're doing this, it has to be tight, accurate, and comprehensive. So you need to do quality control. I'm counting on you."

"I understand."

"I'm serious. Celara fucked us over years ago. Got alternative locked down with our designs. What we have is over one hundred years of proprietary data. Celara can't duplicate it, appropriate it, or fake it cause it's all our own projects. The Consortium wants our data that bad, then that's our lever. The only one we got."

"I get it."

"That's how important this is. You did good work with this. So stay on it. Remember that chance I gave you."

"I remember, boss."

"No excuses, Kowalski. I mean it."

"Yes sir."

***

Her previous visits to Lake City prepared Marietta for re-entry into the street hustle and bustle of fast walkers and talkers, pickpockets, and local color. She'd become rather small town since her relocation to Wayfarer and then the university town, but she was sure she could adapt. She had to adapt in order to do what she came to do.

Today, the time to do it arrived. Marietta took no chances. She decided to present herself as the opposite in order to disguise her real appearance. She twisted her naturally expansive dark brown curls into two strand twists of long ropes. These ropes she pinned beneath a sleek, black wig that fell down to her shoulder blades. The opposite.

She covered her skin in makeup two shades darker than her natural complexion. She lined her eyes and brows in brown pencil so dark, it might as well be black. She didn't bother about her height or weight, because both fell into mid-range. Average.

Even more careful to not stand out, she dressed in black slacks, blue blazer, and a snowy white button down shirt. She wore silver earrings with a matching necklace, bracelet and watch. She also purchased a pair of non-prescription glasses with silver frames. Black flats completed her boring contribution to Lake City's fashion world. If she had to adjust her wardrobe later, she would, but what she wore today had to find acceptance by the gatekeepers at Cadis Industries.

She needed to blend in. As she strolled down the sidewalks of downtown Lake City, she concluded that black, was indeed, the color of choice for most office workers. She pivoted.

Downtown Lake City rose to the heavens, majestic with classic skyscraper architecture. Tan and dark brown bricks blocked the sun. Patches of cold shadow alternated between sunny warmth. Steel and glass grew from concrete infrastructure, crisscrossed by multiple drawbridges over Lake City's main river that drained into the lake. From where she stood on one of the bridges over the river, the urban center seemed a fantastic world that reflected light so bright off sleek, silvery, glittery mirrors that it hurt the eyes. She could barely see the tops of the buildings as they disappeared like secrets into the clouds.

The Cadis Industries building combined the best of both classic and modern styles. The hard dark brown brick loomed over Marietta like a hulking colossus. Modern touches of steel and silver-coated mirrored surfaces flashed in the light and attacked her optic nerves. She shivered under the long shadow the building cast over her. The reflective glass bounced back the street scene almost in self-defense, allowing no insight into the inner workings. She knew from research that a few satellite offices dotted the surrounding suburbs while this building housed the headquarters.

Inside, the cavernous front lobby the sounds of industry echoed off clean, cold marble, and glass. Cadis Industries apparently earned enough money over the years to remodel and modernize the interior as well as the exterior. The large windows allowed those who dwelt inside to inspect the passersby and the doings on the street while remaining concealed. One set of windows provided an envious front row view of the river and the flow of traffic and pedestrians across the bridges. Tourists lined the rails over the bridges and took pictures of Lake City's urban dreamscape.

Marietta walked across the ice cavern of a lobby towards the security desk. According to Ashley at the employment agency, she needed to find Kal Jackson.

Marietta's heart beat faster. Her head swam a little. Almost twenty-five years ago, Stephanie walked across this same floor. Back in the day, Stephanie desired to prove her worth to her parents, her sister, her brother-in-law and lover, and maybe herself. Intelligent and gifted, she had been younger and far more vulnerable than Marietta was today. Stephanie had just submitted to family pressure to relinquish her only child to her sister's possession. And so, she arrived to Cadis Industries, to seek her worth as a professional in the business world.

She must have been full of promise about reaching her goals and optimistic for a second chance at life. Inside this monster-sized headquarters of Cadis Industries, Stephanie believed anything was possible. If Marietta did not know any better, she would believe the same as her birth mother.

But instead, inside these walls of cold steel and hard brick, something went horribly wrong with Stephanie's life. She destroyed not only herself, but also the people around her. Something or someone drove Stephanie to madness and murder. Someone in this building knew the reasons why. The compulsion to know and to discover and to avenge propelled a determined Marietta forward.

Still, the way the other employees walked around today drinking their caramel toffee mocha lattes, you wouldn't think this fortress of evil held secrets. The way these robots tossed their designer haircuts behind their ears, it was like nothing else mattered but money and the comforts money could buy. In the meantime, the cell phones they clutched like religious talismans in the opposite hand sucked away their life force and maybe caused them to believe anything was possible too. Did no one remember what happened here years ago? Marietta wanted to shout Stephanie's story to these zombies through a bullhorn like the religious fanatics she passed in the street on the way to her first day at work. Did no one remember Stephanie?

Marietta's eyes darted towards all four corners on the approach to the security desk. She noted multiple surveillance cameras, electronic gates that required a pass key, and several guards. One such attractive dark-skinned man glanced up from the security desk and waved her closer. They introduced themselves and then Kal Jackson led her to the elevators. Kal was handsome, only slightly taller than her, but stocky. Strong across the shoulders and chest and small in the waist, he had a wrestler's build.

"I have to turn this key for you each morning," he told her once they entered the elevator.

"Oh. Sorry about that."

"Nah, that's my job. The day no one shows up for me to turn the key, I get concerned about my pension and insurance plan." He had dark-brown eyes and a charming smile.

"We're going to the basement?" she asked him as the doors closed.

"Oh yeah. All the way down. You hit the big time, kid."

The elevator door reopened to dark wood trim, plain white walls, and random groups of outdated furniture that cast sinister shadows on the concrete floor.

"As you can see, all the money gets spent upstairs."

"They don't want to remodel down here?"

"Nah. Just the fancy parts the public sees. That might change soon, though."

Of course, Marietta thought as she cataloged the surroundings. The lower level, not open to public access and scrutiny, was Kate's old arena. And if it remained untouched all these years...

"People used to file their documents down here. But now, everyone saves and backs up current documents to the central computer system. No one comes down here anymore. Mostly just us in security and maintenance."

Kal gave her the grand tour and as he led Marietta around, she gathered that the previous generation of his family migrated from the South. He grew up in Lake City and fully embraced the lifestyle of a survivor who played to win. If Marietta were to guess, Kal was a multi-generational blue collar man with education maybe to the community college level. Possibly, a four-year degree on a football or wrestling scholarship.

"This is the guard station," her guide announced. "That's the parking garage. Are you driving to work? No?"

Marietta shook her head. "No, I take the train."

"Okay never mind. Anyway, here's maintenance and all of their stuff. Basically, all this is Operations. Bathroom, lockers, break room, supply closet. This door, I don't know what that is, but it stays locked." The faded letters on the door tried their best to spell out EDUCATION ROOM.

Marietta followed Kal further into the hidden recesses of the basement labyrinth. She wondered if she would ever learn her way back to the elevators. Finally, at the end of another long corridor, Kal stopped.

"Okay, this is your work area."

Stone gray file cabinets lined three walls. The cabinets were about five feet tall, three feet wide, one foot deep. About the height of Marietta's shoulders.

A small wooden desk sat at the fourth wall. Beneath their feet, a shabby threadbare carpet, the color of dirt, covered the concrete floor. Or maybe it was actual dirt. No, it was carpet with multiple cable lines duct-taped to it.

"It's hard to get cables down here since it's so distant from everything and the walls are brick, but we rigged up this computer station for you."

Marietta noted that the computer, an older model and obvious reject from the floors above, had standard accessories including a scanner/fax/copier/printer. Pens, pencils, scissors, and paper clips sat in a plastic tray. No desk telephone, but here in this subterranean crypt where secrets and furniture and business files came to die, Marietta decided that she would hold tight to her cell phone. Even more noteworthy, she saw no surveillance cameras here. Hard to run cables, as Kal said. And who, besides herself, wanted old files anyway?

Beside the computer keyboard lay a laminated list of instructions. Kal picked these up with the well-practiced smile of a charmer and put them in her hand, brushing his fingers across hers.

"Kowalski told me to make sure you read this. Basically, you have to digitize every single document in this room, and then pull information from the document to create a searchable online file. Then you shred every document in the room."

"Do they need the space down here, or something?"

"Mmm. Or something. I think they plan to remodel down here too. Trick it out with more electronic connections and bring in more computers. Maybe set up wireless for the whole building. But you didn't hear that from me."

"Hear what?" Marietta asked.

Kal laughed while she surveyed the metal file cabinets that lined the three walls and tried to estimate the work load. It would depend upon whether the cabinets were full. She tried to imagine Kate in this room, first inserting and then yanking Stephanie's files under direct orders from Derek Robinette, concealing them somewhere nearby. But where?

"Hello? Wake up."

"Oh sorry." Marietta blinked. She realized that Kal was trying to get her attention again.

"You'll meet Kowalski this evening before you leave. He's pretty big on things being done the way he wants them done. Just do what he says, all what's on his list, and you'll be fine."

"No problem."

"See? Then it's easy! Okay, you'll be supervised by us security guards. I'm first shift from seven to three. Kowalski's second shift from three to eleven. Then another guy does the graveyard shift from eleven to seven. You probably won't meet him. The three of us are full time, and then we got some part-timers who rotate upstairs. We'll check up on you from time to time to make sure you're not down here sleeping on the job." Kal winked and laughed.

"Why do I get the feeling you actually found someone sleeping on the job?"

"It happens. The guard on the graveyard shift zones out sometimes, like you did just now." He laughed. "I'm kidding! But seriously, Derek Robinette has ended careers over things like that. That guy's been lucky so far. Just saying though. Don't let it be you."

"Right. Thank you."

He handed her a set of small keys on a huge ring. "Okay, you need these keys to unlock the cabinets. Make sure to relock them when you're done at night. I've got to get back up to the lobby to keep track of the part-timers."

He left.

Marietta immediately used the cabinet keys to check under M for Madison and S for Stephanie. She found nothing except ordinary business files. Until she figured out Kate's filing system, she would have to go through every file in order to find what she needed in order to understand Stephanie's meltdown and all the destruction that followed in its wake. In the meantime, she should get started.

Marietta kept Kal's warnings in mind and followed Kowalski's instructions to the letter. She had two full bags of shred by the time Kal returned to check on her at ten sharp.

"Yeah, I finished my rounds upstairs. I check in with the guards on every floor and hang out in the lobby. By the time that's done, I come down here to pick up what you shred. It works out. Kowalski's gonna do the same this afternoon. How was it?"

"It's okay. It's pretty much what the temp agency described. Not a problem."

"At least we know your baseline now, don't we?"

"I guess. I did spend some time on the instructions to make sure I had everything right."

"Good deal. You're off and running. Kowalski's okay, but he can be a bit particular. And he can be kinda suspicious towards new people. But you seem to be doing fine to me."

"Thanks, I appreciate it."

Kal relaxed against the doorway. "This is one of those jobs that needs to get done, but no one has time to do it, or so they claim."

Marietta laughed. "It's okay."

"Oh yeah, I forgot to tell you to take a half hour for lunch. You remember where the break room is?"

She nodded.

"And look, here's a pass key for you. You can get yourself downstairs each morning. I approved it myself." He brushed his fingers across hers again. Then he drew himself up with expectation.

She obliged him with a smile. "Thank you!"

Marietta ate a sandwich at her desk in the file room. She decided to establish a pattern of eating her lunch at her desk rather than in the break room so no one looked for her or wondered what she was up to.

After lunch, she continued to digitize documents with the scanner. Handling old paper and folders and cardboard boxes proved to be a dusty and dirty, but manageable job. She removed her blazer then stood on a ladder to reach for a cardboard box marked North Shore Blueprints 2003 that sat on top of the metal file cabinet beside her desk. Still balanced on the ladder, she opened the box to see inside.

Several accordion files held blueprints, transparencies, and random handwritten notes. She had to scan it all. But first, she would sort them. She grabbed one of the accordion files, but lost her grip. The transparencies slid out of the top of the folder in a clear stream past her clumsy fingers then behind the metal file cabinet.

Shit! Marietta debated. She could ignore them, pretend she never saw them. But she could not afford to screw up this job, not on the first day. Certainly not before she found the information on Stephanie. She needed the goodwill of her supervisors in order to maintain access to the building.

So she puzzled her way back through the labyrinth and found a long carpenter's ruler in the supply closet. Then she returned to the file room to balance on the top step of the ladder while she scraped and fished for the transparencies. She could see them, but she could only get the ruler close enough to just barely touch them. She couldn't slide the slick sheets of plastic towards her. Plus, the long wig of black hair swung forward and blocked her view. Not good. She would have to move the file cabinet to retrieve the transparencies. She got off the ladder and tugged at the heavy metal box, which did not budge.

She pulled stacks of files out of the cabinet until it was half empty and tried again. This time, the cabinet slid across the thin brown carpet towards her. Behind the cabinet, on the wall in front of her, she saw a small, rusted metal door. INCINERATOR, the door said, marked in faded yellow print.

Marietta's heart pounded. She swallowed. *They told me to put all of her files into the incinerator. Her files and a bunch of other stuff. And I did put her files in the incinerator.*

Of course! She'd forgotten what Kate told her. The files weren't inside any of the file cabinets. Kate removed them at Derek Robinette's instructions. She said so. The prickles traveled down both of Marietta's arms.

She glanced over her shoulder at the door to the file room. She didn't see anyone. She didn't hear any footsteps on the concrete of the hallway either. Go! She tugged at the incinerator door handle. Locked. Marietta sighed and bit her lip. Kate's keys, dammit.

Come on, Marietta! Focus!

She pulled the set of four keys out of her pocket and tried one. It didn't fit. She tried the next key. Negative. Feeling somewhat suspicious of Kate, Marietta tried the third key. This key fit the lock, but she couldn't turn it. If she twisted too hard, the key would break. Marietta pulled the third key out of the lock and tried the fourth key, which didn't fit at all. Marietta exhaled. Then it had to be the third key.

She snatched up all of the transparencies that littered the floor and then struggled to move the file cabinet back into place. She would have to work on the files she piled up from this cabinet. Get those out of the way. Then, since the cabinet was now half-empty, she could move it back and forth whenever she needed. Because she absolutely had to look behind that door. She had to know! So far, everything Kate told her checked out. Marietta felt a small lick of excitement.

According to Kal, Will Kowalski the head of security and the guard who hired her would arrive for second shift at three this afternoon. Marietta got back to work on the digitization to make up for the time she lost during her explorations.

Kowalski showed up to the file room at exactly five o'clock, the end of Marietta's first work day to pick up two bags of shred. To her eye, Kowalski appeared probably ten years older than herself and Kal. It was hard to tell his age. His hair, cut short to the scalp had more salt than pepper. His skin was sallow under the fluorescent basement lights. But his eyes, a grey so pale it was like looking into the rain, scanned over her, alert and intense. Marietta guessed he was about the same age or slightly younger than Derek Robinette.

Without any greeting, he told her, "I'm Kowalski. I need to check the database to see if you followed specifications."

Marietta obediently stepped to the side while Kowalski clicked here and there with the computer's mouse. She already knew that she followed instructions to the letter.

"Okay." With reluctance, Kowalski straightened. "Just so you know, I'm gonna check your work from time to time. Mr. Robinette is a dangerous man when he's crossed. He doesn't tolerate excuses from anyone. Okay?"

"Okay." Marietta wondered if she'd just been threatened.

"That's how Cadis works. Robinette's from the hardscrabble side of Lake City. His father built this company from nothing and now he's taking it to the next level. He and I are from the same place, you see. He brings his people along with him. He's loyal like that. I've been with Cadis for about twenty-five years now."

Marietta nodded, wordless. The pale, grey eyes stared at her with a slight frown bending the black brows above them.

"That's a long time," she quickly added.

"It's a lifetime. Anyway, he knows for a fact that I get him what he wants. What he wants is this database. Accurate. Efficient. Precise. Got that?"

"Got it."

"Okay, keep going just like that. Remember, you're on a deadline."

***

Kowalski used his own key to ride the elevator to the very top floor of Cadis. He entered first one door, then another... all of these gauntlets to enter the dragon's lair. Though expected, Kowalski still knocked on Robinette's door. It made no sense to sneak up on a beast that never slept.

"How's the temp?"

"Taking her longer than we thought, sir. She's only filling four bags of shred per day."

"Well, you hired her. It's your responsibility to stay on her ass. We need that database together by the end of the month and it has to be right. I need the Consortium deal to move Cadis ahead."

"Okay, I'll talk to her."

"Damn right you will. That's a hard deadline the Consortium put down. No if, ands, or buts. No fucking nuts. Get on it!"

"Will do."

CHAPTER 16   ROBINETTE

Early the next morning, Marietta continued to work on the files she piled up from yesterday. Dirt and dust coated her hands so she kept a container of wipes from the supply cabinet on the little wooden desk.

She had to figure out the purpose of each document in the file, its title (or create a title), date, department, add any necessary notes, and then scan each page. Then she entered the data into a spreadsheet. Then she exported the spreadsheet into the expanding database. Then she shredded the original.

Kal Jackson poked his head into the file room. She nodded back at him while she performed the data entry. She worked two more minutes after Kal's footsteps faded down the concrete floor of the hallway. Then she walked over to the first metal file cabinet and yanked it forward.

If anyone asked her about the file cabinet sitting out of alignment, she had her story all set. Some papers slipped out of her hand and fell behind the cabinets. She had to pull the cabinet forward to retrieve the papers because she believed in doing a thorough job. The story had plausibility because didn't it already happen on the first day? Yes, it sure did. However, she had no reasonable explanation for opening the incinerator door. She glanced over her shoulder and listened again. She heard not one sound. Time to test the second part of Kate's story.

She sprayed the oil lubricant that she purchased at a nearby drugstore into the lock. Heart pounding, she stuck in the third key and twisted. *Click.*

Marietta hesitated, and then sprayed lubricant on the metal hinges of the rusty door. No need to announce her entry into the incinerator to the whole building. She traded the spray can for the flashlight in her backpack. She walked back to the incinerator door, pulled on the handle and tugged it forward.

Stale, dry, dusty air emanated from the black square in front of her as though from a crypt. A metal shaft disappeared down into darkness. She shined the flashlight inside and hoped that no animal or spirit life lurked below. Across, another shaft declined on a diagonal like a garbage chute similar to the one in her apartment building. For sure, objects for burning went down that chute.

A metal ladder, welded to the side of the shaft below the door, went straight down, about eight feet, she judged as she moved the flashlight around. Another black square at the base of the ladder indicated another tunnel.

Okay. It's on.

Marietta pulled away and closed the incinerator door. She locked it with a firm twist of the key and moved the file cabinet across the carpet back into place. Then she filled up two bags of shred for Kal, two more for Kowalski.

The next day, she filled two more bags of shred for Kal, which he retrieved just before lunch.

"So what do you think about Kowalski?" he asked with a sly smirk.

"I think Kowalski's the one who hired me and who authorizes my paychecks. That's what I think."

Kal laughed. "Smart girl. He's a true believer, you know. He and Derek Robinette have a lot in common, so he says."

"Does that make you feel like a third wheel?"

"Nah," Kal answered, thoughtful. "Sometimes opposites attract more so than similar attracts. I have my own line of communication with Robinette so..." he trailed off.

"Is Kowalski ex-military?"

"Why do you ask?"

"Well, his haircut and the way he stands, it seems like he's had training. And he's so organized and disciplined with these instructions."

"Well, I don't know about all that. But I wouldn't be surprised if he's killed a few people. Anyway, how about lunch?"

Marietta replied with a blank stare until her mind caught up to the switch in conversation topic. "I brought mine today." She held up her sack of peanut butter sandwich.

"Oh. By the way, I meant to ask, ah, are you with anybody in particular?"

"I... I am, actually. I have a good thing going."

Kal nodded. "Yeah, I figured. Smart, pretty girl like you."

Marietta smiled.

"Well, at least I don't have to worry about Kowalski putting the moves on you. And neither do you."

Marietta laughed. "No, I don't think that's gonna happen."

"Not that he would. He's too focused on ambition to worry about anything else."

"You really think so?"

"Kowalski wants to come up higher in the food chain. He's all tense lately because Robinette's trying to best Celara and settle some kind of mystery feud."

"Who?"

"Celara Solar. You heard of them? No? Well, it's some kind of rivalry thing with the two of them. Robinette wants to join this Consortium that's forming. Anyone who joins, benefits, but Robinette wants the top position."

"Oh."

"So that's why you're here. Robinette needs the database to streamline operations at Cadis and he needs to bring the content with him in order to join the Consortium. That's the word anyway. There's just a limited number of slots available and so Robinette's kind of anxious about that. Whenever Robinette's anxious, he really gets into Kowalski's... I mean, he gives Kowalski a hard time."

"Okay, I think I get it now."

"See what I mean? A lot of things will change around here after the Consortium deal goes through. Robinette will run the city. Remember I told you about all the technology they wanted to put down here to pretty things up?" Kal winked at her.

"Play your cards right, Mary, and you might get on permanently with Cadis once Robinette hits the big time."

**

After Kal left, Marietta crammed the hours-old dry sandwich into her face and chewed it as fast as she could. Most people went out for lunch on the noon hour to the multitude of restaurants that lined the river walk. Others sat at their desks like Marietta or ate in the break room by the security guards. The building remained pretty quiet for now.

As far as Marietta knew, she hadn't done anything out of the ordinary that would attract attention, at least nothing that anyone knew about. She'd dressed for today's occasion in sleek black knit pants with flared legs and a matching knit shirt and cardigan. She removed the cardigan and laid it on the back of her chair. Then she pulled back the long wig of black hair and tucked the ends into an elastic band.

She moved the file cabinet aside. She got the keys and the flashlight ready and opened the small metal door.

This time, Marietta listened. She heard rhythmic mechanical noises coming from the dark square before her, like ventilation machinery. She thought she heard voices, maybe from somewhere in the building, Definitely, this didn't sound like Narnia, or Middle Earth, or Oz. More like a secret evil dimension created by Stephen King rather than a magical wonderworld built by Lewis, or Tolkien, or Baum.

Two tunnels led to the incinerator. The diagonal that resembled the trash chute in her apartment building was where things for burning went. The main shaft with the ladder was for humans. The ones who repaired and serviced the incinerator. *Only... her files didn't burn.*

Kate did not send the files the direct route on the diagonal to the incinerator, Marietta decided. Otherwise, they would have burned before the fire department decommissioned the furnace. Therefore, she hid the files somewhere inside the service tunnel. Tomorrow.

Marietta pushed the cabinet back and continued to shred until five o'clock.

"Why are you behind?" was the first incredulous question Kowalski asked her. "There's usually two full bags. This one is full, but this other one," he shook it at her, "Is only half full. What's the problem, Mary?"

"The shredder jammed on me and I had to disconnect it and dig some paper out. How old is it, anyway?"

This time when Kowalski frowned, a vertical line separated the dark brows bending over his narrow eyes. "Still new. Got it last year."

"Hmm. The basement's kind of damp though."

Kowalski's small pale eyes narrowed further until they nearly disappeared. Marietta stared back at him, transfixed by the gray on silver on gray ensemble of his persona. She wondered whether he might shapeshift into a wolf. Then she wondered why she didn't just trot out the paper behind the cabinet story like she was supposed to. Nerves.

**

On the third day, Marietta heard ponderous footsteps drag along concrete in the hallway, like that of a dinosaur's approach. A heavyset Caucasian man entered the doorway to the file room. She had no doubt whatsoever in whom's presence she stood. She'd heard the whispers.

Rough patches of red, puckered skin covered Robinette's craggy face. His hair remained dark, though most of it had abandoned his balding head. Large and tall, she noted that his suit was tailored especially for his heavy frame. A former athlete stood before her, football player with a bull neck, who let himself go, for whatever reason.

"Mary Madison, is it?" The deep, hoarse rumble emanated from the depths of his diaphragm. "I'm Derek Robinette. I own and operate Cadis Industries."

"Thank you for this opportunity. How do you do?" She noted that the whites of his eyes, surrounding blue irises, were lined with thin red veins, as though in a perpetual state of irritation.

"Extremely well, Mary." Heavy eyelids hung halfway, hiding most of his real expression. "Because I pay attention."

Only the small desk at her back prevented Marietta from taking a step backward. The jig was up then. Just because she couldn't see a camera, that didn't mean there wasn't a camera. She waited.

"I wanted to see how things were coming along down here." Hooded blue eyes waited for her answer.

Marietta swallowed. If Robinette decided to rip her throat from her neck, no doubt Kowalski would help to dispose of her body once five o'clock came around.

"Things are coming along," she said. "I believe I'm still on schedule." Marietta gripped the cell phone in her pocket and wondered whether she would have time to punch in 911 on her keypad before the bad things happened to her. Was there cell phone reception down here? She didn't check, did she? Would she at least have time to scream?

"You believe?" Robinette repeated, and then waited again. He said nothing, just stared at her like an unmovable mountain she could never traverse.

"Yes, I do. Everything's moving right along." Even if she had time to scream, would anyone hear her call for help so far underground? And if someone heard her call for help, like maintenance staff, would they bother to respond?

A silent moment stretched thin and close to breaking like a rubber band. Robinette's heavy gaze remained upon her. Mesmerized, as if she still was not quite sure whether he was human, Marietta wondered whether Robinette would alert to her last name. Madison was a common name in such a large metropolis. How many Madisons per square mile lived in Lake City?

Still, she thanked God that she altered her appearance. Her natural features looked nothing like Stephanie's. At night, when she pulled off the wig and washed off the makeup, she saw the feminine version of Roy Brazil looking back at her. She resembled her father.

This morning, she'd slathered on the usual dark brown makeup. She'd pulled the long wig back into a bun to prepare for the next round of spelunking beneath Cadis Industries. She should be fine. Unless...

"Okay," Robinette said, finally. "Show me what you've done so far."

Marietta exhaled. She was safe, for now. She tried not to cry. Instead, she moved aside to show Robinette the database in progress. His titanic bulk slid closer. Marietta forced herself not to shove past him and run screaming from the room. She clicked with the mouse and scrolled through various windows on the computer screen, narrating her progress. Robinette gazed in silence. Then he reached to take the mouse from her and gave the database another onceover, without any change of expression.

"Okay," he said. He then turned and left.

For half a minute after his departure, Marietta stood stock still, benumbed by the encounter. Then she sagged with relief against the wooden desk. But not for long. She scanned and shredded and indexed as fast as she dared. She made extra sure to have two full bags of shred ready and waiting for Kal at ten.

Kal didn't linger. The unheard of basement visit from Robinette had entered the office grapevine and thereby altered the ecosystem, forcing aberrant behavior from everyone, including Marietta. Driven by an urgent sense of menace, and the feeling that she would never emerge alive from the file room, let alone the basement, and certainly not the building if Robinette ever discovered her real purpose, she told herself that it wasn't too late to abort. She could finish the job and walk away. She could forget all about Stephanie, all the family secrets, all the deaths and *walk away*, as Kate advised.

Because this was the City. The metropolis sparkled and shined like diamonds above, while graft huddled and lurked like dirty coal below. Luck, pluck, money, and connections made the City go. The strong went from rags to riches. The rich used any means necessary to remain so. As for the weak? Well, the law of the jungle remained the rule, not the exception for them. The fit survived. What was Marietta in the scheme of things? Fit? Marietta bit her lip. She needed to remember why she was here.

The dragon and his pet wolf watched her so closely... Robinette gave nothing away during his visit. He might give her a raise. He might burn her to a crisp. She couldn't tell whether he was pleased or displeased. Kowalski would carry out whatever instruction Robinette gave him and feel no remorse for doing so.

After a quick lunch held in a shaky hand, Marietta returned to the ladder, thankful that she wore her usual attire of all-black today. Not only did black clothing blend in with clothing worn by other employees, it also ensured that no dark smudges would reveal her activities. Because if Robinette suspected, if he knew, she wouldn't still be here. Would she?

That decided, Marietta climbed down the ladder with the flash light in one hand. When she reached the bottom of the shaft, she bent forward to shine the light down the service tunnel that led to the incinerator. A distant light from an unknown source heightened the black gloom to dull gray. Her flashlight sharpened the features of the tunnel even more.

Marietta's heart sank. The tunnel was empty. Someone must have found whatever Kate hid down here. Or maybe Kate lied. Marietta shook her head. She would not cry! Besides, she had to be absolutely sure. She had come too far to give up now. She was not a punk.

She got down on her hands and knees and crawled two feet inside the tunnel. Again, she shined the light. For some reason, she smelled the distinct aroma of coffee. She wondered whether a ventilation shaft carried the smell to her from somewhere inside the building. Or, somewhere in the vicinity of Cadis Industries, a coffee shop boiled up caffeine to serve as fuel for downtown workers. All those caramel toffee mocha lattes she saw in the Cadis lobby had to come from somewhere. But she didn't see anything else.

Marietta's heart sank in disappointment. Tears pricked her eyes. It was all for nothing. Damn you, Kate! She started to ease backwards towards the ladder that led up to the file room when she noticed something on her left. A thin dark line outlined a square set flush to the metal wall of the shaft. Inside the square, yellow block writing spelled, SAFETY EQUIPMENT. A small keyhole sat under the letters in the middle of the square.

The prickles dancing on Marietta's arms felt like a swarm of insects. She blinked back the tears. By the glow of the flashlight, she looked at the keys on her ring. She scarcely dared to breathe as she picked one and inserted it into the lock. *Only... her files didn't burn.*

The key fit.

She twisted with a gentle touch. *Click.*

Then she heard voices, distorted only slightly by a hollow metallic quality. In fact, Kowalski sounded as though he were somewhere inside the tunnel with her.

"She better not be slacking off again. I came in early just to check on her because..."

Jackson said something in response that she couldn't hear because in a blizzard of motion, she yanked the key from the lock and grabbed the flashlight.

She slithered backward and then raced up the ladder hand-over-hand. She locked the metal door behind her. She heard the fast march of Kowalski's footsteps on concrete. She pushed against the file cabinet, which snagged on a piece of the threadbare dirt-like carpet. The steps became louder. Beyond frazzled, she tugged the cabinet back and forth across the carpet until it slid into place. Then she grabbed a random stack of documents from her desk and flipped through them with such concentration that they might contain the secrets of the entire universe.

A figure materialized in the doorway. Marietta looked up with complete surprise. Kowalski stood there with his arms folded.

"Looks like you're behind again," he said.

"Not really. I ran into a batch of hard-to-read documents and I lost my place while I scanned and so I had to..."

"Even though you're sweating."

"It's kind of hot in here."

Marietta tucked a few strands of the wig that fell out of the bun behind her ear. She fanned herself.

"Don't you feel hot too?" she asked him.

"No. Yesterday, you said it was damp." Flat gray eyes traveled over her torso. Marietta was too nervous to feel offended by the calm, entitled, masculine perusal.

"Well, I'm working too hard then. Or maybe I'm having a private summer." She chuckled a little. "You know, some of us ladies my age..."

"Yeah."

"Well, at certain times..."

"Yeah, okay." Kowalski turned his back on her and left.

Marietta sagged back onto her chair with relief until she looked down to see what so fascinated Kowalski about her. She gasped. Oh shit. On each knee of her pants leg, a pale circle of gray dust contrasted against the black color of her clothing. On top of that, she felt the sweat on her face and neck. She grabbed the wipes from her desk and tried to straighten herself out.

Kowalski could not miss the fact that she'd been down on her knees, sweating. Oh God. What must he think? Not good.

Not good at all. Why didn't she just tell him the story she practiced? This made the second time she got flustered today. Marietta tried to come up with another explanation to casually toss over her shoulder to Kowalski on her way out of the building. Okay, now practice and get it right!

Oh silly me! I dropped a bunch of files behind my desk and I had to reach under the desk pick them up and the carpet... Or, how about, oh how I wish I knew these boxes were so dusty. I stood against them and got dust on my best work pants. Oh dear!

Those sounded pretty good. Basically, whichever explanation came out of her mouth first, she'd commit to it. Certainly better than, I broke into your incinerator looking for documents to steal.

***

"She's up to something. I think she might be on drugs."

"Are you fucking kidding? Drugs." The rumble from inside Robinette's barrel of a chest held a tone of disgust. "Why is she on fucking drugs, Kowalski? Tell me that."

"She was sweaty and out of breath when I saw her. And she had dirt on her knees."

Robinette stared at Kowalski for a long moment, trying to process what he just heard, which didn't make any sense. "What the fuck are you talking about?" he snapped. "Dirt on her goddamned knees."

Kowalski shrugged.

Robinette flicked a huge hand under Kowalski's nose. Kowalski didn't flinch, he simply waited for the order. "Let me see her background from the temp agency."

"I already checked it. There's nothing there."

The half-closed lids on Robinette's eyes lifted only a trifle. "What do I pay you for, Kowalski? Why are you here?"

Chastened, Kowalski opened his mouth to answer.

"Never mind!" Robinette shouted. He thrust his meaty hand further under Kowalski's nose. "Give me the damn file!"

Without another word, Kowalski turned and found Mary Madison's file inside a desk drawer. He placed the file in Robinette's thick hand which finally withdrew from under his nose. He waited while his employer flicked through three half-empty pages. With obvious contempt, Robinette allowed the file to drop from his hand to Kowalski's desk.

"Jesus Christ, the two-bit temp firms you use. There's hardly anything here! Give her the Cadis special. Do it now. Like you shoulda done before."

"Right, boss."

"And I want a camera on her. Shoulda already had one down there."

"It's just hard to run the cables down there."

"What!"

"And then the wireless from upstairs doesn't reach..."

"Get it rigged up before tomorrow. If she's up to something, we'll know whatever it is before the end of business."

Robinette thought back to Mary Madison's height and build. Her long, black hair tucked into the bun. For some reason, even though he just met the girl, he didn't like her. He didn't know what it was that had him spooked. But something about her... wasn't right.

"Never mind!" he shouted after Kowalski. "I want her gone. Get rid of her. I gotta bad vibe."

Kowalski shook his head, uncertain. "But what about the Consortium deadline?"

Robinette answered that with the resonant bellow of a waking bear, disturbed by the intrusion of inadequacy into his cavern. "Get rid of her! Get her out of the building!"

Though Marietta had her soundbite and a light-hearted chuckle prepared for Kowalski at the end of her work shift, he never showed to pick up the bags of shred. Instead, he called her into his office when she passed by the guard station on the way to the elevator.

Once inside his office, she heard Ashley's cheerful voice on Kowalski's speaker phone.

"Ms. Madison? Hiiiiii! I just wanted to let you know that this is your last day at Cadis Industries."

"It is?" Marietta looked at Kowalski who said nothing but appeared unsurprised.

"Riiiiiiight. We're gonna ask you to gather whatever belongs to you and head on out. Okay?"

"There's still a lot of digitizing left to do."

"I realize that. But sometimes, changes occur unexpectedly and we as professionals just adjust to current situations. Now... your paycheck..." Marietta's mind faded as she realized the implication. She no longer had access to the building, the basement, the files, and the truth.

"Okay, Ms. Madison?"

"Oh. Um, okay."

Ashley ended the call on her end. Kowalski pushed a button that ended on his and Marietta's end. Then he looked at Marietta with clear dislike through eyes that no longer looked like rain. His eyes looked like pieces of ice. He flicked his hand under her nose.

"I'm gonna need the pass key, the work badge, and the keys to the file cabinet. Now." The sinewy, veiny hand waited.

Marietta pressed her lips together. She had no choice but to do as he asked. She turned over everything Kowalski requested to him.

CHAPTER 17   THE POLICE

Marietta never felt more embarrassed and humiliated than during her walk of shame across the ice cave of a lobby. Though it was the end of the work day, the curious gaze of several dozen black clad employees and a few security guards milling about slid over her. But when nothing of significance happened other than Will Kowalski opening the front entrance of Cadis and guiding Marietta through, they returned to their cell phones and continued to negotiate rides home and plans for the evening.

Marietta could almost picture Kowalski slapping the dust from his hands in an all done gesture behind the mirrored glass. And what would he tell Kal about her sweaty face and dusty pants? Marietta's face flamed.

Tears of frustration stung her eyes. She put her hands in her pockets and started a slow walk to the subway station. The evening shadows cast by the towers that guarded Lake City's urban center stalked her down the sidewalk. She clutched the keys that Kate gave her inside a fist. She'd been so close. She had the key in the lock. It fit! The files had to be inside the safety door. Why else had Kate put the key on the ring?

How long would it take for Robinette or Kowalski to figure out what she'd really been up to inside the file room? Had she left scrape marks on the carpet when she moved the file cabinet back and forth? What about when the file cabinet snagged on something the last time she moved it? She didn't bother fix the carpet, did she? No. She didn't.

She definitely left fingerprints... everywhere. If security or maintenance ever looked behind the file cabinet, they would see fresh oil on the hinges of the incinerator door. They would see smudges and handprints inside the metal shaft and knee prints in the tunnel.

Never in her life would she ever want to meet either Robinette or Kowalski at the end of a long, dark street. Nor even within a crowd of people in the full light of day. The way that both men looked at her made her feel... not quite human. It was as if they viewed her as a plate of food to devour. Like prey. She'd felt so alone and so far away from the rest of the world in the file room whenever they came to check on her. She'd felt cornered.

Marietta paid the train fare and headed down to the platform to wait. If Robinette decided to remodel the lower level as part of the Consortium deal as Kal predicted, then they would eventually find Stephanie's files. It was just a matter of time. Would they destroy the files? Yes. And then Marietta would lose the last link to the mystery of her birth mother, plus the answer to her family's destruction.

All just a matter of time. How much time? She didn't know. But soon. She leaned against the wall of the subway station, depressed. The train roared into the station with a mighty wind and Marietta slumped into a seat.

If she were slow or incompetent on the job, that was one thing. Someone, Kowalski likely, would say, "I'm sorry, but it doesn't seem to be working out," or "we decided to move in another direction." Or maybe even, "well, funding for this project has been cut so... sorry."

No need to march a slowpoke to the front door and toss her out into the cold. So something developed from her background check, maybe something Kowalski missed when he hired her. The real trouble started right after she met Derek Robinette. Maybe that meant Robinette discovered something about her that Kowalski didn't realize. Robinette figured something out after he visited the file room to check on her. When he saw her face-to-face.

Perhaps Robinette figured out her connection to Stephanie, the domestic terrorist who attacked his building and killed his father twenty-four years ago. That was the only area of her background that might pose a problem. But how? She didn't look like herself. Marietta pushed the long black strands of her wig out of her face. She couldn't wait to take it off because long black hair reminded her of Susan...

Marietta stared out of the train window. Then she adjusted her gaze to stare at her reflection in the window. Nothing else could have triggered Robinette's reaction. She grabbed the long strands of the wig and rubbed them between her fingers. The hair, combined with the last name Madison, sparked Robinette. She'd overthought her disguise. While she looked nothing like her regular self, she now looked something like Susan. Therefore, she also looked like Stephanie, who Robinette knew quite well. Of course he would remember his father's killer, no matter how common the name.

Oh Marietta!

If Robinette did not realize that Mary Madison was really Marietta Brazil at the time he met her in the file room, then he surely knew by now, especially after he saw her hair. Stephanie used to work for him. Even after almost twenty-five years, he would remember her appearance.

Marietta got off the train and walked to her studio apartment. She had to figure out her next move. A check of her mailbox revealed yet another cold exposition of her finances forwarded from Tony.

Marietta sighed and waited for the elevator to the fourth floor. Inside her tiny studio, she threw down her backpack and yanked off the wig. She washed her hair and scrubbed the thick makeup off her face. She showered off all the sweat and basement dust. Depressed, she fell across her bed in a bathrobe. After all her tough talk to Kate, she'd failed. She choked and stumbled just short of reaching her ultimate goal.

She felt more alone now than she ever had in her life. She couldn't return back to her house because she'd subleased it and taken a leave of absence. Even in the city of her birth, she had no friends and no family. So what? Where? If Marietta really put her mind to it, she might find some old acquaintances from high school with social media.

But what would she tell them? She'd never been really close to anyone at school. Grandpa pulled her from her Lake City high school before junior year was over. No one had seen her since. Certainly Kate wasn't going to talk to her. Tony saw her only as an awkward and unpleasant task he had to accomplish once per month like an insurance payment.

Three hard knocks on her apartment door snapped Marietta from her lethargy.

"Mary Madison. This is Lake City Police. We would like to speak to you about some missing electronics from the building of your former employer, Cadis Industries. We have the understanding that you may have knowledge of their current location."

What?

Marietta's jaw dropped open. She blinked and stared at the television, wondering if she'd left it on and forgot to turn it off. The television screen was dark though. She didn't have a radio.

The police rapped three more times, even louder. "Ms. Madison! This is Lake City Police Department. We need to speak with you immediately."

Marietta didn't answer. Maybe they'd go away. She clutched her bathrobe tighter and waited to see if they would.

Her cell phone's cheerful ringtone sounded merrily in the silence. Frantic to shut it off, she grabbed at it. While she fumbled in her panic, the ringtone sounded over and over, loud and clear, the number of the call restricted. Marietta fiddled with the settings, her fingers jittery on the tiny keys.

The police knocked again. "Miss! This is Lake City Police! We can hear your cell phone ringing. We know you're in there. We strongly encourage you to cooperate with us and cease your hindrance of an official investigation."

Marietta backed away from the door. She backed away from her phone. She backed away until she found herself stuck in the corner furthest from her front door. She sank to the floor with her head on her knees. What the hell had just happened to her life?

She heard a quieter knock this time. A more persuasive tone of voice said, "Ma'am, we're just asking if we could come in to speak with you for just a few minutes about the missing laptops and cameras. Some other equipment too. If you could just indicate some goodwill effort on your part to assist with our investigation, we'd appreciate it. Please don't obstruct our investigation, ma'am. We'll ask you a few questions and then we'll be on our way."

First bad cop. Now good cop. Again, Marietta didn't respond. She simply sat and waited with confusion to see what would happen to her next. Evening shadows traveled across the walls around her until darkness at dusk engulfed the whole room. She knew for a fact that she needed to do something, but she didn't know what. She dare not turn on a light.

While Marietta pondered her dilemma, she heard another knock at the door. This time, she recognized the voice of her landlord, the elderly dark-skinned Indian man who'd rented her the room a week ago.

"Miss Madison, you must vacate this residence immediately. We have received complaints about your behavior."

Marietta shot up from the floor like a jack-in-the-box and hurried to her front door. "My behavior? What behavior? I just got here a week ago. There's been no behavior."

"Yes, there is behavior. I have received reports of strange men at all hours knocking on this door."

"Those were policemen."

"Miss, we do not allow drugs or prostitution here."

"What!"

"It is on your lease."

"But..."

"Miss, I am the landlord here. My family owns this building. We work very hard to keep this building clean and safe for everyone. You disturb the peace, you leave."

"But that wasn't me."

"You are very definitely disorderly, Miss."

"No, I'm not!"

"Yes, you have been."

"I have not! And you can't just throw me into the street with no notice."

"The police talked to me about you. They say you steal where you work. You cannot bring things you steal here."

"That's a lie!"

"That's very bad behavior. You bring trouble here. We don't want trouble."

"But I didn't."

"You have to leave this residence tonight, Miss."

"Well, then you have to refund my deposit and pro-rate my rent."

"Noooo. No! No refund, Miss. You bring trouble, you leave. No refund."

"That's a pile of crap. I'm not going anywhere without a refund."

"Oh, I must tell you. The police will kick this door down. That's what they told me. They will get a warrant. They will get permission and they will kick down this door and arrest you. Because you steal from work. That's what they say."

"It's not true!"

"You cannot prostitute here and do your drugs."

"Give me my refund!"

"Are you going to pay me for a new door when they kick it down? No, you will not pay me for a new door. So you don't get your deposit back. No refund. Get out, Miss!"

"You can't do that!"

"Get out of my building now!" he shouted.

"You get out!" she shrieked back.

"Miss, you better leave! Take your trouble with you!"

Marietta checked the sole window which faced the parking lot. A cop car idled behind her SUV, blocking her in. Oh boy. How would she take her trouble past that?

Earlier, she heard two voices at her door. One officer in the back. That meant at least one officer waited at the front entrance. They would wait for her to respond to the threat they communicated to the landlord. Then, of course, she would run out of either the front or back door to flee the building. One or both of the officers would intercept her and then turn her over to Robinette.

Marietta took a deep breath. Was she prepared to do whatever it took to evade Robinette and his people? Things hadn't gone so well today. How far did she want to take this?

She took another calming breath. Did she want to see this thing through? Make up your mind now, Marietta.

Yes.

After all, she'd run most of her life, hadn't she? But this time, she would run to a strategic position. And then she would launch her offensive.

So let's go!

Marietta got dressed. Then she rushed around the dark room with her flashlight, careful not to aim it at the window. She gathered up the papers and research she accumulated on Stephanie, her laptop and cell phone (now set to silent mode), and a few essentials. She had her backpack and two suitcases. Everything else was replaceable. Kiss it good-bye.

So now what? Not the back entrance. A cop waited for her there. The elevator faced the front entrance. She had to assume the other cop stood guard there, same as in the back. She could take the stairs and try to figure something out, but how could she exercise any level of discretion while she hauled two suitcases down four flights?

Okay. Then think. Think!

She could sling the luggage down the trash chute. Wait for a crowd of people to leave the building, then walk out with them, then circle back around for the luggage, then... Marietta's head felt scrambled. Try again.

Option three still had yet to form. But as precious seconds passed, it emerged from a faraway unspoken whisper to the top of the list... the trash chute. Yes, she would sling her luggage down the chute so she didn't have to carry it. Did the cops have enough personnel to watch the dumpster? No, Marietta decided, more because she needed something to believe in rather than she knew that for a fact. But she had to do something.

Marietta shined the flashlight around her apartment once more to make sure she had what she needed and that she left nothing of importance behind. In fact, she probably carried too much with her, but she couldn't take the time to unpack now.

She crept to her front door and checked the peephole. She didn't see anyone. She listened at the crack. She couldn't hear anything. Her neighbors, typical of Lake City, elected to mind their own business whenever police arrived. Inch by inch, she opened her door and stuck her head out. Nothing.

On the quietest of shuffles, she slid across the landlord's precious wafer thin budget carpet, down the hallway towards the closet that contained the trash chute. She opened the closet door, and then closed it behind her. Wasting no more time, she shoved one suitcase down the chute and listened.

She didn't hear it land, so something soft was down there. She shoved the smaller suitcase down the chute. This time, she heard a smack. It landed on top of the first suitcase.

This left her with the backpack which contained all of her research and documents, her purse, cell phone, and laptop. She could maneuver with her backpack and come back for the suitcases before trash pickup when the landlord pushed the dumpster outside through the utility door. That's what she saw him do last week. She would ask, pretty please, if she could have her suitcases back or she would find them her damn self.

Now, she just needed to join a crowd of... college students, maybe. She would slide out of the apartment building with them, laughing it up and joking around. That sounded like a good plan. Marietta felt proud and productive.

But through the closet door, she heard the familiar sound of the elevator grind to a halt on the fourth floor. Someone was coming. One of her neighbors, probably the twenty-something woman who lived next door, had just finished a day of classes. The elevator bell dinged. She heard the elevator doors open and then the squawk of police radios. Uh oh.

Marietta took off her backpack. If they took her into custody, she didn't want them to get their hands on her research materials. The research on Stephanie's attack and her concentrated focus on Cadis Industries incriminated her far more than Robinette's false charges.

Authoritarian male voices repeated command codes. Marietta dropped her backpack down the trash chute. She might have to beg the landlord's forgiveness in order to get it back, especially if the police kicked down the door to her studio. Multiple footsteps stomped down the hallway and stopped somewhere close to her studio door. She heard the sound of fists on wood and angry shouts. Then she heard the crunch of metal on wood.

No!

She didn't want to go to jail!

Marietta clambered up to position herself over the chute. The police would knock down her door, or the landlord would open it for them. She closed her eyes. If this was all a mistake, it still wasn't too late to call this off and give herself up.

"I wanna lawyer!" she would insist amidst tears to her kidnappers once they held her hostage and demanded a ransom.

She heard a loud crash and more shouts. For sure, she would not get her security deposit back.

Marietta released her hold on the opening of the trash chute and fell backward into darkness.

CHAPTER 18   THE ESCAPE

T his didn't happen.

Did this happen? Really?
 It couldn't possibly have happened.
 Did she really just send herself down a trash chute like a pile of banana peels and used coffee filters? She must have, because here she now sat in the middle of a garbage dumpster on the first floor of her apartment building on top of a pile of banana peels and used coffee filters.

She could feel them and smell them and a lot of other things too. She heard something besides herself moving around. How many viruses and amoebas in this stinking pile looked for just the right opening in her skin to claim her body as their own for colonization?

I can't do this.

Only three minutes on the run and Marietta decided to give herself up to the police rather than endure even another moment of... this. She imagined her landlord's indignation in the face of her humiliation. Are you going to pay me for a new garbage dumpster? No, you are not going to pay for a new dumpster. *Get out, Miss!*

She felt around for her suitcases and backpack. She slung them over the side of the dumpster. She heard something in the garbage react to her movements.

Marietta froze. She tried not to panic while she listened again. Was it a small sound like a mouse? Or a big sound like a rat? Rats had rabies. They bit. What if it was a snake? Should she stand still so it lost interest or wave her arms around and make noise to scare it off?

"I can't do snakes," she announced to no one.

By now, the police knew she wasn't home. They would fan out to search for her. She couldn't hide here.

More trash fell on top of her, wet and disgusting. Why was she here? Didn't she have a doctorate? Then why was she down here?

The thing in the dumpster moved again. Marietta screamed and scrambled to grab the side of the huge metal container. Her feet made sucking noises. Move Marietta! Cry about it later!

"I can't do snakes!"

With a whimper, she threw herself over the side and landed on top of her suitcases like a ragdoll.

After catching her breath, she stood and ran her hands over her body. "I can't do snakes!"

In a sudden burst of hysteria, she smacked at herself over and over to get rid of all the snakes she imagined writhing beneath her clothes.

Marietta tried to refocus on strategy. She bought herself maybe ten more minutes. The interior dumpster, she'd already violated. The exterior dumpster sat in a fenced area on the side of the building near the parking lot. On the days that the garbage trucks rolled through the neighborhood, the landlord pushed both dumpsters outside the fence. Welp, then she knew her exit.

She strapped on her backpack. Then she stacked her suitcases one on top of the other so that she could roll them forward. She crept to the utility door and listened. She couldn't hear anything through the heavy steel. She turned the knob and took a peek. She didn't see anyone inside the fenced area.

Go!

The utility door swung shut behind her with a loud, decisive click. She escaped the building, but she wasn't home free yet.

The reflection of police lights flashed and strobed through the gaps in the wooden fence. She could see her SUV, boxed in by three cop cars now. The cars sat close enough to the fenced area that she could hear the radio chatter. How much did Robinette want her? That damn much? She should get out of town. But first, she had to escape this fenced area.

Marietta stood still. Her shoulders sagged. She leaned against the fence. No way she could get past all of them. Maybe one or two cops, yes. But three cop cars sat in the parking lot at the back entrance. How many sat in front? Too many.

Marietta rocked side to side. Her nervousness heightened to actual fear. She would go to jail tonight. How many charges? Many. Mugshot and fingerprints. They would beat her with phone books and shout at her. They would hurt her feelings and she would cry. Then they would delouse her and put her in a cell with a shared toilet with no rim and no toilet paper. Or maybe they would skip all that drama and throw her into the Lake City River.

What could she do? What should she do? Stephanie...

A shout went up on the police radios. Marietta peeked through the fence again. The uniformed men gestured to each other. The cops in the parking lot ran around the other side of the building towards the front entrance. Two of them drove their cars to join the action. She heard screams ricochet from the front of the building.

Go!

Marietta slid from the fenced area. One cop car, no driver in sight, still strobed its lights like the lonely attendee of a Friday night rave. It blocked her in on a diagonal. Well, who told him to do that?

Quick as quick, Marietta unlocked her car doors. She slid in and started the engine. She rammed her front wheels up the curb, then across the curb. She backed up. Then she changed gears. Up the curb, then away from the curb. She accelerated and drove off, leaving quite an impression on the bumper of the cop car, and some rubber on the parking lot pavement.

She needed an automatic teller machine so that she had cash for emergencies on the road out of town. She withdrew the limit on her bank card, four hundred dollars. Coated with the foul-smelling refuse and detritus of her former neighbors, she drove towards an overnight parking garage in downtown Lake City. She stopped mid-level to give herself time to calm down and think. She was too tired and filled with anxiety to drive tonight. She barely made it downtown, her hands shook so from the adrenaline surge. Maybe she should wait to drive until morning.

But if she checked into a hotel with her identification, the police would pick her up for questioning. However, if she waited until midnight, she could withdraw another four hundred dollars. But even if she paid cash, the hotel might require a credit card for security. On top of that, she smelled like the inside of a garbage dumpster. Depending on the hotel, she might fit in quite well. Or, she might raise a red flag. Well, then she would sleep inside her car.

Marietta tried not to cry. Only a few weeks ago, she lived the normal existence that she always craved. Now she not only looked and smelled homeless, she was homeless. And, on top of that, she now had a criminal record. No way she took electronics from Cadis. They couldn't prove that she did because it never happened. Or could they?

If she returned to her apartment building just to let bygones be bygones, what would she find? Crime scene tape strung across the landlord's shattered door? Would she find an array of laptops and cameras and cell phones scattered about her bedroom? How about her confession letter written with the shaky, guilty hand of a serial killer on the kitchen counter? How easy would it be for Lake City police to set her up? Child's play. This was Lake City.

God, she'd never felt so scared. She could still hear the wail of sirens echoing in her head. Almost as if police cars surrounded her on all sides again. She even heard the squawk of authoritarian commands over police radios and running feet.

Wait a minute.

They'd used her cell phone against her once before when they called her and made it ring. How hard would it be to track the current location of her cell phone? Again, child's play. For all she knew, her SUV had a new accessory it didn't have before, like a GPS locator.

Oh Marietta, Marietta! You have to be smarter than this!

Robinette isolated her by branding her a criminal. That, combined with events from her past would blur any perspective Lake City's finest would take on the story of her persecution by Robinette. No one would believe her, not even her own public defender.

Marietta exited the car with her backpack and luggage. She left the cell phone on the front seat. She heard voices. Feet approached closer.

She ducked behind a row of vehicles then hefted her luggage down a shadowed staircase to street level. Exhausted, she slid behind a row of tall evergreen bushes that also seemed to serve as a public toilet. Cop cars parked at haphazard angles in the street. A few uniforms stood around talking. Above her, from the upper levels of the parking garage, she heard triumphant shouts. They found her SUV, then. The uniforms on the street spoke into their radios. Two of them entered the parking structure at a run, eager as cowboys to be part of the take down. One uniform remained on the street facing the entrance.

Inch by inch, Marietta slid in the shadows behind the row of evergreens, pushing and pulling her luggage along with her. When she reached the opposite end, she eased out of the bushes and melted into the chill of a late summer Lake City evening.

CHAPTER 19   THE UNDERWORLD

The next morning, on the back steps of an enormous cathedral, Marietta shook herself awake and pulled out her laptop to search for schedules and fares. Too much security at the airport. The train didn't leave until mid-afternoon. A bus was cheaper and would depart in two hours, but it was completely booked. Okay, so mid-afternoon on the train then. At another automatic teller machine, she attempted to withdraw her cash limit for the day. Insufficient funds, the receipt said. That couldn't be right.

She shoved her bank card inside the slot for another go. Then another. And another. And then the machine swallowed her bank card. No!

Marietta shook her head, dumbfounded. No way. She had at least six thousand dollars in her bank account. The university professor paid her six months' worth of rent. On top of that, she should have received a direct deposit of her last paycheck. Where was her money?

Marietta fought down panic. A couple of glasses of white wine would really smooth down the ragged edges right about now. But she had to keep her head straight and her thoughts razor-sharp, because Robinette's people wanted or really needed to herd her in his direction. Her SUV had likely been towed by now. She definitely could not afford airfare. That left the train. Could she lay low until mid-afternoon? Where?

And also... pay attention, Marietta. Marietta! This ATM just recorded your face, the time, the date, and the location. Move!

Head down, Marietta walked amongst the office workers who marched in ragged formation towards another day on the grind. Quite a few of them jostled her to the side since she couldn't keep pace with all of her luggage. A few others looked upon her with the strangest combination of pity and revulsion. Marietta recognized those expressions because she remembered wearing that same mask on her own face whenever she saw a homeless person.

After the second block, Marietta decided that two suitcases plus a backpack were too awkward to maneuver in a life on the run. She abandoned the larger suitcase, mostly clothes and shoes, in favor of the smaller suitcase and her backpack.

At 7:30 am, she bought another wig, blonde and short and wavy this time (the opposite), as well as sunglasses, and travel wipes. Inside the bathroom stall of the train station, she sponged the garbage dumpster remnants off of her body. Then she changed into a sleek, black fleece warmup suit. Much better.

She went through her remaining suitcase with an even more critical eye and pulled out only the essentials. These she stuffed into her backpack with her laptop and Stephanie's Bible and other research she'd done on Cadis Industries. Then she left her small suitcase in the bathroom stall with the leftovers as a gift for the next woman on the run.

At 8:30 am, Marietta exited the bathroom stall. She touched her wig and sunglasses to make sure they were on straight. Organized, she looked forward to buying her train ticket out of town. She would buy the ticket now to guarantee her seat for this afternoon. What a shame two uniformed police and several plainclothes cops surrounded the ticket counter.

Glancing down at an imaginary watch for cover, Marietta detoured through the door to the street and walked away. She could still buy a ticket online. But the cops would also watch boarding passengers, wouldn't they? Marietta learned during high school how to fade even in the midst of a crowd of people. High school classmates were one thing. But law enforcement presented quite another challenge. Also, maybe she should make at least a little bit of effort to avoid surveillance cameras?

Marietta felt starved. Her stomach moaned and moved around like it wanted to escape her body and feed itself. But she decided not to buy breakfast at a nearby convenience store or restaurant due to the cameras. During her walk from the cathedral to the train station, she'd noticed a long line of people that wrapped around the sidewalk of the church block. She knew why the hard luck and trouble folks waited. She also knew that she qualified.

Hadn't she put in time on the back steps of the cathedral last night? Oh yeah.

By the time Marietta walked back to the church, only five people remained in line. She stepped in behind the last person. She and her backpack fit in pretty well here and no one asked her questions. She pushed her sunglasses on top of her head and found an empty space at a long table. Most people already finished eating although a couple of men lingered over coffee like it was a sidewalk cafe on the streets of Paris.

As Marietta chewed, she dimmed her eyes and gazed into the middle distance. She looked but didn't see. She heard but didn't listen. She certainly didn't eavesdrop.

"Yeah, I sleep there under the bridge. I don't got a bit of shame about it. I don't get no trouble. Trouble don't want none of me no more no how. Trouble done with me."

"I dunno, this shelter's all right."

"Too many rules here. Everybody in your business. Try to get what you got."

"Least it's warm here. It's cold down by the river."

Marietta slopped up some more food from her plate and stared into space while she chewed, not listening at all.

"Yeah, well it's warm there too in places. Cause of all the boiler rooms. And it don't rain either 'cause of all the bridges."

"Nah."

"Stay one night. You'll see. Better than this jail."

"Jail's warm too. And they got ping pong..."

The men got up and continued their discussion on life in the big city as they walked out the door. Marietta finished up her own meal. She had a busy day to plan in the big city herself.

At 9:15 am, Marietta held the newspaper around her face just to see if she'd become famous overnight. Not so much. Apparently, last night, Lake City police arrested two women in the same block as her former apartment building.

In the first incident, the police officers questioned a twenty-eight-year-old Black woman during a standard investigation of drug conspiracy. The officers arrested the woman on charges of obstruction, resisting, and assault. Marietta frowned. That sounded like her fourth floor neighbor, for sure a college student, not a drug conspirator.

Though the police heard Marietta's cell phone ring, they couldn't be sure she waited inside for them to return, could they? Even if they questioned the landlord again and he confirmed her presence, she might have run to a nearby apartment to avoid the return of law enforcement. Right? If they broke into her apartment and found it empty... then logic demanded that they speak to her neighbors.

Police also arrested a fifty-year-old Black grandmother of three who they stopped on suspicion of solicitation. They charged her with disorderly conduct and resisting arrest. Marietta didn't know who the grandmother was, but that sounded like the scuffle and screams from the front of her building which allowed her to make her getaway from the utility area.

The demographic of the two people the police rousted let her know that Robinette had sufficient pull to order the police to attack first, and then ask questions later, if at all. If Lake City police wanted a legitimate investigation, they wouldn't have attacked and roughed up women who looked like her.

Marietta folded the newspaper with a heavy sigh. She felt terrible that she'd used the other women as decoys. If she had to do it all again... what? What would she have done? Stayed at the university? Well...

Her eyes darted all directions now. She could never return to her apartment building. What's more, she couldn't approach the police for help. Nor could she leave town. Not today, for sure. She was highly wanted and desired by law enforcement. More than that, she had to get off the street before someone spotted her. The police knew she was somewhere downtown. But just to be sure, she again checked the situation at the train station. The same.

At 9:45 am, with great reluctance, Marietta peeled off enough cash from her stash to purchase three tickets for 10:30 am, 1:00 pm, and 3:00 pm movie showings. Under the cover of darkness, in the middle of the small matinee crowd, Marietta dozed. In between blackouts of the sleep-deprived, she went over what she knew or suspected. (1)   Robinette knows that Mary Madison is Marietta Brazil, the "niece" of Stephanie Madison... the terrorist who killed four people, including his father, and ruined his face. (2) Robinette will do whatever it takes to neutralize Mary/Marietta either out of fear or revenge for his father's death. (3) Assume that Robinette will lie, cheat, steal, maybe kill and destroy Mary/Marietta.

And how much death had Marietta known in her life? But why did he want Mary/Marietta so badly? For what real reason? The woman who killed his father and caused his disfigurement died twenty-four years ago!

At 12:45 pm, Marietta changed theaters for the next movie. She had to get organized and think things through. She came up with:

(1) You cannot let Robinette capture you. (2) Lake City police will not help you. (3) Instead, Lake City police will immobilize you for Robinette. (4) You cannot let anyone know your location in Lake City. See Rule 1. (5) But you cannot leave Lake City without learning the truth or it will never be over. (6) You need evidence. (7) The only evidence lays inside the incinerator at Cadis. (8) To get the evidence, you have to re-enter Cadis and the incinerator. (9) You'll never get past the front lobby with its cluster of security. See again Rule 1. (10) Kowalski knows your face and he doesn't like you. Kal likes you. He's friendly and sympathetic. But it wouldn't be just Kal, would it? See again Rule 1.

Marietta's head began to hurt. She lay back and dozed again.

***

Tony returned his mother's call from his cell phone. "Mama, what did you say about the Madison property? I didn't understand the message."

"I came back from walking Abbie and I saw someone over there trying to look over the fence."

"Well, was it one of the guys who works there?"

"No, it wasn't them. I know what they look like."

"It's about time for the meter reading on our street, so..."

"No, I know what the meter man looks like too. It wasn't him. And he wasn't anywhere near the meter."

"Maybe it was the mailman."

"Tony Jennings, do not make fun of your mother. I know what everybody looks like on this street."

"Yes, ma'am, you do," Tony sighed.

"Well?"

"Well what?"

"Ain't you gonna do something?"

"Is he still there? Do you see him now?"

"Nah. He's gone. Maybe you should call Marietta to see if she sent someone."

Tony allowed a long pause to go by while he thought of a reply to that. So that's what this was about. His mother never ceased her matchmaking. He'd be damned if called Marietta for any reason. He just didn't feel like talking to her ever again even though she was his client.

"Uhm, instead of that, I'll check it out myself when I get back. I'll take a look around the property to make sure everything's okay."

"If you say so." His mother's doubts about his judgement warmed the heart.

"But Mama, if you see the guy again, don't talk to him. Just call Sheriff Riggs to handle it, okay?"

***

At 5:00 pm, Marietta woke up during the closing credits for some mindless kid flick. She'd blacked out during the previews so she had no idea what the movie was about. All she knew was that she sat under a pile of popcorn that some little brats must have thrown on her like rice at a wedding while she slept.

The lights brightened. She remained the only person still seated in a pile of popcorn confetti. She felt torn between the need to remain in the company of witnesses and the desire to scurry into a small dark corner where no one could find her.

Marietta decided to leave the movie house after she received a sour look from the usher, not at all pleased with the mess the future leaders of Lake City tossed all around her.

At 5:30 pm, Marietta sat on a bench on the subway platform during evening rush. She noted that she wasn't the only worn down weary traveler who didn't board any trains because she didn't have any place to go.

But when she noted a security guard headed her direction, she got up to board a train anyway. She circled Lake City north to south twice. Then she boarded another train to circle back and forth to the airport, a pretty long ride.

She considered her miraculous escape through the trash chute of her apartment building. She hadn't known where she would end up when she fell down the metal shaft, but she knew it was the only way. Better than a ride in the back of a police car charged with obstruction, disorderly, resisting, assault, and theft. Or even drug conspiracy and prostitution since those options also seemed to be on the table.

Her adventure down the rabbit hole ended in a soft landing rather than a headfirst strike onto a concrete floor or into a brick wall. Wait. Say again?

She tried to concentrate as the train clacked and swayed along the tracks. In the basement at Cadis, inside the tunnel at the base of the metal shaft, hadn't she heard street noise? Didn't she smell coffee? Then why couldn't she find the street entrance to the incinerator tunnel?

Well?

Marietta dug the keys that Kate gave her out of her pocket. One key fit the incinerator door that led to the file room. One key fit the lock to the safety door. That left two keys. Marietta clutched the keys inside her fist. She tucked them back into her pocket on the ride back into downtown Lake City.

At 7:45 pm, Marietta deboarded the train, no longer helpless and confused. No longer on defense, she had a plan. She knew what she had to do. But could she do it? That part, she didn't know.

She already wore cat burglary fashion. The black fleece of the sleek warmup suit and her black tennis shoes would serve. She still had the flashlight and spray lubricant. All she needed was a cape and she was ready for a night of vigilantism with Batman.

Instead of that, at 8:00 pm, Marietta sat with an enormous crowd at an outdoor blues concert. On the cusp of autumn, Lake City fought hard against its icy destiny with a series of music festivals. The City would party with vigor until the blizzards came and whipped all the people back into their steel and brick cages like animals. But for now, the skyscrapers emptied. The worker bees, tourists, hippies, yuppies, bikers, bankers, rockers, hip hoppers, crackheads, meth heads, and others gathered into one merry, intoxicated hive.

Kowalski's shift ended at eleven tonight. She didn't want to run into him, for sure. She'd never met the third security guard who worked the graveyard shift. But he couldn't possibly be worse than Kowalski. And maybe, as Kal hinted, he would feel sleepy tonight.

Though light pollution from streetlamps and skyscrapers washed away any view of the moon and stars, the night was beautiful, though a tad chill. Despite her unease and desperation, Marietta enjoyed the show. That's Lake City, she thought. So bad that it was good.

The concert came to a reluctant end despite the protests and pouts from the rhapsodic drunken crowd at ten o'clock. It was still too early to break into Cadis. Because by now, Marietta had definitely committed to breaking and entering through the incinerator tunnel. Oh yeah. It was about to go down. The mistake that Robinette made when he threw her under the bus was that he gave her nothing more to lose. By God, if she went down, she would swing for the fence and laugh all the way back to home plate. Go big or go home, wherever that was these days.

She would use this hour before the end of Kowalski's shift to locate and reconnoiter the street entrance to the incinerator. Inebriated festival goers stumbled with her past the street level business offices and clothing stores. The tipsy tourists peeled off at the high-end restaurants and hotel bars. The surbanites fell down the subway stairs to catch the last train out of the city.

Marietta walked with the rowdy locals to the next level down that abutted the river. Here, the hole in the wall bars and after hour clubs offered revelry for the regular folks. The secret venues filled with blue collar workers and college-aged hipsters. Intoxicated men catcalled to Marietta and shouted insults at each other. Underneath the odor of burnt grease, car exhaust, and liquor, she smelled coffee. She remembered this street!

There! Marietta spotted the coffee shop where she sat and plotted with Kate what seemed like ages ago. She strolled past garbage dumpsters, employee entrances, and half-full parking lots. But she saw no ventilation openings. She needed to find the next level down.

At 10:45pm, she circled again to find the next level, but met with no success. Tired and discouraged by the heavy pack on her back, she decided not to circle again. Much as she wanted to double-check access to the third level down, the men standing outside the bars kept giving her strange looks. So, instead, she went back up to street level. She sat in the park where Kate chain-smoked and croaked out her fantastic tales about Stephanie. Kate's cigarette butts still littered the ground along with newer litter that park visitors re-gifted to Mother Nature.

Marietta sighed. She looked around at the trees. So much beauty in this place. But the beauty covered a dirty layer of corruption and rot. She twisted on the bench. Look at these chrysanthemums, she thought. Someone took time out to plant these, and then someone else takes time to throw beer cans...

She spotted it then underneath the tree canopy. An iron gate ran along the back of the park which abutted the ramps that the commuter trains used to pull into the main station. Attached to the gate, an iron ladder descended. Marietta cut her eyes left and right. As far as she could see, she sat alone in the park. She rose and eased back towards the gate. She bent underneath the tree canopy.

Marietta pulled her flashlight out of the pack and strobed it downward, on and off quick as quick. She saw enough. She secured her backpack and climbed down the iron ladder. This time, she made it past the second level of streets. Down and further down she descended to the underworld below the level of the river, held back by a wall of concrete. She remembered hearing whispers about this place where homeless, prostitutes, drug addicts and their associates resided, but she never quite believed the rumors.

Broken pavement littered with shattered liquor bottles and syringes served as a floor. Freeway overpasses, pedestrian bridges, and train tracks provided the roof. Marietta saw all of this only because occasional street light and neon cut through the murk via openings in the roof. She saw random rusted car engine parts, broken furniture, old mattresses and other detritus. Some would call this place a dump. But others called it home. When Marietta walked forward, she saw a few human forms huddled down for a night's rest. She passed without a word.

Trucks and buses and trains roared overhead like an ominous heavy metal soundtrack. If she screamed, no one would hear her. But neither would they hear her breaking into Cadis. Focus on the positive.

Actually, Marietta focused her thoughts on geography. She needed to find the old incinerator for Cadis. But how? All the foulness of Lake City ran down here via sewage lines, ventilation ducts, and random pipes. This area served as one big trash dump. Well then, that was no big deal at all for Marietta. You see one trash chute or incinerator tunnel or garbage dumpster, you've seen them all. Somewhere close by, Cadis Industries used to provide an access point for maintenance people to enter and do their jobs until the fire department shut it down.

Marietta felt eyes. Two men watched her. They whispered together. She continued forward and hoped that trouble wouldn't follow behind.

The boiler rooms and HVAC systems ground and chugged, still hard at work while everyone above-ground went home. Heated air whispered past. The air smelled of coffee. Then she was close!

Marietta passed a large pillar that supported one of the busier and louder overpasses. Behind the pillar, a weed-choked, sickly tree grew in front of a rusty grate. The tree's roots invaded the broken concrete like long, knobby alien fingers. The trunk twisted upward around metal protrusions o the pillar. The unnatural tree, an abomination, fought for its right to exist all the way upward from the dank, dark underworld cellar towards a narrow slit that provided its leaves a stingy dose of sun by day and a cold dose of moonlight at night.

But that grate, could it be?

From the smell that emanated behind the pillar, this area doubled as an outhouse, maybe also a crack house, and possibly a whore house. Even the coffee aroma couldn't cover the assault on her nose. Unsure, Marietta shifted. A syringe broke under her foot. And then, from behind her, another syringe broke.

She froze. Someone walked with her. Marietta thought about the men who whispered when she passed. She had to continue forward because she couldn't stay here. Who knew what waited back there. As she walked, the wind shifted. She smelled coffee again.

That grate, dammit, it had to be the grate!

Marietta slid into the shadows and crept behind the broken husks of old furniture. After some time, she found herself back at the ladder to the park. She'd walked in a circle.

Maybe she should go back up the ladder. Maybe she should hitchhike her way out of Lake City and find a quiet place to recover her senses.

Or maybe, she could use her flashlight as a weapon? Because she'd come too far. She wanted what she wanted when she wanted it. She would get it even if it killed her. What the "it" was, no longer even mattered. She had to have it.

Marietta retraced her steps. This time, she didn't see the two men who'd watched and whispered before. Maybe she lost them.

Moonlight from the small opening for the twisted tree gave her just enough gloom to see as she sprayed the lock and hinges on the grate with oil lubricant. She inserted the largest key on the ring into the lock and twisted. *Click.* She looked over her shoulder. She didn't see or hear anything. She grabbed the trunk of the thin, sickly tree and yanked it to the side, breaking the knobby alien fingers. The trunk was dead and moved with little resistance. The few greenish leaves at the top hadn't yet figured out how little time remained of mortal life.

Marietta held the trunk with one hand and then pulled the grate open with the other. She crawled inside the metal tunnel, and then closed the grate behind her. The mostly-dead tree snapped back into position, concealing her entry.

Two strobes of the flashlight let her know that the tunnel was empty. She crawled forward, glancing behind her at the opening once in a while. Her body blocked another quick strobe of the flashlight. Three feet ahead of her, she saw a metal ladder. To the right, she saw the safety door.

Excited, she scrambled forward into darkness. She tried the safety key again and twisted, gently now...

Click.

Fearful of yet another failure, she almost didn't want to tug the door open. Again, she used her body to block another quick strobe. A medium-sized metal strong box nestled inside along with safety googles, a few gas masks, bandages, and other random bit and pieces of safety equipment from twenty-four years ago.

The strong box was locked, of course. Last key. Sure enough, the key fit. She twisted the key in the lock. *Click.*

A low shhhhhh, a hissing noise, crawled from somewhere deep inside the darkness of the metal structure. What made a noise like that? A snake? In the middle of the city? A cat? More like... a rat! Or maybe a raccoon?

Stop thinking, Marietta. Why are you thinking? Get out of here!

Marietta flipped the lid of the strong box open and felt inside. She didn't bother with the flashlight because she recognized the familiar shape and feel of the bulky file folders.

The hiss seemed louder.

Marietta grabbed handfuls of everything from the box and stuffed it all into her backpack.

She smelled something else now. Not coffee. Not urine or feces. She smelled... gas. Marietta grabbed a gas mask from the supply cabinet and put it on. Something fell down the ladder from the file room. Something that glowed. *Recognize and remember that you were warned.*

Marietta scrambled for the street entrance of the incinerator. The shhhhhh followed her. Through the gas mask, the smell of gas grew stronger. She could almost taste it.

Move!

Now she heard shouts from beyond the grate. No choice. She would have to deal with whoever waited out there for her because the gas behind her would never listen to her sob story. She certainly wouldn't try to re-enter Cadis Industries through the file room. She couldn't remain inside the tunnel much longer. She had to get out before the gas poisoned her. She reached the grate, touched it with her hand.

Whoosh!

Smokey particles filled the tunnel. She could barely see. She pushed at the grate, which didn't move because of the tree. The air inside the tunnel erupted into an inferno.

CHAPTER 20　　THE RUN

Marietta braced against the back pack behind her and kicked twice at the grate. On a scream and a howl, she kicked a third time. This time, the grate opened. She knocked the mostly dead tree aside. An explosion belched her and the backpack from the metal shaft as if from a dragon's throat. She collapsed on the ground. The tunnel spit more flames above her head.

So much for staying under the radar, she thought, too stunned to move. Someone started the gas. It didn't just happen. Someone dropped that incendiary device on purpose. She needed to get out of here. While she thought about that, more fire roared from the tunnel above where she lay.

Marietta turned her head. Again, she really needed to get out of here. Smoke poured and flames licked from the dragon's mouth.

She stood up and swayed. The bodies of two men lay at her feet. A third man stood a few feet away, as if he waited for her to notice him. She and he had a brief face-off. Then he approached.

Marietta backed away. He matched her steps. Neon light moved with the shadows across his face, too quick for her to see...

"Somebody help me!" she screamed. But the mask muffled her voice.

The man pounced. She couldn't move fast enough to evade him because she was still disoriented from the hard landing and the gas that seeped into the mask. He grabbed her by the arm and tugged at her face mask. Then he collapsed.

The two men she thought were dead stood in front of her. One of them held a metal pipe in his hand.

"Run, lady! Get out of here!" the one holding the pipe shouted.

"Get out of here!" yelled the other.

Marietta snatched up her backpack, strapped it on, and then ran. She got out of there. She and her backpack bounced at an awkward gallop back to the ladder that led up to the park. Up the ladder she climbed. Through the park she ran. She bounced until she reached the subway. She paused to catch her breath. She took a quick look behind her. She didn't see anyone.

Just in time, before others at the train station noticed and got upset, she removed the gas mask and dropped them into a trash can. She took the train to an all-night casino with garish pink and purple and white neon signs. She disembarked and laughed it up with a group of women wearing outlandish church hats who put their faith and paychecks into the hands of the money changers that welcomed them into the temple. Everyone, including Marietta, made it past security.

Marietta peeled away and stepped into the ladies room. She needed to shake the dust and smoke off her clothes, plus swab the dirt and sweat off her face. She broke out the travel wipes from a side pocket of her backpack.

After her adrenaline slowed, she re-entered the casino and purchased an order of French fries and a soda at one of the fast food restaurants. Her eyes darted all directions, but she saw no one that seemed particularly interested in her.

She opened the main compartment of her backpack with trepidation, and then hesitated. Should she do this? Could be anything in here. She swallowed, cut her eyes around the restaurant again, then reached in her hand and pulled out a file folder.

Stephanie...

The ink of the typewritten pages faded to brown, but she could still read the words.

> Additional considerations we give that minimize security risks of Sundae's exposure--posthypnotic suggestibility, intelligence, reasoning, morality, superstitions, social index, and weakness of the primary support system (her family and romantic attachments). Long periods of REM sleep deprivation and post-hypnotic suggestions increase cooperation and have broken her will, confidence, self-reliance, and moral values. We continue to isolate Sundae from peer groups and we note the following results--depression, apathy, and thorough social failure. Continuous financial failure has increased her dependence upon her owner. Isolation has caused increased anxiety in Sundae, also hostility, tension, discomfort. The owner and the handler use triggers similar to the controller to engineer and program...

Sundae. *I hate Sundays.* Sundae. *I hate Sundays.* Stephanie wrote her hatred of Sundays over and over throughout her journal. But was Stephanie... Sundae? Stephanie hid her journal where she thought certain people wouldn't look, inside her Bible. From whom did she hide the journal? The handler? The owner? Or the controller? Someone owned and handled Stephanie. Her birth mother had been controlled. But then... that meant... the document slid from Marietta's fingers onto the table... that her mother was... a... a slave.

Marietta didn't want to accept that she had in her possession, potential proof of Stephanie's systematic torture and trauma programming. She had found such proof deep within the labyrinthine depths of Cadis Industries. Not a military or government organization, but a commercial corporate enterprise. Cadis Industries owned her mother?

With a new-found sense of hyper-vigilance, Marietta decided too many cameras and eyes circled around her. Too many bells and whistles sounded off. Too many people jibber-jabbered. She couldn't take it. She saw no immediate threat, but she felt so very afraid.

Earlier, Marietta thought multiple cameras and a crowd of people would keep her safe. But now, after learning of this new evil, she realized that she didn't know anything. She just knew that she couldn't remain still while Robinette's forces hunted her down and treed her like an animal.

Like she shouted to her former landlord yesterday, she had been innocent of wrong-doing. But no longer. Technically, she broke into Robinette's building and stole business intelligence. She was burned in Lake City in every sense of the word. More than ever, she needed to find a way out of town. If she had to walk, then she would walk. But where would she go?

She couldn't return to her house near the university. The professor and his wife and children lived there now. Besides, Robinette had her previous address from her background check. She already knew why a hotel wouldn't work. As soon as she showed her identification, the police and then Robinette would have her location.

How about her old house, just overnight until she could try again for a train ticket? If someone like the nosy neighbor saw her sneaking around, then maybe he'd assume she was a ghost come back to haunt potential renters. Boy, he'd love that. The idea had its appeal, but no. She never wanted to see that house again. Besides, Robinette knew that address too and the realty company probably had security installed.

Possibly, she could persuade Tony to tap into her accounts and send funds so that she could rent something else. But how? Anywhere she received those funds, she had to show identification. Even if she managed to pick up the funds without raising a red flag, any apartment manager and hotelier of repute would require that she identify herself. The minute her new address showed up on a credit report, Robinette would have her location.

Her grandfather warned her about Lake City and its ways. Despite the myriad professional opportunities, the City destroyed Stephanie and then the rest of Marietta's family. Now, the City wanted to destroy Marietta. For many years, she obeyed Grandpa's warning. But she just couldn't allow the mystery surrounding Stephanie, her real mother, to stand any longer.

And now, here we are.

Wayfarer. When nowhere else would do... Wayfarer. She still had a home. She was safe there before. Tony controlled her accounts under his name for his convenience. He might hate her, might think she was an ungrateful and self-centered brat... Think? He'd come right out and told her so. But as far as she could see, he'd never cheated her. Steady as he goes.

He told her straight up that his loyalty was to her grandfather, not to her. But at this point, she'd take whatever support she could get. Good thing she didn't fire him, as she'd kept meaning to.

Marietta shoved the insidious file folder into her backpack. She peered at the other contents. Similar file folders chock full of papers and documents lay between VHS and cassette tapes. This technology from the early 90s may or may not still function, but she'd take it along with her.

She dug for Tony's old letter about her grandfather's death years ago that described how he left his entire estate to her, Mary Madison. The cold tone of barely concealed hostility resounded in every paragraph and punctuation mark. His contempt for her rose off the pages in a bitter miasma. Thank God she hadn't left any of this paperwork behind when she fled her studio apartment the previous evening. She never saved any of Tony's emails either. Delete, delete, delete...

Wayfarer.

She had no secure way to warn Tony of her unexpected homecoming. She dared not use email. She had no cell phone and who knew where to find a public phone these days? First class mail wasn't quick enough. She'd arrive to his doorstep before a letter. Tony did not like her, never seemed glad to see her, but he could not deny her birthright.

Marietta headed back into Lake City proper.

CHAPTER 21   WAYFARER

Dawn and delivery trucks woke Marietta out of her stiff-legged stupor on the back steps of the cathedral. All of her energy focused upon leaving Lake City for good, for bad, forever. She used almost all her remaining cash to purchase a disposable credit card.

She used that and her laptop to purchase a train ticket online in the name of "Janet Smith," because the bus was completely booked again. Maybe other people needed to flee for their own reasons.

She sidled into the train station in order to print her ticket at a free-standing kiosk. Yes! She gripped the paper ticket in her hand and folded it carefully into her pocket. She wouldn't feel safe until she actually sat on a train seat as the train rolled over the state line.

Her eyes moved around the train station's lobby. She noted security, but not as much as yesterday. She would have to figure out some kind of way to board this afternoon without being spotted. She had three hours until departure, while she figured out the second part of her plan. She sure didn't like her chances for safety hanging around the train station, not the way things had been going.

She walked outside. Her stomach sent loud and persistent hunger signals to her brain. She didn't have a lot of money left now, so back at the soup kitchen, she ate breakfast with the gusto of a ferocious beast. She came up for air to scan the crowd.

Two men, her fellow travelers from yesterday stood across the room. It looked as though they had already decided their itinerary.

Marietta stood as fast as she could and crossed the room towards them. Startled, they stiffened.

"Miss, are you all right?" one of them asked, glancing at her blonde wig.

"I have to leave town."

"Yeah Miss. That's probably best," the other said.

Then they all looked at each other.

"You probably won't see me again, but... here," Marietta said and held out her laptop. "This is for you. I can't take it with me. It's too heavy and I've got too much stuff."

"What? Nah!" they protested together.

"Maybe you can share it. Sell it or pass it on to someone else if you can't use it. Okay?"

Uncertain, the men looked at each other.

"Please," Marietta said. "I can never pay you back for what you did. You saved my life last night."

"Last who? Don't know what you're talking about, lady."

"Miss, you don't have to..."

"Right." Marietta smiled because she didn't have time to argue. "Well, anyway, somebody told me to get away from here and that's good advice. I'm sure gonna go."

She smiled and set the laptop down on the table next to the two men. She shook first one man's hand then the other. Then she gathered up her backpack and left the church without a backward glance, but with two granola bars in her pocket.

She spent the next two hours in the last stall of the train station's bathroom. Not until she heard the last call for her train's departure, did she join the line of boarding passengers. A mother and a father with a screaming baby and three restless toddlers helped her to bypass close inspection of her identification. One quick glance and an impatient wave and "Janet Smith" boarded the train.

I'm on the train. Oh thank you, thank you Jesus, I'm on the train. Marietta eye-balled the train car. She didn't see anything out of the ordinary, but when would the train move? When would she leave Lake City limits? Why wasn't the train moving?

Marietta looked at the platform through the window and balled her hands into fists. Fear speared through her. A guard on the platform turned her direction. Marietta ran a casual hand across her short blonde wig and leaned away from the window. If he pulled out his radio and made a call...

The train slid forward and gathered speed. The wheels glided over the rails like ice skates. Marietta sank back into her seat. She made it!

***

Early in the morning, the train's conductor announced Wayfarer. Rested now, Marietta already stood at the door with her backpack, anxious to deboard. By the time the conductor arrived, she'd fogged the window. He opened the doors and waved her off with a polite tip of the hat. The Madison home was less than a mile away from the train station. Come to think of it, almost everything in a town this small was less than a mile away. Not much had changed.

Still in her dark knit fleece, but sans wig, Marietta hiked from the train station towards her grandparents' old house. In the South, September was high summer with drought conditions. The heavy pack along with her clothing made her perspire.

A police car swooped into the vacant lot ahead of her. The officer exited his car and walked towards her. Marietta stopped. Okay. Well, Marietta, forty years was a hell of a good run. You had some laughs...

"Hi there," the young and blonde officer said behind mirrored sunglasses. "We just received a call that a deranged woman was walking down this street talking to herself."

Marietta looked around. She didn't see anyone.

"Do you know anything about that?" the cop asked with a small, tight grin, his arms akimbo.

She looked around again and shrugged, mystified. "No."

A second police car pulled in beside them. The second officer, actually, the sheriff, didn't bother with a smile. He and his jar headed salt and pepper buzz cut along with potbelly exited the vehicle and stood, grim-faced and arms crossed.

Marietta stared back at both of them. Whatever happens, happens, she thought. Still, the police stop in Wayfarer where her family had owned property for more than one hundred years surprised her. Although, if Robinette called ahead, if Lake City police shared information, then...

"May I ask where you're going?" The first officer asked. He seemed embarrassed but remained purposeful.

"I'm going home."

"And where is that?" The officer made a slow and deliberate perusal of her clothing.

Marietta told him the address and waited. An awkward pause descended. She and the young officer stared at each other. The silence stretched. He appeared puzzled as if unsure why both he and she were even talking to each other. Marietta decided not to say anything to help out.

"Is that the orchard?" the officer finally asked.

"Yes." Marietta waited again. She hoped he didn't run her name. Lord only knew what would come up in the system. Don't run my name. Don't run my name!

"Well, you seem okay to me." The officer laughed.

Marietta raised her eyebrows and waited some more. Much as she wanted to insert a snarky comment into the conversation, Wayfarer remained the Deep South. Black women who used snark and irony and sarcasm with law enforcement have had the "attitude" beaten out of them more than once. The aggressive behavior of Lake City's police already had her spooked. And the stiff-bodied, big-bellied sheriff appeared as though more than anything else the world offered, he really wanted Marietta to give him a reason.

So she waited.

"Okay then. Stay safe and have a nice day." The first officer tried on a grin.

Marietta didn't trust it. "Am I free to go?" she asked.

The officer waved her away with the bored imperiousness of the heir apparent to the sheriff's throne. Marietta hitched the backpack higher and continued her hike.

At the Madison home, she threw her pack onto the porch. She flexed her tired, hot, sweaty back. A cop car whizzed past the house, the officer inside gave her yet another once over and a friendly wave. But she didn't care anymore.

She was here!

She had not one dime, well maybe a dime, but not much else to her name. She didn't bother with the front door this time because the gate to the orchard stood open. So she walked around the side of the house. And there she saw Tony, as ever, gauntlets on both arms, raking straw from the dirt floor of the falcon house.

He turned a still lean and lithe frame around to look at her for a long moment. Marietta felt self-consciously aware of her disheveled appearance, but oh well. What could she do?

Without a word, Tony walked with her over to the Jennings house where Miss Annette hugged her while Tony retrieved the keys. She already knew, because she did read her statements, dammit, that the utilities--water, gas, electric--still operated in Tony's name, though he paid the bills from her accounts.

This time, he didn't bother to walk her back to the front door. He simply gave her the keys and waited for her to leave his presence.

***

When she took too long to vacate his doorstep, Tony made a point to throw the lock home on his front door as loudly as possible. To his satisfaction, her back stiffened. She got the message.

"Riggs just called to check on her. I vouched for her though. Riggs is always doing too much in this heat. He wanted to know if I was still feeding my monster."

"Your what?"

"Abbie, cause she's so big..." Miss Annette bent to rub behind Abbie's ears. "Yes you are you big baby. That's why mommy wuvs you..." Abbie's tail thumped against the floor.

"All anyone needs to know about Marietta is that she's a sugar-frosted flake. She always has been. She always will be."

"Tony! Are you still mad about the prom?"

"No!"

"Are you sure? Cause you sound mad."

"Mama, it's not about that anymore. It's about how she treats people all the time."

"People like you?"

"Mama, please give it up."

"She's not Carla, Tony."

"I know she's not Carla. She's much worse."

"Son, don't you think it's time you..."

Tony walked out of the room.

CHAPTER 22   TONY

Marietta felt hot and frazzled, just plain bothered by the cops, by Tony, by everything. She went up to the attic and quickly located her clothes from years ago that she'd left in her room. Someone boxed them up and put them in the attic. Fashion trends changed in the meantime, but some of the jeans still fit, barely. She bathed and got to work pulling herself back together. Then she found cleaning supplies under the kitchen sink and started wiping off counters and snapping open window shades. Then she dusted and swept.

The house seemed so hollow and empty of life. Not haunted like the Brazil house in Lake City, but it was a house of shadows, alone and unloved. Summers past, the Madison house filled with the laughter and the voices of the people Marietta loved, or it seemed that way back when she was younger. Now, of them all, only she remained.

Satisfied with a lick and a promise for now, she moved into the orchard to take a look around. The trees matured into a dense canopy that created a fruity, spicy, nutty emerald jungle. She unlocked the old tool house to find the gardening implements she needed. As she worked to rake up rotted fallen fruit for compost, she reviewed the logistics of her situation. She had ten dollars to her name. She had no bank card. Who knows what happened to the money in her personal savings and checking accounts? But she just couldn't make herself walk back across the street and request access to her business accounts that Tony controlled. Not after that hostile display of his. Pride and irritation with his judgmental, haughty attitude remained an obstacle that Marietta did not care to hurdle any time soon. He really needed to be fired, and soon. Real soon.

In mid-September, the orchard brimmed with fruit. A few late peaches and plums hung in clusters here and there. She saw a few early apples too. Marietta got the ladder and picked fruit from a few trees to eat. Now, if she could just find last year's pecans, she had a full meal. This year's wouldn't drop until November. She found some in a barrel and scooped them out and used a hammer to crack them open.

If she tried to locate employment, she would have to identify herself. And besides, jobs were notoriously scarce for those not connected to the local power structure. Unless... well, why not? Marietta got back on the ladder to pick more produce.

The falcons circled overhead. Quick as she could, Marietta strapped on the gauntlets that Tony left inside the falcon house and continued with her work.

***

"So what brings you back to good ole Wayfarer today, Marietta?" Tony asked her while he sat behind his desk in the law office. He wore a crisp white cotton button-down shirt now

Marietta crossed her arms while she stood in front of him in her jeans and t-shirt from long ago because he didn't offer her a chair. Unlike Oliver Twist begging for another bowl of gruel, however, she faced him with defiance.

"I'm going to set up the old produce stand for Wayfarer Orchards."

"You... came all the way down here to set up a produce stand."

"That's right."

Tony stared at her and waited. She stared back and waited.

"And for how long are you gonna do that?" he finally asked.

Marietta narrowed her eyes. "Tell whoever's been working the orchard that I'll work the rest of the harvest this year, and then we'll see for next year."

Tony's eyes flickered, as if he tried to figure out the game. "That's what you want?"

"That's what I want." Marietta decided that she would scream at him if she had to. Break his eardrums. Maybe rip the curtains from the windows of his law office and throw them on the floor so that he understood that she was serious.

"Okay."

They stared at each other some more. So preoccupied with their face-off they were that neither Marietta nor Tony noticed Miss Annette engaged in a slow southern stroll past the open doorway.

***

It took Marietta the rest of that morning to locate all that she needed to set up the produce stand in the vacant lot. A few people in the neighborhood lingered to chat, surprised to see her back in business. Word, apparently, spread. More people came to shoot the breeze, gather some gossip, and then be on their way. By dusk, Marietta had $157 cash in hand.

Just as she was about to start packing up, Tony's mother crossed the street. To pick up a big ole bag of peaches, she said.

"Whoo, Marietta! I got on the phone and called everybody! I told them to come on over if they want fresh and organic today."

"That was you?" Marietta laughed. "Thanks, I appreciate it, Miss Annette. To tell the truth, I wondered where that crowd came from."

"I sent 'em over here! Did all them starved something or others leave me some peaches? I got my mind on peaches."

"Uhm, well, I just ran out of fruit. All I have left are these pecans."

"Oh, those are for me. Imma take those. I need to make me a pecan pie tonight or tomorrow. That's my grandbaby's favorite and my grandbaby gets whatever he wants when he wants it."

"Grandbaby?"

"Oh! Tony didn't tell you?" Miss Annette seemed shocked. "That boy of mine, I swear. Tony Jr was at school when you came by earlier."

"Oh." Marietta didn't know what to say. "Congratulations." She started scooping pecans into a paper sack

"Yes, I love my little baby. He looks just like Tony. Carla was his mama."

Marietta dropped the pecan scoop, which fell on the table with a loud clatter. She grabbed it again for one last go at the pecans. She handed a full paper sack to Miss Annette who slid her a few bills. Marietta held up a hand.

"On the house today, Miss Annette. Thanks for the referrals."

Miss Annette beamed. She turned to walk back home, but then turned back to Marietta as if she just thought of something.

"Oh yes, I been meaning to ask you. You know what? Me and Tony have been looking for just the right person to take care of Tony Jr and Abbie while his father and I run errands and take care of family business."

Marietta looked at the majestic crape myrtle in the front yard of the Madison home, middle-aged, just like her. "Oh, his mother's not around? Carla, you said?"

Miss Annette shook her head. "Now that's a story for you, right there. But it's not mine to tell. Tony might tell you someday. But I just wanted to ask you if you have a few extra hours of time, we could both of us use a break. A little breathing room to get other things done."

Miss Annette looked off to the side. "I'm gonna pay you $15 per hour for both, if that's okay. Cash."

"I don't know. Tony might not like that. He doesn't..." Marietta looked off to the other side and didn't finish.

Miss Annette shifted the bag of pecans to her other hand. "You know, Marietta, I never did tell you how your granddaddy helped us Jennings out years ago. My man... Tony's father, well, he got into some trouble years back. Had to leave us. Things was so bad, Mr. Madison stepped in a few times. He gave Tony his first job so I wouldn't have to go on welfare." She sighed at the memory and then settled into the chair that Marietta abandoned for her.

"Either that or give up my house and move in with relatives. We kept our house over there because Mister Michael Madison gave my son an opportunity. Not many of the gossips around here know this, but Wayfarer Orchards paid Tony's expenses through undergraduate school, what his track scholarship didn't cover. He didn't have loans or nothing. He paid everything out of pocket... from what he earned working for your granddaddy."

Annette lifted her head, fiercely proud. "Did a good job too. Then he used those earnings for law school. After a while, Mr. Madison trusted him to run the orchards. Made him a manager, yes he did. He trusted Tony to take care of your affairs too. Tony would have moved heaven and Earth for your granddaddy if he asked him to. Would have got the wheelbarrow and the dolly and just started hauling. They was real close. He told Tony to always watch out for you as a favor to him."

Marietta looked at the table in front of her, not trusting herself to speak. To cover her emotional reaction, she began to pack up the produce stand.

"Anyway," Miss Annette told her as she stood, "I don't know everything that's going on over here, but I pay cash. If you could help me out with Tony's son and Abbie, it'll give me time to work with my church committees, things like that. I can spend some time on my own which I need every now and then. I'm not as young as I used to be, you know. Tomorrow, okay?"

She winked at Marietta and walked back across the street with a light step, swinging her bag of pecans.

***

The next day, Marietta got up early to purchase some toiletries and groceries. Then she returned to the orchard to set up the roadside stand. Tony brought Abbie over while Marietta arranged the fruit just so. Man and dog supervised her work for a few minutes.

"So where's Carla?" she asked Tony because she felt bitchy about him watching her and she was still irritable after their confrontation in his law office. Also, because without tension, she and he had nothing whatsoever to say to each other.

"Tony Jr's mother?" The lawyer stood as still as a statue with his hands in his pockets.

Marietta shrugged.

"My... uhm," Tony cleared his throat. "Tony's mother, she..."

"Um hm." Marietta stared at him, waiting for the rest. Payback was a mother, Tony, she thought.

"She... left us."

The morning air thickened all around them. "Oh," Marietta said, deflated.

"But we're doing fine," Tony finished. Then he turned, walked to his car, and drove off. Marietta felt a terrible coldness inside. Susan's dark influence on her early life still left its mark. She actually felt sick to her stomach at what she said. As much as Tony angered her, he didn't deserve that.

The brisk sales continued, partly because of curiosity, partly because Abbie had so much charm, and the rest of the sales came from people who just wanted fresh produce. Marietta ate a quick lunch, filled a bottle with water, and returned to find more customers waiting for her.

After school let out, Abbie spotted Tony Jr first and ran to greet him with barks and tail wags and kisses. Miss Annette told no lies. Tony Jr looked like a miniature version of his father.

"Hi Miss Marietta!" He waved at her as he ran up the sidewalk with Abbie at his heels. "My granny told me I better be good today. Or else!"

"Or else what?" Marietta laughed.

Mystified, Tony Jr., shrugged. "She didn't say."

After Marietta burst out laughing again, she castigated herself for the way she spoke to Tony earlier that morning. As his son took Abbie's leash and ran with her into the orchard, he looked so much like how Tony used to look when she and he rode their bikes and roller-skated and explored together.

Carefree, back when both of their lives were a lot less complicated.

By late afternoon, Marietta had accumulated a little over $200. She was lost in thought, waiting for the next customer. Grateful for the shadow of the huge crape myrtle thrown by the sun headed for the tree line and a small lull in customer traffic, she preoccupied her thoughts with what she read in the typewritten pages in Stephanie's old files from Cadis:

> Isolation from peer group and family creates distress and hostility, sometimes resulting in violent behavior as observed by the Controller. Subject's violence viewed as irrational, sometimes criminal. The subject is encouraged to commit acts of violence with spouses, friends, employers for further isolation and shame. Isolation, sleep deprivation, poor nutrition, dehydration, drugs, alcohol, forced sexual intercourse provide additional means of control.

"How much are the plums?" a deep male voice asked. A large duffle bag dropped to the ground, right at her feet. And then Marietta looked up because Kal Jackson blocked the sun.

"Oh my God, Kal." Marietta stood and gave him a surprised half hug after they greeted each other. "What are you doing in Wayfarer?"

"It's not coincidence."

Marietta's brows shot up with trepidation.

"Cadis let me go after I spoke up for you, Mary. I knew you didn't steal anything and I said so over and over."

"Oh Kal, thank you. It's a real crazy situation. But I'm sorry you lost your job too behind this. It doesn't seem right."

"Yeah it's crazy all right." He moved closer to her. "But I came down here to warn you that Robinette's still after you."

"What?" Marietta gasped. She thought it had all ended once she left town.

"He thinks you set that explosion in the incinerator to get back at him, or you know who did."

"But I didn't."

"Of course not!" Kal exclaimed. "If you didn't steal anything, then you certainly didn't set any explosives."

Marietta's gaze faltered when she thought about underworld, which Kal noted. With a keen look, he told her, "Robinette thinks you're involved in something strange. He's been talking to people."

"What... kind of people?" Marietta asked in a small voice.

Kal shook his head. "People," he said ominously. "I like you, Mary. You know that I do. You're a sweet girl. Too nice for Lake City, for sure. I came down here to warn you that, it's not quite over. Whatever is going on, you need to watch your back. Okay?"

Marietta nodded. "Kal, you traveled all the way down here just for me?

"Well, I got people in Rollins, just over the state line. That's where my family's from."

"Oh yeah. I remember you told me that."

"And so, since I had some free time, thanks to Kowalski, I thought I'd look you up on my way to my folks. I know that you were done wrong. I'm a witness. I can help you clear your name. And protect you in the meantime until you do."

Kal stepped closer and leaned against the stand, his eyes focused on Marietta's face. "Now that I think about it, maybe we can help each other," he suggested.

"What do you mean?" Marietta asked as a warning prickled on her arms.

"Well, I decided that maybe it's a good time for me to take a break from Lake City. It's a good life up there, but it can be kind of rough going sometimes. I'm gonna launch my job search from Rollins."

"Oh. Really?"

"Yeah, you know fresh start."

"Oh, I know," Marietta laughed. "Trust me, I know. That's why I'm here too."

"Yeah, you got a nice set-up here." Kal glanced over the produce spread before him and the large house hidden behind the crape myrtle. "But like I said, I can protect you until you figure out your next move dealing with Robinette and all that drama."

"You can protect me how?"

"I'm a licensed and trained security professional between gigs, remember? A storm's headed your way, Mary. I can help you get ready."

CHAPTER 23   KAL

During her and Kal's negotiation, Abbie left Tony Jr in the orchard and padded back to the roadside stand to sit next to Marietta, as though ready to help charm a few more dollars from another customer. But Marietta noticed that Abbie seemed restless this time. Even though the Catahoula fidgeted this way and that, her eyes remained trained on Kal while he and Marietta talked.

Marietta finally figured out that for some reason, Abbie didn't like Kal's body language, how he leaned over Marietta, maybe his facial expression. Unlike with earlier customers, Abbie stood stiff-legged and rigid. Every once in a while, she huffed deep in her throat.

But when Tony's car pulled to a stop across the street, Abbie forgot about Kal and began to really dance. Tony parked, and then walked over to collect his son. Abbie jumped up to lick his face. Tony greeted Kal with a handshake and a quick hello, and then turned to Marietta in inquiry.

"Tony Jr's in the orchard," she told him. When Tony raised his brows at that, she continued, "He stayed back there because it's cooler."

Tony's eyes shifted from Marietta to Kal, then back to Marietta. But rather than pursue that line of questioning, he retrieved Tony Jr from the orchard. Everyone waved at each other as Tony walked his son back to Miss Annette.

"Aren't you taking Abbie?" Marietta called after him. The Catahoula seemed uncertain too, not knowing whether to stay or go. She chose stay.

Tony didn't answer. Instead, he ushered his son into the house, lingered at the door, then headed back to the produce stand. Again, Abbie greeted him with a loud bark.

"Oh yeah, I guess I did forgot Abbie," Tony said in response to Marietta's curious gaze while the man leaning over her sized him up. But he didn't really forget, did he? He left Abbie so he had a reason to come back and figure out why the big city slicker stood so close to Marietta, as if he owned her. And what was with the duffel bag?

"Yes, you forgot Abbie," Marietta replied.

Tony nodded at the stranger by Marietta's side. "So... this a friend from Lake City?"

When Marietta offered no explanation, the man shifted his wrestler's build towards Tony, stuck out a hand and said, "I'm Kal. I'm here to help Mary out."

"Really? Here to help her out? How so?" Tony lifted his eyebrows with a questioning look at Marietta. Her eyes sort of skittered over his shoulder. She knew exactly what he was talking about. Tony and only Tony took care of Marietta's business affairs. If she hired someone, he would know, or he should. Because he would pay their salary.

Kal's voice deepened, "I'm moving in to provide her with protection."

Marietta flinched. Her face seemed redder all of a sudden.

"Moving in... to provide her protection." Tony repeated in a tone flattened by disapproval. He waited for Marietta to either deny or clarify. She did neither.

The two men stared at each other.

"Marietta?" Tony prompted. No answer. He didn't like it.

Abbie growled low in her throat, not appreciating the tension amongst the humans. She stood at stiff attention next to Tony.

"Wow." Tony cocked his head at Abbie. "My dog sure doesn't like you, Kal."

"Guess not," Kal answered.

"She usually likes everybody."

The men stared at each other some more. Tony could do this all day. Law school trained him in the subtle art and science of fucking with people's minds for hours on end.

"So, if not Lake City, where are you from?" Tony asked, prolonging the confrontation. Since Marietta seemed zoned out, he would ask the questions.

"Rollins."

"Rollins, eh?"

"Yeah. Know it?"

"Somewhat. A law buddy of mine is from Rollins. Dhan Grant. He's about our age, maybe you went to school with him?"

"You a lawyer?"

"Yeah. I also protect Marietta. Her business interests, at least."

"I see."

Tony gestured towards the Madison property. "Her grandfather set all this up. He was a good man." Tony looked right at Marietta while speaking to Kal. "You have some big shoes to fill."

She stared back at him, anger in her eyes, but Tony wasn't nearly done. All day, he could do this.

"I know she wouldn't just ask anyone for help."

"Imagine not," Kal said.

"Me and Dhan give each other referrals. We met as undergrads."

"Mmm."

"So, do you know the Grants?" All day...

Kal answered with an unconcerned shrug of his massive shoulders.

"They're a pretty large family," Tony insisted. "They're all over that area. They own a lot of businesses. Beauty salon, bookstore, restaurant. Big family farm too. They're pretty hard to miss." Tony paused. "If you're from around there."

"I'm originally from Lake City."

"Oh. That explains the accent. For some reason, I thought you said Rollins."

"My family's from Rollins. But I was born in Lake City. So Rollins by way of Lake City."

"Hmm. So you wouldn't know the Grants then." Tony allowed the win to linger in the hot afternoon air for a bit. He could tell Kal didn't like that in front of Marietta.

"Heard of them. I don't think my family gets along with theirs though."

"Really? I wonder why? They're pretty nice." Tony, also trained in the art of debate decided he wanted to force the guy on defense. Because he didn't like him.

"They're respecters of persons," Kal responded. "So I'm told."

"Uh hunh," Tony said. "Small world."

"Yeah," Kal replied.

Tony opened his mouth to start another round, but Marietta leaned her head in her hand with a loud sigh. She clearly wanted the uncomfortable conversation to end with Tony's immediate departure.

"Let's go, Abbie." Tony patted his thigh with a lazy hand. Man and dog returned across the street. Round one went to the home team, but Tony still did not care for the fact that Kal would actually stay overnight inside Marietta's house. Not. At. All.

***

Marietta walked into the Madison house with Kal who brought his duffel bag inside with him.

"Kal, there's a bathroom on the second floor, first door on the left, okay?"

Once he headed upstairs, she retrieved a set of clean linens from the attic. For some reason, she didn't want him to know about the attic entry just yet. She met Kal in the living room. "Oh yes, just help yourself to whatever you find in the kitchen. I'm gonna go ahead and make up a bed for you. I'll take your bag up too."

"No, don't trouble about the bag. It's much heavier than it looks."

"Is it?"

"Steel-toe boots. You don't want none of that, girl. Trust me."

"Oh yeah." Marietta laughed. "I'll take your word for it then."

He easily sung the huge duffel across his back and followed her up to her grandparent's old bedroom. While Marietta made his bed, she emphasized the separate sleeping arrangements to which Kal agreed. Kal would train her in self-defense. He would help her to come up with a strategy to immunize her from Robinette's retaliation. At the same time, Kal would also help her with heavy work around the orchard.

Since it was a temporary position, Kal would continue to look for a full-time gig while Marietta figured out her plans and until she felt safe. They would give it a month. It seemed like a win-win situation for both.

But she shuddered when she remembered the look on Tony's face when Kal told him that he would stay with Marietta. She didn't even have a chance to work up a good story to explain Kal's presence before Kal blurted it out. Besides all that, Tony would make her pay for what she said to him this morning.

After a light dinner, Kal got started in the orchard gathering produce for tomorrow's adventures at the produce stand while Marietta cleaned up the kitchen.

"Oh Kal," she called from the kitchen doorway.

"Yeah?"

"Make sure to lock the front gate before you come back in the house. It bolts from the inside."

"Sure thing." He continued on to the tool house to find the ladder.

Marietta ran water into the kitchen sink and got started on the dishes. She had no memories of Stephanie other than those planted by Susan, her fake mother. That was Susan's dark legacy that endured after her death. Stephanie was crazy. That's what Susan always said. Grandma implied the same. But was Stephanie crazy? Kate said no. And for all of Kate's tough, brittle Lake City attitude, the facts upheld her story. Certainly, she told the truth about the documents regarding Stephanie's tenure with Cadis. But some things, not even Kate could tell her.

Once upon a time, surely Stephanie held Marietta in her arms. Surely Stephanie kissed her and babbled baby talk while Marietta smiled and touched her face, and gurgled. Stephanie claimed to have loved her in her journal, even though she called Marietta 'Alicia' back then.

And how Marietta wanted to believe in that love. If only she could remember feeling it. That's what Grandma and Susan stole from her. But if Stephanie truly loved Marietta as a mother loved a daughter then how could anyone, including Grandma, have ever forced Stephanie to relinquish custody to Susan?

She knew that Stephanie tried more than once to reach out to her. She remembered Stephanie's wild hair, and disheveled clothes, standing and staring at her from across the street of her high school. She remembered the fanaticism that glittered from Stephanie's eyes. Marietta had pretended not to know Stephanie. She walked away from her birth mother, embarrassed of Stephanie in front of all her classmates.

She felt great shame... and pain now. She'd had a chance, actually several chances to speak to Stephanie.

Marietta sighed. If only she knew then what she knew now. If she'd been a braver and stronger person and not submissive to peer pressure and her fake mother's manipulation, she would have stopped to talk to Stephanie. She could have asked Stephanie what she wanted. And if Marietta had done that, then what would Stephanie have said in response? What if... what if... she could have talked Stephanie out of the fatal attack on Cadis Industries? What if she had insisted on driving Stephanie to a hospital to get the help she obviously needed?

Marietta wiped away the tears and kept washing the dishes.

If only Susan hadn't alienated and twisted their relationship. If only her father hadn't been so... ambivalent. What if Roy had given Marietta Stephanie's journal the day he received it instead of holding it until after the attack on Cadis? Marietta would have had that one extra day to read the journal, figure out Stephanie's misery and maybe stopped her.

What if?

They'd all been under Susan's thumb back then, with Grandma's cooperation. And now, Marietta had no one to ask the question, "Did Stephanie ever love me?" Everyone who knew the answer to that question was dead.

Marietta checked the kitchen window which faced the back yard. Kal stood on a ladder with gauntlets on both arms. Marietta couldn't stifle her giggle. He looked incredibly awkward, dodging this way and that, anticipating an attack from the falcons from every direction. Occasionally, he picked an apple.

The sun had set over the trees. She flicked on the security lights so that he could see in the orchard. She waved back at him when he turned to give her thumbs up.

Now Marietta started a pot of black-eyed peas on low heat on the stove. She diced vegetables to add in later. Dinner had been pretty light. Kal was a big guy to feed so that would be her and Kal's late night supper.

Marietta used her keys to slip back into the kitchen pantry. She'd nearly forgotten about the family keepsakes until she sought the linens for Kal's bed earlier.

She found a box of photos. Then she spotted her original birth certificate. 'Alicia Marie Madison' felt strange and bulky when she said the name aloud. But the name was the final confirmation of her true identity. The certificate listed 'Stephanie Marie Madison' as her mother and 'Roland Bay Brazil' as her father.

And there were photos! In this one, Stephanie held her while lying in a hospital bed. Here, Stephanie held her while seated on the bench in front of the Madison home. In another, Stephanie smiled while teaching her to walk. All this time, all through the years, evidence of Stephanie's love for her, as a mother loved a daughter, lay hidden within Grandma's belongings. Marietta shook her head when she remembered the times she'd begged Grandma for information about

Stephanie and met with the older woman's disdain and obstinance.

She also found photos of Susan with the original Marietta, who would remain forever young. She flipped rapidly through those, not really looking.

Marietta poked around some more. She recognized other knick knacks from her grandmother's side of the main bedroom. She found older photos in those albums. In these, she saw her mother and Stephanie as children and teenagers.

Once upon a time, Stephanie enjoyed life. She roller-skated. She pointed to a Christmas tree. She wore pigtails, both she and Susan.

Then Stephanie had an affair with her sister's husband. Then she dropped her sister's child by accident, killing her. Then she gave up her own child and applied to work at Cadis Industries. And then, no accident this time, she killed herself and four colleagues. If not for Stephanie's extreme efforts to please others, thereby selling her soul to Cadis and the Robinettes, she might be alive today. My mother, Marietta thought. My real mother.

She dug around some more and found the local paper's obituary on Stephanie Marie Madison's death. Marietta picked up the funeral program and the guestbook. The gathering for her service seemed pitifully small. The spookiness that surrounded Stephanie's killings, plus resentment at Stephanie's big city ways maybe had their effect. That pained Marietta. Susan Brazil attended and signed her name. Marietta recalled that, according to the women at the beauty salon, Susan shed not one tear.

Her grandparents attended, of course. Annette Jennings and Tony attended and signed their names. Not too many others from Wayfarer paid their respects. And which one of these others at the funeral was the big mouth that bore witness to Susan's cold demeanor? Marietta had felt so offended when she overheard, but truth is truth. Much as it still hurt to think about, she believed the gossips now. Her fake mother returned to Lake City in such a strange mood after the funeral service.

Marietta set the box of memories down. She paced the attic floor. She checked on Kal again through the window. Under the security lights, he used the wide shoulders and heavy upper body musculature to wrestle the ladder to another apple tree full of fruit.

As Marietta walked back and forth, she thought back. She'd remained in Lake City with Roy during Stephanie's funeral service. Roy distracted her with trips around the city and then dinner. Susan and Roy kept her from her birth mother's funeral. But did Roy know that Susan and Stephanie switched her? Did he know the secret between the sisters?

He never indicated. She had no way of knowing what Roy knew before someone killed him. Either way, Roland Brazil was her father and Grandpa confirmed that.

She checked for Kal again. This time, she didn't see him or the ladder. Quickly, she grabbed her old television with VCR on top of her grandfather's 8-track and cassette player. With some amount of awkwardness, she locked the attic door behind her and headed down to the kitchen pantry. Then she locked that door. The door to the backyard swung open behind her.

Fortunately, with her back the door, she could call over her shoulder, "Oh Kal. I have to lay down for a bit. I'm exhausted from today. The heat, you know. I'm not quite adjusted to the southern sun. I've been in the Midwest too long."

"Oh yeah. Me too. It's hot as hell."

"Would you mind dumping that bowl of vegetables into that pot on the stove? Go ahead and turn it to low. Bread's already on the table, so whenever you get hungry again, just help yourself." She shifted her load. "Oh, and just flick the switch by the door to turn off the outside lights."

She didn't wait for a response, but instead scurried through the dining and living rooms then up the main stairs. Marietta pulled her backpack from inside her closet and tugged out the VHS tapes, the recording medium of choice in the 80s and early 90s. She tried to remember how to set-up the old entertainment center, complete with huge, doughnut-sized headphones.

CHAPTER 24   THE SLAVE

O pen the door, Sundae."

"Open."
"Sundae... anything. Anytime. Any place. Anyone."
"Anything. Anytime. Any place. Anyone."
   "Or two, or three, however many."
   "Yes."
   "Did you give the package to Celara?"
   "Yes."
   "Where is the package?"
   "I am the package."
   "You did not deliver the package."
   Silence.
   "Sundae! Where is the package?"
   "I am the package."
   "Sundae! Answer the question."
   Silence.

At the handler's signal, an electric volt shot through Stephanie's body, courtesy of the operator.

"Sundae!"

"I..."

"Dose her again. The drug's wearing off."

The operator shifted to comply, then paused. "Wait," he said.

"Do it," the handler insisted.

"I don't think she understands the question."

The handler bent closer to Stephanie's face. "Sundae," the handler asked. "What happened at Celara?"

Stephanie shook her head.

"Sundae!"

"He said... freedom."

"Who said?"

"Ronny."

"What did he say?"

"He said that I would be free. I could live. I could have a family."

"Ronny lied to you, Sundae. We are all the family you ever need. You will never be free." Derek Robinette laughed. An athletic, dark-haired, tall, strong Derek whose face appeared smooth without the stony crags and red, puckered scar tissue.

The operator adjusted dials.

"Sundae, come home," Derek insisted.

"I am home."

"You belong to us."

"Yes."

"Even when you leave us, you are still with us."

"I am still with you."

"Even when it's over, it's not over."

"It's not... over."

"Nothing that you hide, that cannot be found. Nothing that you say, that we cannot hear. Nowhere that you run, that we cannot follow."

"Yes."

***

The vacancy in Stephanie's eyes reminded Marietta of the old abandoned Brazil home. Lifeless. Hopeless. Dead. *She was a robot!*

***

"There will be blood. There will be suffering. But never mind the bad times and the bad things. Never mind them, Sundae. The bad times and the bad people do not exist. You do not need them. They do not exist."

"They do not exist."

"Remember to forget, Sundae."

"I will remember to forget."

"Do not ask. Do not tell. You should be seen. Not heard. Keep the secret."

"I will keep the secret."

"Who do you love?"

"Marietta," Stephanie replied.

***

Marietta gasped to hear Stephanie say her name in a declaration of love amid such monstrous, twisted circumstances.

***

"Keep the secret, or everything you love will disappear," intoned.

"Yes."

"We are the only family you will ever need."

"Yes."

***

Disappear? *When you look back on this conversation, recognize and remember that you were warned.* Kate said that.

Marietta shivered. Derek Robinette ended his sinister re-education of Stephanie. Paul Robinette stepped into camera frame and threatened once again to disappear Marietta if Sundae did not cooperate.

I highly recommend that you leave that door closed because it's not going to end well. Kate said this too.

No, the tape did not end well. Paul Robinette reinforced his dominance over Stephanie in the ways of old. He assaulted her. Marietta fast-forwarded through Paul Robinette, Derek Robinette, then the recorder and operator and security, all of whom took a turn on top of Stephanie.

Throughout the ordeal, Stephanie lay as still as a corpse. She made no sound, nor indicated any emotion, a tormented marionette whose strings lay slack in the hands of the puppeteers who tortured her. All this took place in the Education Room in the basement at Cadis... on Sundays, when no one else was around...

They used her. Used and used her.

Marietta shuddered. Stephanie... Stephanie...

I hate Sundays.

I hate Sundays.

I hate Sundays.

Marietta wanted to gouge out her own eyes. But the knock on her bedroom door was loud enough to cut through the thick doughnut-sized headphones.

CHAPTER 25   ANNETTE

Marietta paused the VHS tape and opened her bedroom door. She tried to angle her body so that Kal didn't notice the television screen.

"Just wanted to let you know that supper's ready whenever you are. Also, you've got a whole mess of apples ready for tomorrow. But, there's still plenty left on the trees for the day after though."

"Thanks so much for the help tonight, Kal."

How could Paul and Derek Robinette have ever happened in modern-day North America?

"No problem. I'm just surprised the tough guy across the street doesn't help you out. What's his problem anyway?"

"What tough guy?" Marietta asked, genuinely confused. She wondered whether he meant Sheriff Riggs.

"The one who got in my face earlier and kept eyeballing me."

"You mean Tony?" She frowned. "The lawyer?"

How quickly had Derek Robinette isolated and criminalized her. Within the blink of an eye, Robinette took away Marietta's job, set Lake City police on her trail, drove her from her apartment, and then cut off her access to money.

Kal shrugged.

Marietta shook her head in disbelief. "I didn't see him eyeball you."

With an idle wave of the hand, Robinette ruined her reputation. And then Marietta was on her way down a trash chute, eating at soup kitchens, walking amongst the denizens of underworld, and fleeing the city. And how about those poor women who got dragged off the streets of Lake City for just looking like her? All Robinette's doing.

"I'm pretty sure you weren't supposed to see that."

"Okay. If you say so. But did he get in your face? I didn't see that either."

"He looked like he wanted to sic that dog on me."

"Abbie? Abbie was just sitting there. She keeps me company while I'm selling produce. I babysit her. I think Tony and Abbie were just nervous because they didn't know you is all. This is a small town with small town ways."

Stephanie fought Robinette and paid the ultimate price. But even then, she didn't cancel the threat. Instead, the deaths of Susan, Roy, and Jesse followed in quick succession.

"Mary. Mary?" Kal snapped his fingers by her eyes. "Where do you go when you fade like that?"

Marietta blinked back to awareness. "Oh. Sorry. I was just... um, Tony does help me in the orchards now and then. But he has his own business to run--the law office."

While Marietta wallowed in guilt and sorrow for over a year about Susan and Roy's deaths, her grandparents, survivors of the Jim Crow South and witnesses to southern justice, remained terrified that someone would try again to take her life. So they kept the secrets too.

"He seemed really annoyed to see me here."

"Like I said, he doesn't know you. Wayfarer's real funny like that. I don't know why, but new faces make people nervous."

Everything looked so much different now that she was older. Marietta had resented her grandparents for keeping so many secrets from her. But then, her grandparents knew from a lifetime of accumulated wisdom and experience the difference between what life should be and what life actually was.

"Is something going on between the two of you?"

Marietta laughed. "Oh no. There's nothing going on. Far from it, in fact."

"Oh. Well, I mean, you keep his dog and his kid."

"Well, the dog belongs to Tony's mother."

The woman who raised her had never loved her. But then, hadn't Marietta always known? When had Susan ever looked at her with warmth in her eyes as though glad to see her?

When Kal didn't say anything, Marietta struggled to focus.

"His son... well, he's just used to playing with the dog. Miss Annette says Abbie's her grandchild too and that she's Tony Jr's only cousin. We're all buddies."

"Okay. If you say so." Kal looked mystified.

"What? It's just a thing around here, Kal. That's just how they are"

"Uh hunh." Kal chuckled at that.

Susan's facial expressions had two settings--satisfied or not satisfied. Pleased. Not pleased. Everyone, including Marietta, had danced to ensure that Susan remained pleased inside her world of nerves. Everyone danced for Susan.

"You know, it's clear to me now that you need a man in your life, Marietta. To help you focus and to make things easier." Kal's smile was gentle, taking the sting out of his words. "Let me help you, Mary. Really help you. I'm here to take care of you now. No one will hurt you when you're with me."

"You want to help me?"

"Yes, I do."

"Then tell me what's happening at Cadis, Kal. What's Robinette going to do? What does he have planned for me?"

Kal sighed. "It's more like he'll give you a really bad reference to make it hard for you to get another job. A lot of bad-mouthing. Things like that. You know, I'd be happy to serve as a reference for you."

"Oh yeah," Marietta replied distracted. "Sure." A bad reference was the least of her worries right now.

"I'm bringing it up because I have to confess the real reason why I'm here."

"The real reason? But you said you were worried about me. You didn't know what Robinette might to do me. What's going on, Kal? You're not here because I might get a bad reference. How'd you find me anyway?"

"No. I mean, I'm still concerned about Robinette. He's an old school Lake City player and he's done a lot of damage to a lot of people."

"Right." Kal didn't know what Marietta already knew, especially about the content of Stephanie's tapes. "Like bad references."

"Guys like that..." Kal shook his head in disgust. "Look, the other part is, I was really attracted to you from the beginning. Ever since you walked into the lobby at Cadis, I don't think straight." Kal took her by the hand. "You see how I came all the way down here, don't you? I could have just called you."

"That's true." Marietta frowned. "Although you didn't have my phone number."

"I just thought there might be something between us that we should explore. That's part of the reason that I was so pissed off at Kowalski for giving you a hard time. You didn't deserve that. But Mary, don't you feel it too? Don't you feel what I feel? You let me inside your house, after all."

"Because you had my address," Marietta said slowly.

He stood up and drew her closer to his body, into an embrace that left no space between them.

Marietta stiffened. "I just need time to work through all my thoughts," she warned.

"I know."

Kal kissed her cheek and then rested his own on hers. "I won't ever let anyone hurt you, Mary."

It had been a long time since Marietta felt the touch of a man. Kal was extremely handsome. But then, so was Derek Robinette once upon a time.

Kal's hands traveled her body. She shivered. Then they both heard barking from the orchard which interrupted Kal's intentions. Marietta gave him a gentle nudge away.

"Is that the dog from across the street?"

"Yes, its Miss Annette's Catahoula, Abbie. I don't know why she's back over here. I can hear her in the orchard, but I don't know how she got in because it should be locked, right? You didn't leave the gate open, did you?"

"No, it should be locked. I didn't touch anything but apples."

Marietta frowned. "Well, sorry Kal. I have to take her back across the street so she doesn't get run over by a car in the dark."

Kal nodded and pulled away. Marietta walked him to her bedroom door. "Look, let me find my shoes to go get her. I'll meet you downstairs in the kitchen for supper when I get back, okay?"

***

"I don't know why Abbie's so jumpy lately, Miss Annette." Marietta walked with Abbie through Miss Annette's screen door.

"She's protective of you because she loves you."

"She's a sweetheart." Abbie's tail beat the floor like a drum.

"Oh, now that she is and she knows it well." Miss Annette cleared her throat. "Marietta, I feel I need to tell you something else. Something I've been thinking about for a while."

"Okay." Marietta sat on a chair. Abbie followed and lay across Marietta's feet.

"Now, your mother moved up North, but she was still our people. She's from here. You're not from here, but your people are from here and you used to visit us every summer, till you stopped."

"I know," Marietta replied with a wince.

"But all that doesn't matter. You're still one of us no matter what anyone else says. If anybody says different, then you tell them to come talk to Miss Annette about it. That's what I told Riggs too."

"Who?"

"The sheriff. He called here asking me questions about you. You know what? I said the same damn thang to him that I'm saying right now."

"Miss Annette, why do people around here say my grandmother was... why do they talk about my family the way they do?"

"What do you mean?"

"Years ago, when I was at the hair salon, getting ready for prom with Tony, I heard them. People said things when they thought I couldn't hear them."

"Ah, I see how it was now." Awareness dawned on Miss Annette's face. She sighed and shook her head. "You know, Marietta, things seemed fine before Stephanie and Susan went North. Then things changed. I don't know what exactly. Something. But that's family business. All I know is Miss Rose seemed so sad... and then after Stephanie and Susan passed so close together, Miss Rose was never the same. The Madisons seemed like... they were afraid of something. You seemed different too, you know."

"I guess I did."

"You used to smile all the time, so pretty and lively. But after your parents passed... you never smiled. Hardly never."

"I guess not."

"I'm sorry about the way people act down here. My God. But ignorant people will be ignorant people no matter where you go."

"Yes. I suppose they will. Speaking of that, Miss Annette, I'm so sorry for how I treated Tony. I was so upset that day. Not with him. There was just so much that happened. My head wasn't where it needed to be."

"You was still in mourning, wasn't you, Marietta?"

Marietta nodded.

"I see how it was now. I always did hope you and Tony would..." The older woman shrugged, "find your way back to each other."

"Tony doesn't like me, Miss Annette."

Miss Annette laughed. "He never got over you, girl. Even after Carla. That's what I told him the other day when we saw your young man looking for you in the orchard."

"What other day? He just got here today."

"No. I saw him about two days before I saw you and I saw you the first day you were back, yesterday morning. I remember because it looked like you came the direction from the train station. You had that big ole heavy black bag on your back. You looked tired. I don't know why you didn't call a taxi.

You could've called me or Tony to pick you up. Either of us would've, you know. Wearing all that black in this heat... I didn't know what you were thinking. Chile, I almost told you to change out of them dark clothes before you fell out with a conniption in the middle of the street... But I said to myself, Marietta grown. She gonna wear what she wanna wear."

Marietta had no words because Miss Annette's observations seemed pretty detailed. Two days before Marietta's arrival, she played hide and seek in Lake City.

"...and I saw him knock on the door," Miss Annette pantomimed, "and then look around the back fence like he thought you were in the orchard. Let me tell you, girl, that's when I almost called Riggs, because I thought he would try to break and enter. And me and Abbie, we don't play that around here. Do we Abbie? Not on our watch. No ma'am. You see this here whistle? I blow on this whistle..."

Marietta frowned, lost in thought.

"And then I thought, maybe he's a real estate agent..."

After she went down the trash chute and got money from the ATM, she abandoned the cell phone and SUV. Robinette lost track of her. He couldn't find her. He assumed that she'd fled back to Wayfarer and sent Kal to track her down. Robinette is how Kal knew how to find her.

"Ya'll shoulda called each other and coordinated your schedules. Don't you have a cell phone? You need to get you one, Marietta. Maybe you can email and instant chat if you get a computer. They have 'em at the library, you know."

Kal flew down to Lake City only to find an empty house. They'd been too far ahead of her in the game of hide and seek.

"But then he left, and I figured it was a good thing I didn't call the sheriff. Riggs can be a bit much sometimes. I wouldn't want to sic him on a friend of yours. You saw how he was with you. I told him to leave you alone because you one of our girls.

Always have been. Always will be. Riggs is so extra. He's always doing too much in this heat. And he's way too fat for that."

Kal reported back to Robinette, who concluded she was still in Lake City, and had watchers stationed around the building. One of them stalked her through the underworld beneath the Cadis Industries and tried to end her. Marietta shivered. How many times now had she escaped death? How many lives did she have left to live?

"I told Riggs, I said Marietta's one of our people. Her family's been across the street longer than anybody's. Now, she's been gone a long time but ain't some travelling allowed? Just foolishness..."

I know she wouldn't ask just anyone to help her.

She'd invited a stranger into her home. Allowed an enemy over the threshold, so thankful that a real man had finally come into her life to protect her. She'd welcomed what she thought was a guardian angel, warm and charming. She wanted another masculine presence nearby to take the sting off Tony's everlasting disgust and rejection.

"I'm glad I didn't get your friend in trouble, dear."

She'd even worried about what Robinette might do to Kal because of his association with her. Everyone close to her paid such a heavy price. In fact, though it didn't happen tonight, because of Abbie's unrest, she might have accepted a more intimate offer from Kal than protection.

CHAPTER 26   KOWALSKI

Marietta's steps dragged on the walk back across the dark street to the Madison home. If the past few days of near escapes taught her nothing else, they taught her to pay attention to instinct. Mr. Johnson, the nosy neighbor of the Brazil home had nothing on Miss Annette for vigilance. Marietta had no doubt whatsoever that Miss Annette saw exactly who she saw when she saw him.

And that meant Kal was a liar.

No matter his excuses and reasons for showing up at her home hundreds of miles away from Lake City, he was connected to the net that closed in tighter around her. She wondered where Kal was inside of her house. Did he spy on her even now through a window like she spied on him in the orchard?

She stopped on the front porch with her hand on the door. For a brief moment, she entertained the thought of taking off again, maybe Mexico this time. Or Brazil. She could blend into the population, learn the languages. But now, she was angry, so angry now. She was tired of running, exhausted and fed up. She would not run tonight or ever again. For better or for worse, her life would change forever this evening.

Marietta opened the front door and entered into silence. She closed and locked the door behind her. Like Stephanie, she had no escape. Her life's early journeys had been decided by others. But this time, she would face life head on. She would decide.

A quick glance informed her that the kitchen, where she'd instructed Kal to meet her for a late supper, was empty. She would go to her bedroom and lock her door. In the morning, she would tell Kal to leave. Kal knew that she had reason to fear Derek Robinette. But what he didn't know was that she no longer considered him her ally. Her knowledge that Kal was dirty served as her sole advantage for now.

In the morning, she would take him by surprise and confront him, learn as much as possible, then order him off her property. She would have Abbie with her and Abbie would back her up. She would have to do this before Tony Jr. came over after school.

Could she threaten Kal with law enforcement? No. Not when her name had smudges on it from her activities in Lake City. Sheriff Riggs hadn't been too friendly at their first meeting. Only her connection to Miss Annette and Tony got Riggs off her back. And what about Tony? No help there. Tony thought she was a total screw-up and a loser. Most likely, he would help Riggs handcuff her. No way he would believe such a fantastic tale. She barely believed it herself and she was the main character in this drama.

Besides, any day now, any hour, heck, any minute, maybe even right now, police chatter would wind its slow way down to small town Wayfarer. By horseback, by Morse code, by sign language, information on her background would emerge, for sure. The accusations against her would land her back into Robinette's evil waiting arms. So, somehow she had to finesse Kal and try not to get hurt in the process.

Marietta climbed the stairs in a house as silent as death. She approached the door of her bedroom as if the gallows awaited within. As soon as she turned the doorknob, her heart sank.

Oh Marietta!

She hadn't locked her bedroom door when she ran downstairs to retrieve Abbie from the orchard. And now... a visitor sat on her bed. Not Susan this time, but Kal, who smiled at her with such cunning triumph, he may well have been possessed by Susan's ghost.

Marietta's eyes darted to the television's VHS player. No tape.

"Looking for this?" Kal held the VHS tape in his hands.

"Give that back to me, Kal. It doesn't belong to you."

"And it doesn't belong to you either, does it? It belongs to Robinette. For a hefty price, since he's starring in it." Kal laughed. "How much do you think I could get?"

Marietta shook her head slowly. "Don't do that, Kal."

"Why not? What price would you pay, Mary?"

"Please."

"So what's the plan here? Tell me how I can be down?"

Again, Marietta shook her head.

"That's the Lake City way though." Kal shrugged. He dropped the tape on her bed, and then rose. He wrapped two muscular arms around her in a hug. "I can protect you Mary, if you let me." He placed his cheek on hers. "You told me you were involved with someone else, but you aren't, are you?"

"I told you that... I'm not... I can't... I'm not ready for a relationship right now."

Kal tightened his embrace and touched his lips to her ear. "You say that like you really have a choice."

Marietta's body went rigid. "I appreciate your help, Kal. Really. But it's getting too weird between us. You need to leave in the morning. I'll handle Robinette by myself."

Kal laughed and relaxed his grip, but he didn't let her go. "Mary, Robinette will chew you to pieces. After he's done with you, there won't be anything left of you for anyone else to identify. You can't beat him at this game. He invented the rules. Not only does he own the team, but he's also the referee, the scorekeeper, and the judge. You may as well join him. Unless... you want to join me?"

"But don't you intend to blackmail him yourself? Hefty price. That's what you said."

Kal looked thoughtful. "I did say that, didn't I? Maybe I should cut you in for half. Let's go." He grabbed the tape. Then he yanked her from the bedroom by the arm, down the hallway towards the stairs.

"I don't want to, Kal," she said, stumbling behind him.

"Again," this time Kal shoved her, "You say that like you have a choice." He grabbed her by the neck as they descended.

"Let me ask you this, Mary," he said when they reached the bottom of the staircase. "Where do you think you can hide that Robinette won't find you? Because, he's looking, you know."

Marietta didn't have an answer for that. Through the front door's window, the moon shone full like a dirty, pitted, rotten orange. She reached for the doorknob.

"No you don't." Kal jerked her away by the neck. "This way."

In front of the living room window with the panoramic view, Kal ground his mouth and body into hers. She couldn't pull away when he balled a fist into the thick brown cloud of her hair and forced her head into whichever angle he desired.

"That's for your nosy neighbors. They won't bother us for a while, I don't think." He licked the side of her face, leaving a trail of rotten-smelling saliva behind.

Marietta recognized the harbinger of her death over Kal's shoulder. Like an eclipse, a shadow passed across the dirty orange moon, and then disappeared into the dark of the crape myrtle.

Still gripping her close, Kal grinned into her wet face then yanked the curtain closed. He threw her towards Grandpa's old recliner and stood above her where she sprawled, arms and legs akimbo.

"That's right, Mary." Kal leaned over her, placing one hand on either arm of the recliner. "You can do things the easy way or," he indicated the VHS tape on the floor, "You can do them the hard way, like she did."

Marietta wanted to cry for herself and her mother.

Kal's sour breath wafted over her. She tried not to breathe it in, not wanting any parts of him inside any parts of her.

"Robinette will not bend you. He will break you. Trust and believe that it will happen."

Marietta felt the familiar prickles travel up and down her arms. She felt hot and cold at the same time. This could not happen to her. Surely not in her own home. It wasn't right. What could she do to stop this? How could she make this end? How could she make this over? She could provoke Kal into killing her, for one. Or, she could force him to knock her unconscious so she didn't feel anything.

"Did he break you, Kal?" She curled her lip. "Is that what made you loyal? Or did he bend you?"

For a split second, Kal looked angry. Marietta braced herself for the hit. But the old grin and charm returned.

"This?" He picked up the VHS tape and tossed it onto the table by the recliner. "This is the PG-13 version. You will not believe the things that you will do, Mary. Or the places that you'll go. Things that you never even knew were possible become possible. You will believe in magic tonight, babe."

"No!"

"Oh yeah."

"You're gonna have to kill me. You'll have my dead body, you degenerate. But you will never have my soul. I won't do it!" Marietta spat into his face.

Kal touched his face and looked at her spittle on his fingers. Marietta drew back, her eyes wide. That did it. She would die. Then he would molest her corpse.

Kal wrapped the same wet hand around her neck. He squeezed. "Well, thank you so much for such a lovely invitation. I love the goddamn southern hospitality around here."

He relaxed his grip and watched as Marietta heaved and coughed. "Since you like it rough, scream if you want to, Mary. Your neighbors already know what we're doing." He grabbed her by the neck again, then glanced over his shoulder. "But maybe later."

"What are you waiting for, you punk?" Marietta's voice was intended as a shout but came out a whisper. "Get it over with."

"He's waiting for me." Kowalski's flat Midwestern accent crawled over Kal's shoulder. The steel gray hair and cold, pale gray eyes followed.

"All yours," Kal told him with a smirk. "Oh yeah." He snapped his fingers as he stepped aside. "Sorry, Mary. I must have left the gate open earlier after all."

"Why don't you ever die?" Kowalski asked her.

"Why don't you ever die!" Marietta screamed back and then started coughing.

"We got a problem, you and me," Kowalski said.

"Get in line, you animal!" Marietta shrieked. She hacked again, and tried to massage her neck. "I need some water."

"Shut up, girl." Kowalski folded his arms. "You made me look bad to Robinette more times than I care to remember. The only thing keeping me off you right now is that Robinette wants you for himself. You should know that whatever Robinette wants, he gets. And right now," Kowalski flicked his eyes with irises so pale, they appeared nearly clear over her, "He wants you. By the way, setting off explosives underneath Cadis?" He actually *tsked tsked* at her. "Naughty. Very naughty. Bad girl!"

Marietta gasped. "You followed me that night. It was you!"

"I followed you because that was my job. You got into Cadis on my watch and I had to make things right for the Boss."

"You tried to kill me. You set off that explosion and tried to burn me alive. What are you? Who does that?"

"Please, with the lies." Kowalski bent over her like Kal did before, an arm on either side of her. "It's not gonna work, Mary. The investigation's headed your direction, sweetheart. Arson, breaking and entering, terrorism." He smiled and straightened up. "Boy, you're dangerous. I'm kinda scared of you myself."

"I didn't do that. You did!"

"Really?" Kowalski snorted with disbelief. "Now, you're gonna try to do this? Right now?" Kowalski turned to Kal. "Listen to her already trying to get her story straight for the cops."

He turned back to Marietta. "So that's how you're gonna play it, eh? Try to throw me under the bus. Well, you sell that fantasy to whoever wants to buy because nobody wants none here. In fact, sell that line to Robinette. He'll fucking love that." Kowalski drew his right hand over his left shoulder then swung down on a diagonal, backhanding her across the face. "That's for lying to me on the job. And for trying to frame me."

Kal grinned and had a seat in Grandma's old recliner to watch the action. "Oh yeah. Like I said, you hit the big time, Mary." He laughed. "You're stomping with the big dogs now. *Rowf!* How do you like it so far?"

"Speaking of dogs, this is for that damn dog running up on me out back." Kowalski chose forehand this time. "You're lucky you pulled it off me in time, otherwise..." He yanked her back into the chair when she coiled to jump out of it.

"Christ, don't you people have any kind of leash law down here?" Kal interjected with disgust.

Kowalski struck her again, forehand. "This is for what those homeless men did to me."

"Stop it! No!" Marietta jumped up from the recliner and turned to run. "Stop it!"

She didn't get far. A cold heat gripped her from behind and brought her to her knees. The electric shock ripped into her like hundreds of falcon talons raking beneath her skin. Her teeth clenched and prevented her from screaming out. And, oh, how she needed to release the pain that violated every nerve ending in her body.

After what seemed like a thousand years, the shock ended. Marietta moaned and fell over on her side. Then she curled into fetal position. "Oh God," she whispered. "Please don't let this happen to me."

Kowalski shocked her again. "And this," he shouted at the top of his lungs, "this, you bitch, is for messing up my first thing for Robinette. Your fuck face father nearly ruined everything for me!"

The beating and the shocks took their toll. Seconds later, when Marietta came to again, she heard the ugly sound of Kowalski's voice still talking, "Now stay there like a good girl, Mary, and wait for Robinette." Behind her back, where she lay dazed on the floor, he had the audacity to sound amused. "Don't make me use this on you again."

Stephanie... Stephanie...

"Well, if you're gonna do all that then I have time to take her upstairs," Kal declared.

Marietta closed her eyes. No. No. No.

"Nah. Robinette's almost here. He wants her first."

"Well fuck. By the time he's done, she'll be too messed up and dirty for anyone else."

"Kal, don't go there."

"You know how he is."

"She probably already shit herself from the shocks anyway."

"Whatever." Kal made an impatient noise. "Well, if I can't have her, then lemme see your phone."

"For fucking what?"

"I wanna play my goddamn game! Fuck!"

The conversation seemed so outrageously mundane. The banality of evil. They'd finished with Marietta as entertainment, at least until Robinette arrived. Maybe she should try to shit herself... now while she still had the chance... before the third round began.

"You need to plug it in because the battery's low."

Marietta heard scuffling noises. One of them found an outlet. Then the landline in the kitchen rang.

"Who's that, Jackson?" Kowalski demanded. "Who's calling here?"

"Who knows?"

"Well, don't answer it."

"Like I was really going to."

"Just let it ring. Where's a bathroom?" Kowalski asked. "She got blood on me."

"Upstairs, first door left."

"Well, I gotta go. Watch her. But keep your paws off her. Robinette's on his way."

The landline rang a second time while Kowalski stomped upstairs.

"Hey bitch!" Kal called out to her.

Marietta made no noise or movement. Something Kowalski said while he tortured her stuck in her head. She messed up Kowalski's first thing for Robinette. Her father nearly ruined everything for him. Her father... her father... the hospital...

"Hey! You awake?" Kal threw one of the sofa pillows at her. It bounced off her head. Still she didn't move. Tears leaked from her eyes and dropped onto the rug as her body purged all fear. She would kill him. She had not one more thing to lose. Not a single thing. Kowalski would die tonight. If she had to die herself in order to take him down, then so be the cost of doing business.

"Whatever," Kal grumbled and got busy with his game.

***

"Sheriff, there's trouble at the Madison house. Marietta's home, but she's not answering her phone. Something funny's going on and my Abbie's going crazy."

"You bet there's trouble."

"What?"

"I'm already on my way to the Madison's."

"You heard my Abbie?"

"Abbie? What are you talking about? No! I need to detain..."

"Abbie! Abbie! Come back here! Dammit! Riggs, I'm getting my shotgun!"

"The hell? Miss Annette... wait!"

"Abbie just pushed past me out the front door again. She's running back over there!"

"Dispatch reported a tip on that girl of yours."

"All I know is I heard screaming. Abbie ran over there like a bat out of torment. This is the second time. I got ammo. I'm ready!"

"Stand down, Miss Annette. That's an order from your sheriff." His voice faded in a muffle.

"Riggs! What'd you say?"

"Miss Annette... Jesus, I'm clear all the way on the other side of the county." Miss Annette heard a siren engage over the telephone.

"...about fifteen minutes and deputy..." he said to someone else in a muffled voice.

"Too much talking, Riggs."

"Annette! I am your sheriff! Your sheriff just told you..."

"Just get here!" With that, Miss Annette dropped the telephone receiver by the cord. "Stay inside, Tony Jr!" she yelled over her shoulder and ran towards the Madison home.

***

From the floor, Marietta heard the sound of barking at the front of the house.

"That dog's back again," Kal called up the stairs to Kowalski. "Jesus, what is up with that thing? Does it have rabies or is it in heat?"

If it was her time to die, then fuck it. It was her time to die. She would take Kowalski into the pit with her and smile for the camera all the way down. Marietta whipped herself off the living room floor and tore through the kitchen's back door. Under the orange-tinted pall cast by the moon through the leaves of the fruit orchard, Marietta saw Abbie charge around the corner of the house. A wild roar rose from Abbie's throat.

With a shout, Kal slammed through the back door behind Marietta. He launched himself from the back steps to tackle

Marietta's legs. Abbie intersected him mid-flight. Man and dog fell to the ground in a jumble of arms, legs, claws, teeth, and fists.

***

Tony stomped his brakes and swerved to avoid hitting his mother who ran past his front bumper with... a shotgun. Of all things. He sat open-mouthed with disbelief for a few seconds.

"Mama! What are you doing?" Tony parked and leapt out of his car.

"That man is up to something with Marietta. Abbie keeps running over there. I heard screams. Oh Lord, help us. Marietta!"

"Wait!" Tony took firm hold of the shotgun and tugged it from her hands. "Get back inside the house, Mama, and watch Tony Jr. Lock the doors and call Riggs!"

***

Marietta stumbled into the falcon house. The loud barks and snarls from Abbie entered with her. The birds stirred and called, not used to night disturbances. She dropped and rolled under a bench.

Kowalski burst into the falcon house in hot pursuit. This time, the falcons screeched and went on the attack. The birds of prey ripped and tore at Kowalski's skin with beak and claw. Their wings beat about his head and disoriented him.

Kowalski ran out of the falcon house, a whirling, screaming dervish of flailing human arms and raptor wings. The birds stayed with him, defending their territory.

Marietta found the gauntlets and crawled out, past the two men. Kal lay huddled in a ball, not moving. Kowalski fell to his knees, locked in a death struggle with the birds. Nobody's fool, Abbie had run underneath the back steps of the house when the falcons went on the attack and she barked from there now. Kowalski managed to pull off his jacket to cover his face, which left his back exposed. The falcons took full advantage of that then rose above the trees to circle the men.

Tony, hearing all the commotion, ran around the side of the house, following Abbie's path.

He saw Marietta crawling towards the house, away from two men who lay prone.

"Marietta, get inside! Lock the doors and call Sheriff Riggs. I'll take care of this."

She nodded, with a dazed look, as if she wasn't sure who he was. The falcons screamed above them.

"Wait!" He ran over to Marietta and snatched the gauntlets off her arms. "Give me those. I have to get the falcons back. Go!"

Abbie barked from beneath the back steps. "Abbie!" Tony called to her and she ran to his side. The falcons wheeled and flew lower, but did not attack. They recognized the one who fed and cared for them.

"Abbie! Guard!"

Abbie snapped to obey. Her lips pulled off her teeth. She stiffened into a crouch over the two prone men."

Tony waited until Marietta entered the back door. All three locks clicked home.

He turned back to the excited Catahoula, the falcons, and the two men who might be dead or alive and tried to figure out what to do first. He needed to immobilize the men and check their condition. But he also had to keep Abbie from ripping out their throats. Then he had to coax the falcons back into their house so they wouldn't go back on the attack whenever law enforcement arrived.

Hopefully, that would be sometime soon.

Marietta tried to catch her breath while she watched Tony through the window on the back door. Then she grabbed a kitchen chair and jammed it under the locks she just engaged.

She would let Tony take care of the men in the back yard. She didn't know if they were dead or alive. She hoped dead. But now, at least, she had help. No getting around it, she had to call the sheriff like Tony told her. The situation was completely out of control at this point.

If she went to prison too, then she went to prison too.

She picked up the phone receiver. A long, thick arm snaked from behind her and ripped the entire phone off the kitchen wall. The arm then hurled the remains of the phone into the kitchen sink.

CHAPTER 27   ABBIE

Marietta turned to look behind her. A hideous monster waited and watched with a bent, amused leer on its face. Yellow teeth like stalactites dripped saliva onto the bottom row of stalagmites inside a black cavern surrounded by red.

Marietta opened her mouth to scream. Derek Robinette snatched her by the wrist, and yanked her back against the large, solid wall of his huge bulk. He covered her mouth with a huge hand. Then he dragged her backward into the living room, the scene of her previous torture.

She bit into his hand. He yelled and shook her.

"You worthless bitch," he growled in her ear, yanking her backwards again. "At least Stephanie pulled her weight."

Breathless, Marietta gasped for air. "I know what you did to her. You're a beast, Robinette. You stole Stephanie's soul from her. That makes you a demon!"

Robinette chuckled. "Beast, eh?"

"Yes."

"Demon?""

"Yes!"

"Well, she took my face from me. Look at what she did!" Robinette turned Marietta to face him. Frankenstein's monster. Marietta shrank away from him. He pushed her down into one of the recliners and bent over her.

"Get a good long look, Mary. Real close now. See what I see every day. Then feel what I feel every day."

"So?" Marietta asked, defiant.

"So, sweetheart, this face is the last thing you'll see before you die tonight."

"I know that."

"Oh, you know that?"

"I know everything. You tortured Stephanie Madison. You're a rapist along with everything else you are."

"She volunteered."

"No. She wouldn't. Never! She turned on you at the end. Didn't she?"

"She came back to us knowing that she would kill us. She killed my father, which was premeditated murder. Stephanie Madison was a terrorist and a murderer. Everyone knows that, except you, for some reason."

"And what about everything you did to her?"

"Stephanie played the game. She knew the rules when she signed up."

Marietta stared at him.

"And those were?"

"Bitch knew the target. But she forgot what team she played for. She wasn't supposed to..."

"Defend herself? And me?"

"She had the package inside her," Robinette whispered in wonder.

"What?"

"It came out of her."

Marietta frowned. "What came out of her?"

"Did you not hear me just tell you that she killed my father? Paul Robinette."

"And then you killed my father! My father was a good man. Remember him? Roy Brazil. You did that!"

Robinette lifted a brow. "So... Kowalski's been talking out of school, has he?" Robinette shrugged. "Turnabout's fair play. He shouldn't have got in Kowalski's way. My way. Besides, Mary, you killed your mother. Now, what does that make you, I wonder?"

***

Annette ran into the orchard.

"Mama! I told you not to leave Tony Jr!"

"I locked him inside the house. I came back to help because Riggs has to drive in from the other side of the county. Where's Marietta?"

"Locked inside too. I told her to make another call to Riggs." Tony looked up into the trees.

"Is she okay?" Miss Annette asked him.

The birds still circled overhead, agitated and screaming. Abbie jumped and snapped at them.

"I don't know. I think so. I... okay, look Mama. The birds are out of control. I need you to take Abbie to the front yard. Every time I try to step anywhere she attacks these guys behind my back. I need to get rope from the tool house to tie them up. Plus, she's keeping the birds excited. I can't get them to land."

Tony watched Annette grab Abbie by the collar and to try to convince over one hundred and twenty pounds of solid resistant muscle to cooperate with her.

"Keep her in the front, Mama. Watch for Riggs and tell him to come back here and take these men into custody."

***

Marietta, I think you better calm down before you end up like Stephanie.

Instead of flying at Robinette with all of her own claws extended, Marietta lifted her head. "No, you killed my mother."

"I could have sworn, you bounced her off the hood of your car."

This time, Marietta flinched. The verbal blow struck home.

Robinette smiled. "That's right. I know about that."

"You fixed my brakes so they failed."

Robinette narrowed his eyes.

"That's right." Marietta mocked him. "I know about that. Lake City police put that in their report." She pointed at him in accusation. "Susan Brazil died because of you."

"Did she?"

"Derek Robinette, you're a serial killer."

Robinette narrowed his eyes. He seemed almost sly. "I've killed no one."

"Just admit it, you coward. Be a man or whatever you are and stop playing games."

"Why would I play a game that I've already won?" he asked, mystified. Then he pulled out a handgun and pointed it at her.

Marietta shook her head. "There's nothing left for you here, Robinette. What more do you want?"

"It's never gonna be enough. And why don't you ever die, by the way?" Robinette with wonder. "I'm sitting here right now with a gun on you, but rather than kill you, I'm thinking maybe I need to recruit you. You owe me a life."

"You're a psychopath," Marietta whispered.

"You're a criminal. Don't you hear those sirens? They're coming for you, not for me. You see, I'm the one who called them. You can't hide from me down here in Mayberry either. They know who you are and everything that you've done."

***

At the curb in front of the Madison house, Abbie continued to resist and growl low in her throat. It was all Annette could do to keep the Catahoula from dashing off again.

"Oh Lord, Abbie, as soon as this is done, I'm gonna give you a sedative and lock the damn door."

She could hear faint sirens now. Finally! Riggs was always where he didn't need to be and took his time getting to where he was supposed to be.

***

"What I've done? Those false charges you put on me about the electronics won't stand. I'll fight you in court."

Robinette threw back his head and opened the dark cavern of his mouth to laugh. "Oh sweetheart, we're so far beyond that, you have no idea. Mary Madison or Marietta Brazil, whoever you are... there's nowhere you can run that you cannot be found. You broke into Cadis Industries after taking a job to surveil your target. Me. After I confronted you about your dubious background, you returned with your terror cell, which remains at large by the way, to set off explosives in the incinerator. An act of revenge and terrorism. Arson. I'll help the cops think of more."

Marietta slowly shook her head. "No one will believe you."

"And apparently, the local police in Lake City have personal beefs with you. Obstruction, evading, vehicular assault... who do you think people will believe?"

Marietta's shoulders sagged.

Robinette chuckled, a rough, phlegmy, wet sound. "The media will believe whatever I tell them to believe. Then they will convince everyone else. The investigation will go in whichever direction I decide it goes. Right now, it's headed straight your direction. You're looking real good for multiple felonies. Real good. They wanna close this case so bad they can taste it. Taste you. They want you, Mary."

Robinette leaned closer.

"Especially when people discover your link to Stephanie Madison, a known and documented terrorist. A madwoman. That'll make good press. The second generation taking up the family business. What will the court of public opinion decide about your vendetta against me? I'm a long time businessman and employer in Lake City. A contributor to various causes and charities. Who are you?"

When Marietta didn't respond, he answered for her. "No one."

Marietta found it hard to breathe, but she managed to form the words. "That's right. I'm no one. So why did you send Kowalski to kill me? I was just a child. I did nothing to you."

***

Tony finally got the men lassoed tight. Kal, he knew from earlier this afternoon, the other man, he never saw before. Both of them were in bad shape, but he still would take no chances.

The sirens got louder, closer. He began landing the falcons. Mama could direct the first responders to the back to get these lowlifes hauled away. But he had to get the birds settled before more people came into the orchard. He hoped Mama sent someone inside to check on Marietta. She seemed so out of it, like she was in shock.

Things were almost under control in the orchard. All seemed quiet in the house.   Maybe too quiet.

***

"Stephanie fucked us big time when she got turned by Celara. We had to send a message to the others that we were serious so..."

"What others?"

Robinette shrugged. "Your father sufficed when he got in the way of Kowalski's first thing. And you got lucky. So did Kowalski, because I nearly ended him for that mistake. By the way, what were you looking for in my incinerator? What was down there? You didn't try to enter the building through the file room."

"You dropped that device and set off the explosions!"

"You got lucky again. Apparently, your little terror cell jumped Kowalski."

"No."

"Then the fire department came out. You would not believe the payoffs I had to make, the bureaucracy and the paperwork. Otherwise, you would have seen me here much sooner."

He burst into laughter. "Good thing we had Kal in place to keep track of you. How's he been treating you, by the way?"

"You brutalized Stephanie until she wasn't even in her right mind anymore. She didn't volunteer for that. I saw what you did to her. Animals! You disgust me. I saw the tape."

"Ah, I see. So that's what you found in my incinerator." Robinette's eyes darted around the room. Still pointing the gun dead center to her chest, he picked up the VHS tape that Kal dropped. "Well, what do you know? This looks familiar."

***

Now, Annette had to hold Abbie with two hands. The older woman's shoulders hurt. The huge dog yanked Annette this way and that.

Her baby really needed to go back inside the house so she wouldn't jump at Riggs. Knowing Riggs, he'd probably try to shoot her. And then Annette would have to shoot him.

Again, she doubled down on Abbie's collar. The dog started up another fit of barking. The sheriff was almost here, just a few blocks away from the sound of it.

Almost upon them.

***

With one meaty hand, Robinette broke the hard plastic. He snatched out the ribbon and crushed that into a ball.

"I made copies. They're all in..."

"A safe place should anything happen to you... yadda yadda... No you didn't. Don't ever threaten me."

"Why not? You threatened me."

"And now here we are. And what do you know? It's no longer a threat. See this gun? It's loaded."

"Stephanie stopped you."

"But she didn't stop me, did she? You need to make a choice right here, right now... Mary. I can make all the bad things go away. You can join me or be thrown to the wolves. I can protect you, but if you cross me, I'll ruin you first, and then I'll hand you over as a felon and a terrorist. What do you think I haven't done in order to hold my position in the City? What do you think I won't do? Or have done for me? Your life won't be worth living after I'm finished, Mary. Besides, you owe me big for what she did.

Join me, Mary. Help me close the Consortium deal like you agreed."

***

"I knew something wasn't right about that girl the minute I saw her," Riggs said, grimly satisfied, his hand on his weapon. "I'm taking her into custody."

"What are you talking about? I just told you she's in trouble," Miss Annette responded, both hands on Abbie's collar.

"Damn right she is. You and Abbie stay behind my car."

"Riggs!" Miss Annette called after him. Abbie yelped her own protest.

Riggs ignored both of them and stalked towards the house, waving for his deputy to head back into the orchard.

***

"Are you crazy?" Marietta finally said, staring at Robinette, with a look of horror at the audacity.

"I have to hand it to you. You played a real good game. You're a smart girl. Creative. Yeah, you made me break a sweat. But now your back's against the wall. You took it as far as you can. You hear them out there, don't you? Wrestling with that damn dog and those birds. After they handle Kowalski and Jackson, they're coming in here. Then it's game over for you... Marietta."

Help was all around, but she never felt so alone. Marietta hated the sound of her name in his ugly mouth, but he wasn't finished.

So what's it gonna be?" the predator asked his prey.

"Deputy, what is your status?" Riggs whispered into his walkie talkie as he approached the porch steps.

"It's a disaster back here. Feathers. Blood all over. Two male perps down. Tony Jennings, you know the lawyer from across the street, is back here. He's got them tied up. Sheriff, he says Mary Madison is locked inside the house. He says she's the vic, sir."

"Okay, stay back there. I'm checking on the female suspect. Over and out."

***

"Kowalski's done. He fucked up one too many times. This is your chance to be greater than what you are now. Everything you ever dreamed. My wife couldn't deal with what happened to me at Cadis. Because of what Stephanie did to me. I don't have any children."

Marietta closed her eyes, willing the harsh voice to stop its insane rambling. But Robinette droned on.

"We can rule Lake City together. You'll have more money than you could ever make here. I'll see to that. Everything can be yours."

Marietta shook her head.

'Because if you don't, your boyfriend across the street and his son..."

Marietta's eyes popped open to witness Robinette drawing a finger across his throat.

"No. Don't."

"The old woman too."

"Don't do it. Please. They're not involved."

"They will be."

Marietta remained silent.

"You will be even greater than she was."

He will not bend you. He will break you. Trust and believe that it will happen.

"I'd rather die."

"Or you can die... because I can't let you live without me. The police will understand that I had to do what I had to do... after you attacked me again."

Then it was over. Marietta understood that this encounter would end exactly how Robinette predicted. No more shields. No one stood between them now. His would be the last face she would see.

Robinette shrugged and raised the gun. "Okay, here we go."

Marietta bowed her head and closed her eyes.

Soon I'll see you again, Stephanie.

***

"Sheriff's Department!" Sheriff Riggs screamed. He threw his shoulder against the front door and bounced off. A streak of outraged muscle and fur shot up the steps and passed him, leaving a bellow in its wake.

***

The glass of the window with the panoramic view shattered inward. Startled, Robinette's bullet went wide.

Marietta froze on the recliner, not understanding why she wasn't dead. And what just happened to the window?

Abbie snarled and wrestled through the curtain. She leaped for Robinette's throat, missed, and yanked him to the floor by the arm. The gun went off in Robinette's hand again when he tried to knock Abbie away. When he dropped the weapon, Marietta dove to retrieve it.

***

At the gunshots, Tony ran for the front of the house, ignoring the deputy's order to "Halt!"

"Sheriff Riggs, it's Tony Jennings!" he shouted as he rounded the corner of the house and dashed up the stairs to the porch. Sheriff Riggs shifted so Tony could knock more of the broken glass away with his shotgun. They both jumped through the window into the living room.

"Marietta!" Tony shouted.

Marietta didn't look. Her hand shook so when she tried to train the gun towards Robinette. He threatened the life of an innocent child she cared about. He ruined the lives of so many others she cared about.

No more. She could finally make it all stop. This might be her last chance.

But she didn't have a clear shot. Abbie was all over him. The gun wobbled in her hand.

"Sheriff's Department! Drop the weapon, Mary!" Sheriff Riggs yelled. He pointed his own firearm her direction. "I said drop it!"

Marietta dropped Robinette's hand gun and raised her hands.

"No!" Tony dropped the shotgun to the floor and ran to pull Abbie away from Robinette while Riggs kept Marietta under guard.

In the melee of trying to control Abbie, Robinette reached out with a large, thick arm and snatched his gun back and shot again, missing Tony who dove to the floor.

"Stop!" Riggs shouted, moving his gun from Marietta towards Robinette. "Drop it!"

But once Tony loosened his grip, Abbie renewed her attack on Robinette. She savaged his face and hands as Robinette tried to use his arms to block his throat.

Robinette dropped the gun again. This time, he wrapped both hands around Abbie's throat. The two beasts, both fighters and predators of dangerous game, wrestled each other. Despite the fact that her ancestors were bred to hunt and bring down wild boar, the Catahoula yelped and struggled within the tight vise of Robinette's huge arms, outdone by the wicked determination of a super predator driven by menace and hatred rather than instinct.

"No!" Tony leaped at Robinette again to save Abbie.

"Get back, Tony, goddamit!" Riggs shouted.

Marietta ignored Riggs and joined Tony, trying to pull Robinette's ham-sized hands from around Abbie's throat. Abbie whimpered. She choked and gagged.

Marietta heard yells from behind her. Someone, Tony, maybe, snatched her back.

She heard multiple shots. Then silence. At last, Robinette released his hold on Abbie. The Catahoula fell limp to the floor. Marietta closed her eyes and turned her head, not wanting to see the loyal girl breathe her last.

"I sure hope that was the bad guy. Anybody who puts wrong hands on Miss Annette's monster's the bad guy."

Riggs looked grim, but also a little uncertain. "You people..."

Marietta collapsed, dazed into her grandfather's old recliner. Too much death. Jesse and now Abbie had given their lives for her.

Sheriff Riggs turned to her. "Miss, I'm told your backyard is a complete mess. I've been meaning to ask you, do you have a permit for those birds? Mr. Madison was a registered falconer and so's Tony, here. But are you?"

Almost in a trance, Marietta replied, "I'm... working on that."

"Well, if you're gonna stay on here, you need to get that taken care of or I'll have to write you up."

CHAPTER 28   THE TRUCE

R iggs is in quite a state," Tony told her. "He's furious that they transported Robinette back to Lake City before he had time to get a good lynch mob going. But there wasn't much he could do. Robinette has friends in high places."

"Robinette belongs in hell, but I guess Lake City will have to do," Marietta replied from her hospital bed.

Tony gave an obligatory laugh, but remained serious. "Marietta, now that we've talked it all through, I can understand things better now that I didn't back then. I missed a lot that was going on with you right in front of me." He took her hand and squeezed it. "I let you down. I let Mr. Madison down too."

"You didn't know, Tony. How could you? No one told you."

"I guess I could have asked, but I had no idea."

"No one did."

"I guess I understand why you kept running away. You had monsters chasing you for most of your life. No wonder Mr. Madison..."

Marietta waited for him to continue, but instead Tony looked away.

"It's over now. I hope," she said at last.

Tony, back on familiar ground straightened and said, "Well, I'm doing my best. I made several calls up to Lake City to consult with a defense lawyer. I'm pretty sure that we can convince the district attorney to drop the charges against you in exchange for your statement." Tony still seemed shaken. "The fact that he threatened my son... I didn't protect you before, Marietta, and... I'm sorry for that.

"Well, I made sure to not make it easy for you, didn't I?" Marietta made a face that forced another chuckle from Tony.

"I... had to lay some of my own ghosts to rest. But I'll damn sure protect you now," he told her.

"What kind of ghosts, Tony?"

Tony scooted his chair closer. "I had some papers to sign. I took care of that earlier this afternoon."

"Your ghosts were unsigned papers?"

"Divorce papers." Tony's words speared through Marietta's light-hearted laughter.

"Oh." Marietta felt chastened.

"It was time for me to let her go."

"Carla?"

"Yeah." Tony nodded.

"I'm sorry, Tony."

He shrugged as if to say, what can you do?

Marietta allowed a moment of silence for the death of Tony's marriage. Then she changed the subject.

"If it makes you feel any better, after Grandpa passed, you were the only real thing in my life, you know. The one thing that never changed."

"Gee, thanks."

"I think that's what kept me from firing you. I didn't want to let go of the one thing I knew that I could count on."

"Funny you say that because that's the very part of me that Carla didn't like."

"Oops. Again, I'm sorry, Tony," Marietta repeated. "But Tony Jr. is a wonderful boy. I think that still makes you the lucky one in this room."

"You know what?" Tony asked her. "You're right. I have full custody of my little man. He's a terrific kid. The best." He smiled, pleased.

"At least we can agree on that, if nothing else. Tony?"

"Yeah?"

"I have to be honest. Part of me resented the relationship you had with my grandfather, you know. You got to spend more time with him than I did."

Tony took her hand again. "Marietta, Mr. Madison saved my life. He saved our home. Me and my mother will be grateful for the rest of our lives for that. There's nothing we wouldn't have done for him. All that stuff I said before, it wasn't fair to you because I left out some important things you deserve to know."

He cleared his throat. "Your grandfather loved you so much. He was so proud of you. For years, he'd go on and on about how hard you worked. How smart you were. How much you helped people...""

Tears sprang into Marietta's eyes. "Tony, I wish I had come back home when you told me to. I should have."

"Don't." Tony moved closer to put his arm around her then changed his mind since she was still covered with bruises just about everywhere. He cleared his throat again, a little uncomfortable now. Finally, he settled for handing her a clean handkerchief.

"So, other than all this, how are you feeling?" he asked, scowling at the dark marks around her neck and arms. The black eyes from Kowalski's handicraft still incensed him.

Marietta had to laugh. Tony was the most hilarious when he didn't even know he was hilarious.

"I've been here for two days now. I think I'm ready to go home. The bruises will fade one of these days. Look, Tony. Do you think you can spring me out of here, or what?"

"Sure." He smiled at her. "Just as soon as you can, though, I need your statement to take with me up to Lake City. Trust me, Derek Robinette's going to try his dirty best to throw you under the bus. He's already turned on Kal Jackson." He hesitated.

"What?"

"Look, Marietta, I don't know if anyone told you yet, but Kowalski didn't make it. Between the birds and Abbie... but mostly the birds..."

Roy Brazil never got to see his remaining daughter grow up. He missed out on every milestone, starting with Marietta's high school graduation, her triumphs overseas, grad school, everything. She still felt so sad whenever she remembered how much he loved her. Even at the end, her father fought to save her from Robinette's hit via Kowalski.

Marietta stared at the hospital wall in front of her without expression, choosing not to admit her satisfaction that the man who killed her father died a horrible, pain-filled death under tooth and beak and claw.

"Um," Tony filled in the silence. "But let's get you home."

While she waited for Tony to return to her hospital room, Marietta struggled to remember her past life, before all of the death and destruction. Once upon a time, she'd thought of her childhood as idyllic--birthdays, holidays, summer vacations in Wayfarer. A semblance of a middle-class childhood with two parents, good schools, stable home life, loving grandparents, etc. But that life was always an illusion. The house of the

Brazils and the Madisons both fell upon Stephanie's death as though constructed from a deck of marked cards.

Marietta had no control over her past. She had no agency over the decisions that other people made for her, the secrets kept, mistakes made, apologized for, forgiven, avenged.

She had been loved. Definitely, her father loved her. If not for Roy Brazil, Kowalski would have slain her in that other hospital bed in Lake City. Stephanie loved her. Even in the midst of her own pain and despair, she killed for Marietta, and then she died for Marietta. Her grandfather loved her. Possibly her grandmother loved her as well on some strange level. Who knew anymore?

The assurance of the love she did receive far outweighed the black hole inside Susan's heart and all the love sucked inside that empty vacuum each time her heart beat. Marietta wasted too many years of her life searching for something that never existed in any space, dimension, or plane of the natural world. Susan didn't have any love inside of her to share with anyone else.

Tony returned quiet and contrite. "I tried my best, but the doctor requested one more night." His nostrils flared when he took her hand again. "You got roughed up pretty bad by those assholes. I'm sorry that guy died, but he brought it on himself. The other one can face the law and get what he deserves from the justice system. As for Robinette..."

Tony squeezed her hand in his. "I have to get back to my son and mother. Everyone's pretty nervous and I'm scared my mother will try to get her gun off again. There'll be two guards on your door because Jackson's still here in recovery. He's chained and cuffed to his bed though. I knew that guy was bad news when I first met him."

"Tony, do you think this story will go public?"

"Too early to tell, but I'm leaning towards yes."

"Yeah, I guess it will. Even in Lake City, the corruption eventually creates too much stench to ignore."

"I found your backpack with all the documents and tapes where you told me. It bears out what you said. Real nasty stuff."

"Stephanie Madison sacrificed herself to stop Cadis Industries from ruining more lives. But Cadis outlived Stephanie and then took out Susan and Roy in return. And came after me."

"Right."

"Paul and Derek Robinette used secrecy and fear and shame to control others. That's what Robinette said. The others."

"Others? You mean more like Stephanie?"

"I'm not sure. I don't know, Tony. That's why we need a review of the case against Stephanie Madison in light of the new evidence. Derek Robinette should undergo investigation for crimes against humanity."

"Yes. He should."

"He can't hurt Stephanie anymore. But he shouldn't be allowed to hurt anyone else either. Especially people I care about."

Tony hesitated.

"Marietta, I know life's been a tough road for you, but the future is yours to decide. You know this, don't you?"

"I know, Tony." Marietta smiled. "I'm not afraid any more. As long as I'm alive, I can focus on the next day and the day after next. No more running, I promise."

"You hanging around?"

"I'm standing my ground this time. For better or for worse, Wayfarer is my home."

"That's good, Marietta. Real good." Tony's smile lit up the hospital room. "I like that."

He looked as though he wanted to say more. Instead, he squeezed her shoulder and left.

"We're staying the night with you, Miss Marietta!"

Marietta's eyes popped open when Tony Jr skipped into the room ahead of this father and grandmother. Miss Annette sailed in like she sailed in everywhere, as though she owned the place.

Abbie brought up the rear, her tail doing a slow wag when she looked up at Marietta.

"Oh, Miss Annette, is Abbie okay?" The brave Catahoula saved Marietta's life several times in the fight against Robinette and his henchmen. In fact, she took on about as many blows as Marietta. "She looks like how I feel."

"She'll make it, now that the vet's stopped bothering her. She hates it there. She misses you, you know. We had a hard time getting out of the door without her, because she's even more protective now."

"She's my hero. You're my hero, Abbie." Marietta reached out and Abbie licked her hand.

"Trust me," Miss Annette replied, "She knows. She's very proud of herself now."

If not for Abbie... if not for everyone who ran to her rescue... Marietta shivered. She didn't even want to finish the thought.

Tony took charge. "Okay everybody! Camp out! We're gonna get comfortable with our blankets and snacks as soon as they bring in the cots."

Steady as she goes, Marietta thought with a smile.

CHAPTER 29　　THE CONFESSION

The red-haired woman walked up the steps to the Madison home and crossed the lawn to sit on the bench next to Marietta. The low branches of the decades-old crape myrtle shaded them from a late September sun that still blazed like hottest July. Marietta didn't greet the woman at first, but instead waved a cheerful hand at a passing car, just barely visible through the leaves.

Kate cleared her throat. "This place is so lovely, I wonder how Stephanie ever left," she rasped.

Marietta shrugged. "Bright lights and big city hold a special allure if you're not from there."

Kate snorted, but she looked pensive. "Do you miss Lake City, Mary?"

"No. Wayfarer is my home now. I'm where I belong. You received my postcard?"

"Well, yeah. A blank postcard arrives to my home address with a Wayfarer postmark, I figure I need to see what that's about."

Marietta waited.

"You should know that I helped her, Mary."

"Marietta."

Kate raised her eyebrows with a small incline of her head.

"I know you helped her, Kate. She was your friend."

"No. I mean..." Kate took a deep breath and then looked away. "Close to the end of things, she told me that they said they would kill you."

"Kill me? Who?"

"Paul and Derek Robinette. If Stephanie wasn't a 'nice girl,' if she didn't close deals like she was told, they said that they would make you disappear. But she just couldn't anymore. The things they did to her. The things they made her do. You know, don't you?"

"I know why Stephanie hated Sundays." Marietta looked down at her hands. "I saw."

Kate shook her head and looked at the passing traffic.

Marietta took a deep breath. "I know that Paul Robinette was Stephanie's 'owner.' She killed him and the recorder, the operator, and security in that so-called Education Room. Derek, her handler, survived. But his face..." Marietta shivered. Abbie's teeth and claws only added to the obscenity of Robinette's twisted visage.

"Right." Kate's lip curled with distaste. "His face."

"Derek used the hit on me to recruit new talent for Cadis-- Kowalski. But what I don't know is what happened to the controller?"

"What?" Kate frowned.

"The day Stephanie attacked Cadis Industries, the controller wasn't in the room. I read the notes on Stephanie's programming. There was a controller, Kate. And the controller wasn't inside the Education Room with everyone else."

"No." Kate said. "She wasn't in the room. She was never in the room."

"She?" Marietta asked, her voice escalating to a higher pitch. "Where was Stephanie's controller? Who was she?"

Tension developed in the long silence between the two women.

"Who was she, Kate?"

Kate stared at the younger woman with shock. "Wait a minute, Marietta. You don't think..."

"Why did Robinette call you, the file clerk of all people, to come in to work on a Sunday?"

Kate's pale skin flushed under the late September sun.

"Well?"

"Okay, Marietta. Just wait a second."

"Why did he call you, Kate? Why were you there?"

"Look, I admit that I didn't tell you everything. But it's not what you think."

"And just what do I think, Kate? I want to know what I think, Kate!" Marietta bit down on Kate's name with such cutting force that the older woman flinched. "Tell me what I think, Kate!"

Kate swallowed. "Okay, I'll tell you the rest." She looked with unseeing eyes at the flowers of the old crape myrtle. "They... wanted you too, Marietta. At first, Paul Robinette threatened to make you take her place. Stephanie's place. They wanted to make you do the things that she did. "

"And? What's the rest of it?"

"And then, he threatened to kill you. And... the controller would have helped them do that."

Marietta blinked at the knowledge of what she'd escaped not only as a teenager, but not even a few days ago when Derek Robinette tried to recruit her. She would never forget the eerie vacancy in Stephanie's eyes, the madness and the despair that sent her careening over the edge. That would have been Marietta's fate, walking the tightrope one too many times, if she took Robinette's deal. Trapped within an evil web, stalked from every direction by the tentacles of a monstrous spider. Dying a slow death while Robinette fed upon her life force.

Kate continued. "Look, I know she's your mother, Marietta, but Susan Brazil was no kind of a sister to Stephanie."

"What does... I already know that." Suddenly, Marietta couldn't breathe. The back of her throat closed and she tried to choke down breaths of air. *She was a robot!* That's what Susan told her about Stephanie.

Marietta stared at Kate. "What... are you saying?" But she already knew. She always knew.

"They recruited Susan Brazil, too, Marietta." *They used her. Used and used her.*

"That's what they do. They use people. Think about it. They needed someone close to Stephanie. Someone who had access to her whenever she was away from her owner and handler. Someone who could modify and control her behavior whenever her owner needed... remote access, no matter where she was. Derek was her handler in-house. Susan controlled Stephanie in the field."

Marietta flinched at each statement. She closed her eyes, sickened. Because she knew it was true. Susan Brazil had assisted in the subjugation of her own sister. All questions finally answered. Was that the real secret behind Susan and Stephanie's twisted relationship? Susan controlled Stephanie. But then, hadn't she always, even prior to Cadis Industries? Paul and Derek Robinette exploited an already unnatural relationship between the sisters to suit their evil purposes.

How Susan must have reveled in her new and more powerful role in Stephanie's life. Meet your new controller, same as your old controller. It meant that Stephanie had nowhere to run and nowhere to hide. Susan was the reason why. If what Kate said was true, then Marietta had been raised by a monster of the utmost cruelty and evil.

"She's not my mother," Marietta stated in a flat tone.

Kate's eyes widened, but she didn't ask for clarification. "Anyway, just the thought of that... of you being hurt..." Kate shook her head in sorrow. "The thought of them hurting you the same way they hurt her, that's how they broke her whenever she resisted what they wanted her to do, whenever she tried to fight the programming. And after the controller forced her to abort a pregnancy..."

Marietta's shoulders slumped. She bent her head, not sure how much more she could take.

"After everything else... she just gave up. She gave in. They had her boxed in on all sides. I couldn't reach her any more. So I..."

Kate's face crumpled. Marietta waited while Kate searched her purse for a tissue.

"When she asked me to help her, I did. Stephanie just wanted... she wanted to go away to the one place that she knew they couldn't reach her. She was supposed to take the gas pellets to Celara Electric the next time she met with Ronny Webster."

"Celara Electric was the original target?"

Kate nodded. "But when she learned what the Robinettes had planned for you, she decided to attack Cadis instead. She sacrificed herself in order to do it."

Marietta doubled over and squeezed her eyes shut.

"She couldn't think of another way. They always searched her," Kate continued.

"He said... that it came from inside her," Marietta whispered.

"She swallowed the gas pellets."

Kate's eyes brimmed with unshed tears. "I repackaged them for her so she could... I could do it because they weren't watching me. I mean, who was I? Nobody. But I'm the one who made it possible. Then I replaced the package for Celara with intelligence from Cadis."

"The photovoltaic designs?"

Kate nodded. "Stephanie delivered intelligence from Cadis instead of the chemical device."

Her voice lowered to a whisper. "I tried to talk her out of it, but she knew that was the only way to end their control, both the father and the son, and to save you. She wanted to destroy Cadis. She swallowed the gas pellets so they wouldn't find them when they searched her. She told me..." Kate paused. "That she would give birth to a new baby."

Marietta shuddered.

"When they used the electric shocks..." Kate swallowed. "Everyone in the room that died with her had a role in her torture. Don't you cry for them, Marietta."

Marietta wiped her eyes. "I'm not."

"That's who she took with her," Kate finished. "Except Derek Robinette, of course."

"And Susan," Marietta finished. She put a hand over her face. Susan forced her own sister to abort a baby, the baby that would have been Marietta's younger sister or brother.

"And me," Kate responded in a low rasp. She bit her lip and didn't bother to wipe the tears that ran down her face, streaking her mascara.

"I'm sorry. I'm so sorry. I don't know what to say, Marietta. I don't even know what it makes me that I helped her to do it. But she wanted to save you and... I did too. When Derek called me into work, I had to come, otherwise he would know that I was involved. He wasn't even dressed when I got down to the basement. He'd been in the men's shower and he was still dripping wet with a towel around him. He screamed at me. I could barely understand him. I ran to find a phone to dial 911 because I could see burns all over his face. But he yelled at me to get the tapes from the Education Room and then burn them with all of her other files. Then he ran back into the men's executive bathroom and I could hear the shower going full force. I was so scared. I ran to do what I could, what I thought was right, for once. And then I just... got myself away. I went home and I watched the news about the attack on Cadis just like everyone else."

"That was quick thinking, hiding everything inside the service tunnel."

"I guess." Kate shivered. "While Derek was in the shower, I went into the Education Room and I saw..." Kate closed her eyes and whimpered. "I saw dead bodies smoldering... the smoke and the smell... and Stephanie..." She shuddered and looked away. "I held something over my mouth and nose. I got the tapes and I held my breath as long as I could, but I accidentally inhaled."

Kate rubbed her throat. "The police questioned me and all the other employees the next day but... I never told anyone what I did. No one figured dumb little me knew anything anyway. And I could barely talk since my throat was burned. Everyone always assumes that I have this voice because of the cigarettes."

Kate looked at her cigarette with distaste and then stubbed it out under her shoe. "The fire department decontaminated the building and decommissioned the incinerator. Locked everything up."

"You copied the keys?"

"Yeah." Kate nodded. "I copied them and returned the originals. The day after that, I started work at Celara Electric and I never looked back. A lot of people resigned Cadis Industries about the same time after that because they were scared of another attack, so no one noticed me. Derek was in the hospital. It was a crazy time."

"It's over now, Kate."

"We can only hope."

"Right. We can only hope. Look, I don't know how all this is going to play out."

Kate's laughter was as brittle as it was bitter. "Whoever does?"

"I don't know if Derek Robinette will ever face justice for what he's done. Maybe even still doing. He's connected. He knows people."

"Tell me something I don't know." Kate shrugged again. "Standard operating procedure in the City is to throw the subordinates under the bus."

"Kal Jackson and Will Kowalski."

"That's who did that to you?" Kate indicated Marietta's bruises. The dark marks had nearly faded.

Marietta nodded, massaging her neck. "Will Kowalski's dead. Kal Jackson will go down. Robinette? Who knows? I'm staying South, just to be safe. I'm selling off all of my property up there. But what about you?"

"What about me?" Kate snorted. "Told you. I'm not fresh off the block anymore. And I'm not dumb like Kowalski. I'm always gonna be okay, Marietta."

Marietta searched Kate's eyes, doubtful. Kate smiled and shook her head at Marietta's concern. "Alex King takes care of me." She eyed Marietta. "Robinette's connected. But I'm protected. How do you think I lasted this long?"

"Alex King?" Marietta searched her memory. "The CEO of Celara Electric?"

"Celara Solar now," Kate corrected. "I always bet on the winning team. You should know that by now."

"Does King know what was really supposed to happen? Does he know that Robinette targeted his company?"

"He knows. He just never had proof." Kate's eyes shifted, then glittered green in the sun. "Until now."

Marietta blinked, stunned. Oh yeah. Kate, a Lake City girl, would always land on her feet.

"Can he prevent Cadis from joining the Consortium? Robinette doesn't need that kind of power."

"He certainly has a better chance of blocking them now than he did before, thanks to you. King knows that he owes you, Marietta. You have friends in Lake City."

"I have friends here. My life is here, Kate. But thank you."

"You deserved the truth. Besides, I needed to tell someone and when you showed up all grown up and full of fire, I knew it was gonna be you. I knew you would do what I couldn't and that's do right by Stephanie."

They sat in silence for almost a minute.

"Look Marietta," Kate said at last. She firmed her lips and squared her shoulders. "I guess you gotta turn me in. I'm ready to face the consequences for what I did and the role I played. I've had a good run, but there's no statute of limitations on murder and... I'm an accessory."

Marietta thought back to her own proud determination to do time for Susan's death and her taciturn grandfather's uncharacteristic roars of protest.

"No." Marietta shook her head. "No. The evidence you helped me to acquire cleared Stephanie's name. Somewhat. I mean, she did what she did. But now, at least, I know why. That's all I ever wanted." She paused. "I already wrote out my statement for the district attorney's office."

Kate stiffened on the bench next to her. "So now you're protected from Robinette too."

"For what that's worth. I told them that I stumbled on all of the torture files while I was working in the file room. That's my story. The beginning. The end."

"They believe you?"

"Well, it's actually the truth."

Marietta held out the set of keys for Kate whose mouth trembled when she took them back. "Thank you."

Marietta nodded.

"Stephanie loved you, Marietta. So much."

"I know."

Kate smiled. "She would have been so proud of how you turned out. I know this. She always said that you were her best thing. She always kept telling me about how smart and popular you were and how all the other kids hung around you in front of the school. How everybody liked you. It was almost like you were her daughter instead of her niece, the way she talked."

Marietta froze.

Kate gasped with a hand over her mouth when she realized. "Oh Marietta."

Marietta tried to form a smile. "Go in peace today, Kate. Okay? That's all. Go in peace."

Kate hugged her and then left her alone on the bench. Marietta stood up and walked into the orchard to cry yet again.

CHAPTER 30   THE DREAMER

That night, the white mist descended again.

Whispering secrets to her. Drowning her. Stealing her breath.

Marietta sat bolt upright in bed. Though Kate dropped enough hints, the tough as nails Lake City broad just couldn't bring herself to reveal the very last piece of the puzzle. Even at the end, Kate tried to protect Stephanie's "best thing."

But no one could protect Marietta from her unconscious mind that sifted, relentless, through the available facts while she dreamed.

Robinette admitted to Stephanie Madison's torture and the hit on Marietta which took Roy Brazil's life instead. He admitted to setting off the explosion in the incinerator beneath Cadis Industries.

But not once had he admitted to fixing the brakes on Marietta's car which resulted in Susan's death. He never admitted to any association with Marietta's car. Only Kowalski's attempt at the hospital. In fact, he seemed startled when she accused him, then sly. But not... guilty.

Kate admitted to repackaging the gas pellets for Stephanie and was willing to take responsibility as an accessory for the chemical attack. But neither did she confess to sabotaging Marietta's brakes either. It was time for Marietta to face what she already knew, what she always knew.

Who did that leave?

Who else had a relationship with Robinette, Stephanie, and Marietta? Who had unquestioned and unfettered access to Marietta's car? Not Kate. Kate with her white skin and red flame of hair would have stood out in Marietta's old neighborhood, her presence noted by neighbors and questioned by police investigators. Besides, Kate, the ex-stripper and file clerk, split and ran whenever the going got tough.

Not Kowalski. The botched hit at the hospital was his "first thing." And, as with Kate, her nosy neighbors would have known he didn't belong and would have mentioned him to police investigators.

Who harbored such hatred in her heart against Stephanie so deep and dark and malicious that she would sacrifice Stephanie's daughter in order to punish Stephanie, even after Stephanie's death?

Who attempted to carry out the very first hit on Marietta's life?

But had Robinette even given the first order? Or did someone... volunteer? Again, he didn't register any particular glee when Marietta accused him about her car's brakes, unlike with the other accusations she hurled at him. Say the name and free yourself, Marietta.

Say it!

Marietta closed her eyes as the familiar prickles ran from the back of her neck down her arms. Her lips trembled. Tears stole from beneath her eyelids. She covered her face with her hands. She swallowed and took shallow breaths and tried to calm herself. But she no longer doubted. Not anymore. She knew. She always knew. Ever since...

Denial isn't just a river in Egypt.

The white mist of clouds smothered her. They suffocated... like a pillow... and then she woke and saw Jesse standing stock-still, barking, distrustful... saving her life.

As much as she had been hated, she had also been loved.

Say it, Marietta.

"Susan."

Two nights later, she searched Susan's room and found the gun that would take Jesse's life. Susan's car lights flashed across the bedroom wall. Marietta used the early warning to turn off the bedroom light and flee to her own room. But a long time passed before the front door opened. A real long time.

It could have happened at night while everyone was asleep.

Susan climbed the stairs and opened Marietta's bedroom door. Marietta slowed her breathing in an imitation of deep slumber. Susan stood in the doorway for an age, watching as Marietta pretended to sleep.

They both pretended that night.

Trembling, Marietta got out of bed. She was safe now at the Madison home. She was in Wayfarer, here to stay.

At long last, she'd forgiven Stephanie. She understood now the terrible truth behind her mother's choices and decisions.

Tony already sent someone to repair the large pane in the living room window. Dedicated, efficient, and loyal, any woman with post-traumatic stress was lucky to have a Tony in her life. And Marietta's life would continue to move forward.

Still, she checked every lock and every window in the house.

ABOUT THE AUTHOR

Lee McQueen enjoys writing, research, water colors, and gardening. She has been a librarian, a bookstore owner, and a substitute teacher and holds an MLS from SUNlY-Buffalo, a BA from Xavier University, and coursework in public affairs at the University of Texas at Austin. Now editor and publisher at McQueen Press, her projects include novels, poetry, short stories, screenplays, and greeting cards.

AUTHOR'S NOTE

"Wild Hazy, Beautiful Crazy," a poem from the *Things I Forgot to Tell You* collection, began the journey to *The Cadis Evening*. "The Confessions of the Dreamers" is a short story from *Imaginarium* published in 2006. *The Cadis Evening* fills in quite a bit of the back story. "Stephanie" is the short screenplay based upon the short story published as part of *The Dark Fantastic: 12 Short Screenplays* in 2013.

The Cadis Evening also shares the fictional worlds of *Celara Sun* and *Windrunner*. Lake City, the fictional metropolis, provides the geographical link while shared characters emerge in key situations. In fact, close readers may also pick up slight references to *Kenzi*.

Though filled with characters that inflict a world of hurt upon each other, the themes of not allowing past mistakes to cripple a future might inspire some much-needed forgiveness from us all.

The events in all of the previously named works are one big fat lie. They never occurred. The characters do not exist. You've never met them. Neither have I. The places do not exist. You have never been. You can never go. Neither can I. All is fiction. Celara Electric, Celara Solar, Cadis Industries are also creations.

The concepts of trauma programming, psychological abuse, mind control, industrial espionage, and alternative energy are real, however.

ACKNOWLEDGMENTS

Thank you to my family, the McQueens, for helping me to live for my dream of writing. The art of the scribble is simply to wonderful to describe with mere words. But still, I allow words to speak for me.

Thank you M.I. McQueen, Quaker McQueen, Homer McQueen, Ora McQueen, Melanie McQueen, Gabon Jamal McQueen, Brandi McQueen, Emily McQueen, Mary McQueen.

For my nieces and nephews, all four of you, I miss you so much as time goes by. I cannot wait to see what you will become when you grow up. I know for a fact that you, Shawntavia McQueen, Larry McQueen, Brandzarya McQueen, and Dreylynn McQueen will always be special in my heart.

Thank you, as well, to University of Arkansas Medical Sciences, Texarkana College, McDonald's, Starbucks. You are wonderful hosts! Destiny Carter of University of Arkansas Medical Sciences, Paul Keener of Texarkana Community Journal, Marvin Williams of Sky Over Yonder Productions, Monica Macon of Texarkana Workforce, thank you for your support.

Short Screenplay Collection
ISBN-13: 978-0-9798515-5-1
2013
These screen-ready tales of dark fantasy, horror, and adventure reflect possible rather than impossible worlds. Great stories for lovers of afro-futurism and speculative fiction. Plenty of monologues and dialogues for drama students and teachers, actors, screenwriters, producers, and directors.

Travel Memoir
ISBN-13: 978-0979851568
2013

In 2012, Lee McQueen traveled from Colorado through Kansas, Oklahoma, Arkansas, Tennessee, Mississippi, Alabama, Georgia, Missouri, Illinois, Iowa, Nebraska, and then back to Colorado to promote her latest romance novel. From Beale Street to Route 66 to the Great River Road, to Colfax Avenue--in the spirit of Jack Kerouac and Johnny Appleseed--she fell in love with the road. This collection of journal entries, blog postings, narration in retrospect, and watercolors reveals surprises on Lee's journey through Middle America.

Suspense/Romance Novel
ISBN-13: 978-0979851575
2012

A cross-country chase carries Tolly Henry and Scott Windrunner on an adventure from Midwestern rolling prairies to southwestern Rocky Mountains. Roadside motels, truck stops, corn silos, and windmills guide Scott's whirlwind rundown of Tolly amid echoes of past military service, domestic violence, and post-traumatic stress.

Action/Adventure Screenplay
ISBN-13:978-0979851599
2nded.
2011

On a Christian mission to redeem slaves in Sudan, a reformed female gang member Davey is kidnapped and sold into slavery herself. She uses her former street experiences and talent for leadership to convince the other slaves to break free and flee to the Ethiopian border. Everything Davey has ever learned will save her life.

Suspense/Drama Novel
ISBN-13: 978-0979851582
2010

As *Dallas* and *Dynasty* showcased the wealth, sex, intrigue, and power that drove the oil industry, so *Celara Sun* reveals the tumultuous world behind solar and wind. Martina Butler matches Alexander King step-for-step in a battle of wills to control Lake City's solar and wind energy markets. During the green revolution, the players realize that life moves forward, never backward—and it certainly doesn't stand still.

Non-fiction/Reference
ISBN-13: 978-0979851544
2008

This non-fiction reference work collects the interviews and submissions of fiction and non-fiction writers who discuss the impact of libraries on their career development. Numerous transcripts, photos, biographies, library quotations, footnotes, a glossary, and an index present the information as a teaching tool for the reader.

Romance/Family Drama Novel
ISBN-13: 978-0979851520
2007
Kenzi, an intelligent, sensitive woman living in small-town Texas, feels alienated from the person she knows she should be and would be if only she truly believed it possible. If Kenzi finds the ability to forgive her own mistakes and the mistakes of others, she may have a chance to meet her destiny head-on.

Things I
Forgot to
Tell You

Lee McQueen

Poetry Collection
ISBN 978-0-978515-3-7
2007
2nded.
Out of Print
Poems speak on uncertainty, sadness, despair, guilt, anger, frustration, love, hope, forgiveness, happiness, joy, and spirituality. Poetry is interactive. The reader or listener meets the author or speaker halfway and fills the poem with their own reality and expectations. A lot like life and diamonds, poetry reflects back an image that depends on where one stands in relation to the expressions.

Imaginarium

Lee McQueen

Short Story Collection
ISBN-13: 978-0979851506
2006

Fourteen short stories describe inner turmoil that drives change. Especially when the characters who inhabit the stories step outside the ordinary for a moment in time. And so, there remains the Imaginarium, where Dreamers know when to take a chance and Heroes know when to make a stand. Because refusing to make a choice is a choice. And sometimes, the least of all has the greatest ability to influence the future of the world.

DREAMS IN ARKANA

The long night is over
Or is it
The nightmare has ended
Or has it
Light fills the empty space
Or does it
Dreams in Arkana